MOTHER KNOWS WORST

www.mascotbooks.com

Mother Knows Worst

This is based on a true story. The names have been changed to protect the guilty.

For more information, please contact:
Mascot Books
620 Herndon Parkway, Suite 320
Herndon, VA 20170
info@mascotbooks.com

Library of Congress Control Number: 2021921789

CPSIA Code: PRV0622A
ISBN-13: 978-1-64543-362-0

Printed in the United States

TO MY SON

SOFIA BELLA ROMA

MOTHER KNOWS WORST

A NOVEL

CHAPTER 1

"I NEVER THOUGHT that I would be sitting here feeling the need to speak with a stranger. I have always seen myself as a strong person, but lately I feel like I'm losing it. Should I start at the beginning?" Rose asked before she cleared her throat.

"I feel like I am paying for a friend," she started again. Rose's voice cracked a bit as she shifted uncomfortably on the couch. "I have never done this before…the therapy thing. Maybe this is a good thing. My mother says everyone should do this, and that even my brother sees one. This will be good for me. A different perspective…right?"

With wide eyes, Rose watched Amy take notes. *What is she writing? We just started. I wonder if she will notice if I try to peek. Ugh, I can't see a thing. I just don't want her to write something bad about me. Shit, I feel so nervous.* She noticed the certificates on the wall and Amy's bare ring finger. There were pictures of Amy with who appeared to be her two older boys. The boys were good-looking and maybe in their twenties. Amy had a sweet smile; she might've been in her late forties or early fifties. She certainly didn't look her age. She had a very young, kind face. Amy's eyes were big, brown almond eyes that had this twinkle in them. They were framed with thick black lashes; Rose could tell she wasn't wearing makeup. She was attractive and obviously spent money on her shoes. There were these cute little colored bows on the top of the shoes that highlighted her purple painted toes. Her hair was thick and brown with soft curls. She was thin but still had a voluptuous figure.

Amy looked up from her notes and smiled at Rose. Rose looked into her warm smile and instantly felt at ease, like this was a safe space to speak. Amy had a nice softness about her.

She smiled at Rose. "Where would you like to start? The beginning might be a good place. Let's start there," Amy directed.

Rose took a deep breath to steady her nerves. "I was born in New York, but when I was seven we moved to Colorado," she began. "I never really adjusted to Colorado. I didn't want to move away from everything and everyone I knew. I had my school and family in New York. Plus, back then the people in Colorado were mean to me. The teachers, kids, and parents were such a bag of dicks. They made fun of my accent and called me terrible names. It is crazy that people can be such assholes to a child because of where they come from." Rose could feel her eyes well up with tears as she remembered the fear and pain. She wiggled in her chair and took a gulp from her water to distract herself and avoid crying.

"But we had to move. My dad's job was transferred, and my mother felt like Colorado may be a better lifestyle for the family. So, we moved away from our big Italian family to a little town in Colorado—Littleton. In the late seventies, Colorado was a little state in terms of population, and the town of Littleton was even smaller. The move was definitely a shock to the senses," Rose explained.

"You have to realize," Rose said, "that most of my family members are from Italy. Some of my them never learned to speak English. My mom and dad are American, but their parents were not born here. I think it must have been hard on them growing up as the children of immigrants. They both grew up with humble means. My mom was raised in the projects, which was the affordable housing for low-income families. My dad moved from house to house because his dad kept losing his job. I heard my grandfather had a drinking problem, but I am not entirely sure of that," Rose shared. Rose leaned back in the chair and smiled at Amy. She took a deep breath as she slid back.

"My parents didn't have a traditional love story. My mom wrote letters to my dad in the war, but not because they were dating or in love. It was because she was friends with my dad's sister, Angelia. My aunt asked my mom to write letters to cheer up my dad. When my dad came home from the war, they all met up and hung out. My understanding is that my dad fell in love with my mom, but she loved someone else. My grandmother didn't approve of the other man, so my grandmother arranged for my mother to marry my father."

Rose cleared her throat. "Maybe that loveless marriage between my parents formed my ideas about love. I don't know, but I think it influenced me. I saw them sleep in separate rooms, and my mother was always sad and unhappy. They fought all the time. Screaming and yelling was a daily occurrence in my home growing up," Rose shared.

"My mom said that my grandmother beat her when she told her

she didn't want to marry my dad. My mother always looks so sad when she tells the story. She never knew love from a man—her father abandoned her family when she was twelve. My mother said that her father never looked back. She told me that one day he came home and packed all his stuff and just left. He left my uncle and her crying while her pregnant mother just watched him leave. My mother said that there were court battles, and that her father won some sort of visitation. My mom believed that he did this out of spite, because my mom and my uncle would wait for their father all day at the curb, and he would never show. That has always made me feel so sad for her. My heart literally hurts for her," Rose said with a shaky voice. She looked down at the floor to keep from crying.

"My dad had two sisters. His father was in construction, and his mother was a stay-at-home mom. My dad never really spoke about his childhood. Everything that I know about my dad's childhood I learned from my mother. Apparently, my dad's father would come home from work drunk every day. My grandfather was abusive to my grandmother—both physically and emotionally."

Rose could feel her stomach turning like a butter churner. It always made her feel a bit queasy. "Growing up, it made my stomach turn that my mom didn't love my dad. My dad loved my mom until the day he died, or at least he thought he loved her. He always said he loved her, but I don't know. Can you know how to love if you never felt that love in return? I do not believe you can. I think they both did the best that they could under the circumstances," Rose shared.

"My mother was only nineteen when she was made to marry my dad, and my dad was twenty-six years old at the time. They got married in a big Catholic Italian wedding. I am sure it was some grand affair by the look of the pictures." Rose smiled as she thought about the photos. In her mind, she could vividly see the sixties hair and dresses. Her mom's long white lacey dress synched at the waist. The vail that trailed behind her mom for what seemed like a mile. Her hair flipping out at the ends, and those eyes with the black liner that made everyone look like Cleopatra.

"My mother always talks about how she wasn't given a bridal shower, and that my grandmother didn't pay for the wedding. I guess that must have really bothered her, because she mentions it all the time. My mom said that was the first big bill my parents had—the bill for their wedding," Rose explained.

"My parents had me two years after they were married. My understanding is that it was hard for my parents to conceive. My mother had a miscarriage, then she had several surgeries. She said she took a cab to and from the hospital by herself every time. She was always alone. I remember being five years old. It was a summer morning, and my mom took me for a walk. I had been bugging my mom for a sister for what seemed like my whole life. I was holding her hand, and she said that the baby went back to heaven. I asked her why, and she gave me some sweet angel explanation. Then we walked back to the house, and she got in the cab and went to the hospital. She was alone."

Rose looked up at Amy and said, "It is funny what we learn from our parents and what we pick up from them. How was I ever supposed to have a decent relationship? I didn't learn how to have a decent relationship. Is that what my husband and I are doing to my son?" Rose reflected.

"Growing up my mom disciplined me the way any normal Italian mother disciplined her child—with a wooden spoon, of course. I had so many spoons broken on my ass," Rose said with an uncomfortable laugh. "I guess it is better than the way she was disciplined. My grandmother used to bite her...Geez, can you imagine that? I remember running through the house with my mother chasing me. I guess it wasn't too bad because I own wooden spoons today, but I have never hit my son."

"That is harsh; it was a very different time," Amy interjected.

"Yes, I know. My dad used the belt on me, and I hated that thing. It still freaks me out," Rose said as she shuttered. "I don't know why, but my dad was always in and out of work. As a result, we had to move from house to house because my father could not keep a home. I hated moving all the time. It was exhausting. My dad was emotionally unavailable, and he really didn't show much of an interest in being a father. He wasn't a bad dad. I think he did the best job he could. My mom told me that his parents never told my dad that they loved him. He did tell me that he loved me often. Beyond that, I can honestly say I do not know who my dad really was or what he enjoyed. I know that he was good with his hands and a wonderful artist and builder. He could paint the most beautiful paintings and carve the most amazing sculptures out of wood. My dad could build anything. He was talented. That is all I know of him," Rose said as she looked down at her hands.

"By the time my little sister and brother were born, my home life was filled with screaming and yelling almost all the time. I thought that by cleaning the house, I could make my mom happy and maybe help her so she wasn't so frustrated. That was a silly child's thoughts.

I think my mom misdirected her anger at me, and my dad would often defend her when I went to him for help. I felt as though no one had my back, and I resented my father for not defending me," Rose explained.

"Because of my declining home life, I began to live in my head, and I did it so well that when my mom and dad were fighting, I didn't even hear them. I didn't hear any of the names that they called me. I didn't hear how I was 'just like' my mother or father. I was so engrossed in my fantasy world that I totally and completely escaped. I got so good at it that I could have an entire conversation with my mom and not even know what we talked about, because I was literally somewhere else. The fighting went on for years. My parents finally divorced when I was seventeen. I was never sad about the divorce; I was relieved. I felt like now maybe they both could be happy," Rose explained.

"In high school, I didn't really date. I had so much going on at home. I didn't have many friends, either. I worked and went to school. I worked for this financial advisor in his dingey basement." Rose shivered as she thought about that basement and her old boss. "He was a creepy bald man, Russ Shive. He looked like a Q-tip. He was always touching me. Eventually, my mom involved herself in my life. She thought it wasn't healthy that I wasn't dating, and she set me up with one of her young coworkers; his name was Adam. He was tall and nice looking. He worked out all the time and liked muscle cars," Rose explained and took a deep breath. Rose shifted in her seat and looked at her hands for a moment, and then stared at the floor.

"But Adam was also abusive and dominating. In the end, he ended up hanging out with my mom more than me. They would sneak around together. I was hurt by her relationship with him, and it put me into a downward spiral. I would yell and scream often when I didn't know how to process what was happening," Rose explained.

"I was enraged that my first love was sneaking around with my mom. I was *more* enraged that I found out about it from my father, and that my father didn't do a thing about it." Rose stopped talking as she stifled tears. She paused for a moment, then chuckled softly. "I would throw these ridiculous tantrums. I remember screaming at my mom and crying. I look back, and I don't even recognize myself. I was sad, pitiful, and pathetic. I would often dissolve on the floor crying. That's not the person I am today. I do not cry. I do not dissolve. I pick myself up and dust myself off," Rose said.

"Maybe that is why Anil was so easy to love. When we met, Anil was fun. He wasn't a screamer, and he had a calm family that never raised their voices. He was full of energy and not judgmental. Maybe that is why? I don't know. All I know is that I fell in love with him, or at least I thought it was love. But what could I know about love? I had never seen it. I guess I needed to get away, and my family was pleased with the idea of me leaving. So when I was twenty-one, I decided to pursue my dream of acting and dancing. I moved to New York. Adam stayed behind in my home, and he lived in my bedroom. He took vacations with my family. He celebrated birthdays with my family. It seemed to me that he took my place," Rose shared.

"I was so excited and at the same time nervous to move to New York all by myself. It was an empowering experience. I was taking my life back. In New York, I ended up taking dance classes and acting classes and managing public relations for a restaurant. I did get a few small parts in movies and commercials, but I ended up doing more partying with the stars then becoming one myself. I also had a few more bad relationships. I never really trusted anyone because of the Adam incident," Rose explained.

"I didn't want to date or meet anyone, and I began hanging out with a group of girls that I worked with in the restaurant. They were all lesbians, and for the first time I had real friends and I felt safe. They looked after me, and they hung out with me. They didn't want anything from me other than friendship. When we hung out, it was mostly laughing and taking these amazing trips. They invited me everywhere. They were fiercely loyal, and I bathed in that loyalty. I drank up that loyalty like a starved cat drinking milk for the first time. I knew they had my back. I enjoyed my time with all of them and look back on that time of my life fondly. Those girls taught me how to be a friend, a girlfriend, a sister, and a mother. I didn't know it then, but they would change my life. They changed me from this negative scared little girl into this fun-loving woman who would give anything a go. They taught me to laugh, love, live, and have fun," Rose explained, a slight smile spreading on her lips and a slight sheen in her eyes, before a sudden, distant look took over.

"I don't know that I want to divorce Anil. I love him. I really do love him. There are so many things undone between us." Rose's eyes began to well up, and her mouth turned downward. "I just don't know that I can take the resentment that has built up between us, the anger and the hurt. I don't know if that is fixable. I don't know that I am fixable."

Amy was watching Rose with the intensity of a cat staring at its prey. Amy smiled, her arms were open, and her hands were flat on her lap. She looked directly into Rose's eyes for a moment and then said, "Most marriages are 'fixable.' You need to heal. Why don't you tell me how you met your husband?"

Rose thought for a moment. "After I decided that acting wasn't in my cards, I went back to school and placed my bets on law school. I wanted to help other women. I wanted to do something good in the world, and I thought law school made sense. Law school gave me an avenue, opportunity, and a sense of purpose. My husband and I met there. We were in the same class, but we didn't start dating until the last two months of school, right before graduation. We had the same circle of friends, and we would study together. We never really spoke to each other much. I was closer to his friends, George and Pruniv. One night the guys called to hang out…" Rose looked up at Amy. Rose smiled as she began to recall the story.

"Hey Rose, we are all getting together to hang out. Wanna come?" George asked. George was kind of creepy. He was one of those guys who couldn't get a girl. George was so smart it was almost annoying, but he was harmless. That night, he told Rose they were going to Sam's for a beer, then back to George's house. At first, Rose said no, but after some begging, she relented and said she'd come along.

When George drank, he became a little inappropriate. He always made sure to tell Rose how she wasn't his type. He would go on and on about how he didn't like big boobs, and that her tiny back made her breasts look bigger. Rose would just roll her eyes; she was secretly grateful she wasn't his type.

Over the phone, George told Rose they were outside in the car waiting for her. Before heading out the door, she gave her dogs fresh water. They were the sweetest dogs. Rose had rescued them before law school. One was a Doberman and the other was a Doberman mix; they were her best friends. She would've rather spent time with them than anyone else.

Sam's was a dive bar, but the beer was cheap, and patrons could play pool. The bar had a dirty, smoky feel, even though there was no smoking inside. Back then, Rose was usually the only girl in the group. The guys liked to hang out with her because they could say anything and she didn't get offended.

When they walked into the bar, the group started playing pool, and the guys immediately started teasing Rose, saying she was "a stick with tits."

Anil was at the bar just having a beer and talking with George. Rose had never really spoken to Anil before that night. He had been in a serious accident over the summer—he was hit by a car while running. He had to take an entire semester off because of the accident; he had to have reconstructive surgery and had bolts put in his leg. By this time, he had just returned to school and was walking with a cane. The surgery was long and took about eight months of recovery time. Anil's mother had ovarian cancer at the same time.

Because Anil missed so much school, he wasn't able to graduate with the class. He had to make up the credits over the summer. The school was letting him walk at graduation, but he would receive his diploma when he finished the credits later that summer.

❦

"It's crazy what attracts you to a person. Anil isn't even close to the type of guy that would turn my head. He is good-looking; don't misunderstand me. I just like those Venetian-looking men. Ya know? Like the guy in that movie, *Under the Tuscan Sun*. What is his name? Oh, Raoul Bova, he is so yummy! Gosh you can just eat him up," Rose said smiling, looking up at Amy.

Amy laughed. "Yes, you can really eat him up. So, why do you think you were attracted to Anil?"

"Right." Rose smiled. "For whatever reason, I walked over to Anil when George left to play pool. I don't know what it was about Anil. I think I admired how he just came back to school after his accident and jumped right back into the heat. He didn't let the accident stop him or slow him down. I think that is what I found attractive at first." Rose took a breath and looked around Amy's office. "Yes, I found that very attractive. I like strong people. The type of people who don't get caught up in what others think about them. They face adversity head on and straight in the eyes. At least he appeared strong," Rose looked around the room. "I tend to be in my head all the time and very cautious. I can be in the room with people and be a million miles away. Anil wasn't like that, he was present. Anil was the kind of guy who was at ease and liked to have fun. He just said how he felt, unlike me. I liked that a lot. The ability to have fun without caring what anyone thinks…how refreshing. It seemed to me that he was like me in that he marched to the beat of his own drum. It's so hard to find a man who isn't caught up in all the societal bullshit."

Rose walked up to Anil at the bar. "Hey, I am glad you are back. How are you doing?" she asked.

Anil looked Rose in the eyes. She noticed he had the most beautiful almond eyes with long, thick eyelashes. He wasn't a large man—about five feet, ten inches with a slender build and creamy brown skin. Rose thought he almost looked Greek or Italian, but he was actually born in India and moved to the United States when he was about nine months old. He was about six or seven years older than the other law school students.

"I'm doing better. Thank you so much for asking," Anil answered with a warm smile. "I was worried that maybe people would be afraid to ask or talk about it. I saw that you signed my get well card that the class sent, and you pitched in on the gift basket. Thanks. It meant a lot to me."

"You noticed I signed the card?" Rose asked, smiling at the floor. Rose was so surprised that he noticed. There were over a hundred signatures on that card. It made her feel special to be remembered; it was a feeling she didn't get often growing up. Rose was finding it hard to look into his intense eyes and not feel shy or filled with butterflies.

"Everyone was really worried about you," Rose said, trying to keep the conversation natural. She could feel her throat drying up. "When we heard you were coming back and that you were okay, we were all so excited for you. You have a lot of support here, Anil. People really like you," Rose explained. Rose took a gulp of beer to clear her throat, staring into his eyes.

George approached the two of them and interrupted their conversation. "Hey, Rose you're coming to my place, right?" he asked. Rose wasn't sure whether he was oblivious or just didn't care that she was interested in talking with Anil alone.

"Yes, George," Rose said with an annoyed look on her face.

"Okay, let's go. I have wine at my place so you can drink there," George said, as if he didn't even notice how irritated Rose was.

"I thought we were going to study. Ya know, finals?" Rose inquired.

"Come on, Rose. You are always studying. One night off isn't going to kill you. We'll study tomorrow," George persisted.

"I'll be there," Anil said. "It would be good for you to get out of your cave," he said with a smile, looking at Rose.

"Okay, I'll come." Rose could hear her inner thoughts screaming at her for saying it like a twelve-year-old girl who was infatuated with Robert Pattinson. *Are you fucking serious? Could you sound any more ridiculous? Why did you say okay? You said it so fast; you sound so desperate.*

The group piled into the car and headed to George's apartment. Rose didn't know it at the time, but Anil was living with George. He needed a place after his accident because he lost his old apartment. It was a simple apartment with two bedrooms. The furniture wasn't bad. They had a navy blue couch and loveseat with a coffee table. The TV was a flat-screen with a nice sound system. Rose was surprised to see that the apartment was relatively clean and neat. The counter was filled with half-drunk liquor bottles.

They were all hanging out laughing and drinking. Then the guys started to look at something on the computer. Rose was sitting on the sofa, and Anil was sitting next to her. He started talking to her. Rose realized Anil didn't speak to hear his own voice; everything he said was so thoughtful. For Rose, everyone faded out into the background.

"You want to be alone for a minute," Anil asked her.

"Sure," she replied nervously. The pair got up and went to his bedroom. Anil closed the door behind him, and they immediately started grabbing and pulling at each another. He slammed her up against the wall and tore off her clothes. They looked like crazy animals tossing each other around the room.

They finally ended up in the bed. Rose fell off the bed, but that didn't stop them. They just started mauling each other on the floor, and she kicked over the lamp. They ended up falling asleep on the floor, wrapped up in his blankets. The next morning, they snuck out of the apartment before George woke up. Anil drove her home; Rose sat in the passenger seat, nervous.

"Okay, well bye," Rose said, her voice cracking as she opened the car door.

He smiled and said softly, "Okay, Rose. I'll see you in class."

Rose blinked, coming back to Amy's office. "I think love is like a stupid pill that you take, and it makes you oblivious to everything around you. I am a clean person to the point of obsessiveness. I line my cans in my cabinets so that all cans face forward and in order. In my closet, my clothes are perfectly spaced and color-coordinated. Anil, not so much. That morning, his car was a fucking disaster. It looked like the inside had been through a tornado. Shit was everywhere. He had piles and piles of crap, old wrappers from food and clothes. But at that time, my brain didn't see a mess. My brain saw a cluttered car. Why do we do that? Why do we make men something they are not? Is it a neurological disorder?" Rose looked at

Amy for clarity.

Amy smiled. "Maybe you just wanted to see what you needed. You said your father was emotionally detached, but it sounds like Anil listened to you and noticed you. Maybe the cans lining up just didn't matter to you anymore," she explained with a soft smile.

"I guess. I never thought of it that way before. It was crazy. I didn't date all through law school, and here I was acting like a crazed sex-deprived person. Admittedly, I was sex deprived and my head hurt from falling on the floor. Anil was an extra-special surprise, because I never thought that I would be in a relationship. Not that I don't like sex. I just… It's just that when I meet a guy and I'm attracted to him, well then, they speak, and I am instantly turned off. I guess I just always saw through the bullshit. My girlfriends in New York taught me to see through the bullshit. They gave me an edge," Rose explained.

Amy just kept listening to Rose's story. Rose appreciated that Amy listened without interruption. She thought, *Amy may be the only person in my life who isn't judging me right now. I guess as a licensed therapist, she probably shouldn't judge. Right? She is supposed to be helpful.*

"Anyway," Rose continued. "It happened. I started having the crazy girl thoughts. *Was that a one-night stand? I don't have one-night stands. Was it not good for him, and that's why we are having a one-night stand? It was because I fell. Why did I fucking fall off the bed? Why can't I just be normal at least during sex? What does that mean, he'll see me in class? Brain, please stay calm. Stay calm. Breathe, breathe,* I kept telling myself," Rose explained, talking quickly while her eyes darted around the room.

"You have to understand," Rose continued. "There's a reason I didn't have sex for three years in law school or even date… It is hard for me to connect with anyone. If I feel like I can have the guy, then I don't want him, and if it is too easy, then it's boring. Also, I am discerning. I can't just be with anyone even if I find them attractive or interesting. There always must be something more, but I can't really describe that 'something.' Plus, the guys in school all looked like walking Q-tips to me. When they spoke to me, I blanked out. I mean, their big Q-tip lips were moving, but I didn't hear a word that they were saying," Rose explained, a bit frustrated. "Sometimes, I'd start to daydream about being on a beach far away or talking with someone else. Sometimes, I'd picture Raoul Bova instead of them. These guys were so boring and arrogant, but Anil was different. Anil was real. Anil was just himself. Now everything has changed, and sometimes I wonder if everything really changed or it is just too much, and I just don't want to do this anymore. This toxic dance that we are doing, Anil and I…"

The next time Rose saw Anil was during finals. She had made up her mind that that type of encounter could not happen again. After gaining a bit of clarity, Rose realized: *I had finals. I am graduating. I must pass a bar exam. I need to focus on my career. This would be my first one-night stand.* In her mind, she had simply slammed the door on the Anil indiscretion. She walked out of the classroom, visualizing herself slamming a door in his face. Just as she was exiting the building, Anil caught up to her.

"Hey," he said.

"Hi," Rose gulped. *Why do I have to keep gulping? Stop fucking gulping.* she thought.

"How do you think you did?" Anil asked, smiling.

"Eh. I always leave tests thinking I failed. You?"

"It was what I expected," he said with a sweet smile.

Anil was frustratingly smart. He never studied. Rose studied her ass off to get a B. He didn't do a thing and would get an A. Rose thought, *This is another immature reason why I should just walk away, right? Who can compete with that?* She found his level of intelligence exciting. He was so beautiful and smart.

"Well, I should go. Ya know…to study." She gestured toward the book.

"Okay, see you later," he said like he knew something that Rose didn't know.

Rose just smiled. *Nope. Nope. Nope.*

NO see you later, she thought. *I must study. I have my career and the bar.*

Rose walked home trying to focus on how she was going to study and pass the bar, except all that really kept creeping into her head were thoughts of Anil and her fucking. That night while she was sitting in her living room, she heard a knock on the door, and her dogs started barking like crazy. She got up and walked over to the door slowly and opened it.

Anil's big brown eyes were looking right at her. She could not believe that he just came to her apartment. Uncontrolled thoughts flooded her head. *Why is he at my house? Maybe this is a mistake? What am I twelve? Just say hi. Say it. Say HI damn it!*

It must have been some time that she was just standing there. He finally said, "Hi."

"Oh, hey. Sorry, I was just…"

"Thinking?" He smiled.

"Yeah. Uh…come in," Rose said, looking at the floor.

"I came to study with you. You seemed stressed last time we spoke," he said. "I love your dogs," he said as he bent down and got right in their faces. "They are beautiful." He smiled.

No one ever did that with Rose's dogs. Most people were terrified, but not Anil. He was playing with them in an instant. They both rolled over on their backs so he could pet their bellies.

"Oh, great," Rose said.

"You sounded worried about the last final, and I thought maybe you could use a study partner," he said, matter-of-factly. *At least he had a book in his hand,* Rose thought.

"You mean, you thought you could help me understand the next subject?" Rose asked, trying to make it sound like they were just friends and she didn't think that he was the most adorable person she had ever seen.

He just smiled and sat on her couch. She sat next to him, and they opened their books. Then they started making out. Then they started tearing at each other again, so much so that they fell off the couch. They were going at it so heavy that she forgot where she was for a moment.

Suddenly, there was a heavy wrap on the door. They both jumped up and scrambled for their clothes. *Shit, I forgot the guys were coming to study*, Rose thought. Anil was putting on his jeans calmly, and Rose was looking for her bra that somehow managed to work its way under the couch.

After they put themselves together, Rose opened the door.

George, Jake, and Pruniv were looking at her and backing up because her dogs were barking so loud.

"Hi, sorry guys. I forgot we were supposed to study today, but good thing Anil remembered. He's here too. I guess he beat you," Rose explained, flushed.

The guys shuffle slowly into her apartment. They brought scotch and started pouring drinks and opening the books.

"Rose, you look like a mess. You nervous about the test? You always worry, and then you do fine," George said.

"Thanks, George," Rose said, stifling a chuckle as she looked over at Anil.

Anil smiled back and said, "I don't think you look like a mess, Rose."

"Why thank you, Anil."

Rose blinked away her blushing. "I don't know why, but I didn't want anyone to know that I was fucking Anil," she told Amy. "I guess I just didn't want any questions or maybe it was that I thought it was only going to last five minutes. I don't know maybe I was worried someone would steal my joy. I knew Anil had been around the block. He wasn't known for his lack of partying and women. So maybe I didn't want anyone to know he had another notch on his bed post… and that that notch was me. Maybe I just didn't want to answer any questions when it went nowhere with Anil. Whatever the reason was, Anil agreed to keep our trysts quiet," Rose explained.

"We got through our finals just fine. By this time, Anil and I had been seeing each other since the beginning of April; by then it was the middle of May. We kept our promise to one another and didn't tell a soul. I appreciated that he was discrete. He totally honored my request for silence, and that made me feel more comfortable around him. He was kind to me and fun to be around," said Rose.

"Anil would come to my home and play guitar and sing. What I came to find out was that he wasn't only smart but also talented. We bonded over our love for music and the arts. He also shared my love for zombie movies and didn't pitch a fit when I made him watch a marathon with me. Anil had a great sense of humor and came up with the craziest sayings out of the blue. He was so funny that sometimes I laughed until I cried. That time with Anil is what I think keeps me going in our relationship—the bonding, the fun and the laughing," Rose shared.

"The week of graduation, I was so excited. My family was preparing to come in for it. I was shopping, cleaning, and preparing my apartment for their arrival. I really liked that old apartment. It was this old Victorian home that had been divided into two apartments. I think it was built around the 1920s, but who knows," Rose explained. "All I know is that it was so old that the home ran on oil, but it was so charming. Some of those doors even had those old big key holes. The ceiling had wooden beams. My apartment had three bedrooms and a nice size kitchen. It was freshly painted a light green, and the sun filled the apartment in the day because the windows were so large. There was a huge front porch where I loved to sit and read. Right in front of the porch sat a large walnut tree," described Rose.

"It felt like graduation day came so fast. I was so happy to be done but sad at the same time to leave. Our graduation was outside in the park across the street from the school. It was such a nice, bright day. The school had set up these big tents outside with a stage for us to walk up and collect our diplomas," she said.

"My family made sure that they had a nice spot in the middle. I could see my mom with her fire red hair. She is shorter than me with green eyes and pale skin. You would never know that she is the Sicilian side of our family. She looks Irish. Her husband, Daniel, sat next to her. He is tall and thin with blonde hair and blue eyes. He is a nice-looking man with a kind soul. My sister sat next to Daniel. She has the biggest, bluest eyes you have ever seen. My sister is tiny. She is pretty, but you can tell she has no idea how pretty she is, and that makes me sad," Rose shared. "Sometimes I feel like it is a waste that she does not know how beautiful she is, because she could rule the world with her looks and brains. Instead, she has the soul of an angel, so soft and sweet. My brother didn't come to my graduation… I guess he was too busy," Rose said, looking a bit sad.

"That day, the ceremony began on time. We walked to the graduation song and took our seats. We had the typical ceremony with speakers and cheers. Anil was seated up front, diagonally from me. I could hear him shout and scream when they called my name. He was so loud that I was pretty sure he was the only person screaming. After the ceremony, the school had set up tables with food and champagne. They had tables filled with cheese, crackers, shrimp, and other fancy hors d'oeuvres. We all gathered under the tents with our families taking pictures and introducing our families to our friends. It was all idle chatter that I hated, but I pulled through all the bullshit. I think I pulled through because I was focused on looking for Anil," Rose admitted.

"I kept looking around for him, but it was like he vanished. It was a little bit of an empty feeling not seeing him. I had spent all morning getting ready so that I could look nice when I met his parents. I mean, I knew he wasn't going to introduce me as his girlfriend, but I figured that I would at least meet them. I wore my hair down with large curls. I highlighted my green eyes. I had this blue dress that showed my lean figure and long legs. I even wore matching heals. I really put effort into my appearance, which I don't ever do, and I did it for him. I was disappointed," Rose explained.

"I didn't see Anil at all that day, but he called me that afternoon," Rose started.

"What happened? I was looking for you after the ceremony," Rose said softly. She didn't want to sound annoying, but inside she was really upset and hurt.

"Oh yeah, my parents wanted to take pictures. Then we left and went to have lunch," Anil said.

"Oh. Well, did they enjoy the ceremony?" Rose half-asked holding back the tears. She could not believe how hurt she felt.

"Yes," Anil answered. "They had a nice time. You looked pretty. Did you hear me scream for you?" he asked sweetly.

"Yes," Rose said with no emotion. *It was so illogical for him to like me and not want to spend time with me*, Rose thought. *Maybe he didn't like me. Maybe it is just a fling and I read too much into it.*

"What are you doing tonight?" he asked.

"I'm driving into Boston with my family to have a nice dinner.

Are you still house-sitting for me while I go to Canada for a week?" Rose asked. Rose's mom and sister were taking her on a graduation trip to Canada. They had rented a condo on a lake. The three of them were driving up all together. It was their first trip just the three of them. They were staying in Montreal and visiting Old Quebec.

"Yes, no problem. I'll stay at your house." He sounded almost relieved that Rose asked, almost like he knew what he did was really fucked up.

"Okay. Well, I'll call you tomorrow," Rose said with disappointment in her voice.

"I guess I should have pressed for why he didn't stick around so that I could meet his family," reflected Rose, "but we had only been dating for two months, and I didn't want to be too emotional or needy. So as usual, I kept it all inside. I just met him the next morning for morning sex before I left for Canada. I pretended that everything was okay, that I didn't care, and that it didn't hurt my feelings. Now I realize that I should have just blurted out how I felt. I should have said to him, 'What you did is fucked up. Why didn't you introduce me? What am I to you?' I should have said all that instead of nothing," Rose said.

"When I got back from Canada, it was time to start studying for the bar. They tell you that when you start studying, the bar should be your *only* focus. You should not start a new project or relationship. You are supposed to study at a minimum for eight hours a day. That isn't exactly what happened when I was studying. I have always had a hard time following the rules, so naturally I kept on seeing Anil and studied for the bar about four hours a day. I did go to the bar class every day and sat at a table for four hours studying for the exam. I listened to those speakers as they tried to make the driest subjects entertaining. No one can make property law interesting. Sorry, but it isn't possible," Rose said, shaking her head.

"Every day after the bar class, I would walk into my apartment and Anil would be waiting. I guess he never returned my key after I returned from Canada, and I never asked for it back. Big surprise, right? I didn't know what he did all day, but judging by his eyes I'd say he smoked pot," Rose said flatly.

"When I'd walk in, we'd immediately began going at it. I don't think I ever ate lunch. We just started having sex from the moment I walked in the door until the next morning when that horrible bar course would start. I guess we ate here and there. I did get really skinny, so maybe we just ate each other. I think we ordered take-out a lot. What I hadn't noticed—and I don't know how I didn't notice—is that Anil never went back to his apartment. We were just suddenly living together, and I never noticed. Is that possible? I mean he slowly moved in; suddenly all his stuff was there. My friends all say that I was oblivious, and I just saw what I wanted to see. Is that true? Do you think I just ignored the situation? Do you think I hid in my head?" Rose questioned.

Amy looked up from her notepad. "What do you think?" she asked with a knowing smile.

"I see now that I just see what I want to be there," admitted Rose. "I create my own story in my head. I live there, ya know, in my head."

"That is your escape, Rose. Everyone has a defense," Amy

explained. "You would hide in your head when your parents fought or did things to hurt you, and now it is just automatic." Amy said it in a way that reassured Rose she would be just fine.

"He and I partied pretty hard, but just together. I spent the morning studying the bar, and every night and weekend I was studying Anil. In all that time, he never really spoke about his family. He didn't say much except that they were from India," shared Rose.

"Late one night, he and I were drinking a bottle of Crown and eating Chinese food. His mom called and I could hear her because he was sitting next to me. I remember that night like it was a minute ago. I think it impressed me so much," Rose started.

"Hi, Anil," his mother said on the other end of the phone. Her voice was so loud and high pitched.

"Hi, Mom," Anil said. It is surprising how well he could speak after drinking so much.

"What are you doing? Are you studying?" she asked with a heavy Indian accent.

"Yes. I am studying every day," he said. He sounded irritated.

"Are you studying with friends? Are you focusing? You know you have to get a good job," she pressed.

Anil got up and poured himself another glass of Crown. Rose could hear his voice crack; it was almost childlike. By this time the two of them had more than enough to drink.

"Mom, I am dating someone." He blurted it out, almost like ripping off the Band-Aid.

"Oh. Who Anil?" Rose could hear what sounded like surprise in her voice. "How are you going to study if you are distracted?" she asked in what seemed like protest.

"Mom, you would like her," Anil explained, almost like he didn't hear what she was asking. "She graduated law school with me. She is smart and very pretty." He tried to go on, but his mother interrupted and asked, "Is she Indian? Are you going to marry her? You know you must get married?" she continued.

"No, Mom. She isn't Indian," he sighed, "but she is like you. She is smart and kind. You are going to really like her. She is helping me study for the bar," he explained like he was trying to convince her.

I was helping him study? Really? thought Rose.

"Is she American? Where are you now? Anil?" She questioned and her voice grew louder. She almost squawked when she spoke. It was like she knew he was with Rose.

"Yes, she is American," he said.

"Anil, American girls sleep around. They are manipulators." She stated like this was a fact.

"Mom, I'll call you tomorrow," he said. It sounded as if he had given up on the conversation.

"Are you drinking, Anil?" she questioned.

"No, Mom. I have to study." He looked annoyed.

"You shouldn't drink, Anil. It isn't good for you. American women tell you what you want to hear. They manipulate. That is how they use sex." She was so persistent, and she sounded so strong in her convictions.

"Mom, love you. Talk to you tomorrow," he said. She started to talk, but he hung up on her.

Anil looked at Rose. "She is so cute. She is so interested in who you are. She seems excited to meet you," he said.

Rose questioned what he was saying. She was wondering if she'd missed something. To her, it sounded like an interrogation. It was one question after another. She was horrified. Her head was spinning. Anil noticed her distress. He looked at her and said, "It is hard to like my mom, but please try."

"I guess that was my warning…that statement. That red flag that people talk about all the time. Well, he held that flag high in the air, but I missed it completely. I mean who says that their mom is really hard to like? Really? Who says that? I play that moment in my head over and over, but instead of saying to Anil, 'Are you fucking kidding me? That conversation was insane, and this is insane,' I opted for the better approach of burying my head in the sand. I said, 'Oh babe, your mom and I are going to be best friends.' Clearly, I make well-thought-out choices, but love isn't a choice, right? Or is it?" Rose asked.

Amy just looked up and smiled.

"Who knows, maybe it is a choice? I don't know," Rose continued. "I can choose what is best for me. I didn't see it at the time, or I didn't want to see it, but this wasn't best for me. Now when I replay that moment in my mind, I see Anil holding that big red flag high in the air above his head. I picture myself running through the door like some cartoon character, with smoke under my feet and that outline of myself in the wall. I guess, as women, we really try to make it work, and we become totally blind to the inevitable—therapy, couples therapy, a child, and maybe divorce."

Amy just continued listening quietly, and Rose continued her story.

"It was July quick enough, and the exam started to creep up on us. We were all feeling the stress and pressure. Our exam would be at the end of the month. Anil went home to Indiana to visit his family for the Fourth of July. His grandmother had flown in from India, and he wanted to spend some time with her. I just stayed at the apartment and studied with friends," Rose explained.

"Anil texted me, but not nearly as often as when I was in Canada or when he was at my apartment and I was at the bar classes. I guess that was to be expected. He only called early in the morning or late at night while he was visiting his family. The difference wasn't noticeable," Rose reflected.

"I heard my cell ring, and I saw his name pop up on my screen. I got butterflies at once. It was noon on the last day he was there, so I was really surprised to hear from him," Rose began.

"Hi, babe," Rose said with clear excitement. "How are you doing?"

"I'm good. I miss you," he said in almost a whisper. It was as if he was trying not to whisper, but at the same time not be heard.

"I miss you, too. I can't wait until you come home," Rose replied sweetly.

"What are you doing for the fourth?" he asked.

"I think I am just going to study," Rose said.

"You always study, Rose. Why don't you do something fun for a change? You are going to pass that exam, babe." He said it like he just knew it was going to happen. The truth was, Rose was really nervous, and inside she was completely panicked. She knew she had not been focusing on that exam nearly enough. She had been focusing on how many blowjobs she could give Anil a day instead.

"I'm not like you, Anil," Rose explained. "I really must study. It does not come natural to me," she started giggling. "You are like a super genius."

He laughed. "Okay, Rose. If you say so."

"Well, you are good at everything you do," Rose said, trying to be sexy. She tried to be like Angelina Jolie, but then she just felt awkward. Rose thought he found her quirkiness endearing, and that made her feel at ease.

Rose was about to continue when she heard his mom screeching in the background.

"Anil!" she squawked. "Where are you? What are you doing outside?" Her voice was so loud.

"I'm on the phone, Mom," Anil answered, obviously irritated.

"It is lunchtime. Come inside," she ordered indignantly.

"Okay, Mom. I'll be there in a second," he yelled back.

"Hey, babe. I'm sorry. I guess it is lunchtime. I should..."

Rose heard his mother again screaming in the background.

"Anil. Get off the phone. Your Nana ji is waiting to have lunch with you. Who are you talking to? Get off *now*!" she screamed.

"Okay!" he yelled obediently. "Bye, I'll call you later," he said in that low voice. Rose didn't get to return the goodbye before he hung up. He didn't call her later, either. She didn't hear from him until the next morning.

❦

"Anil came home July 5. I was so excited to see him, because at this point it was the longest we had been away from each other. He walked through the door, and we just started to make out. His lips were so juicy. I really loved kissing him," Rose reflected, her eyes floating around Amy's office in a happy daze. "We laid in bed that night talking. I honestly don't remember what we were talking about. I do remember we had just had sex when he turned to me and took a deep breath and said, 'I love you, I really love you.' He said it with such intensity that it took me a moment before I understood what he was saying. I never heard anyone say it the way he said *I love you* before. What I didn't realize and what I know now is that you can be a man's love…and he can still have no problem being completely selfish. I think I hung around those lesbians too long, because when they loved it was forever," Rose said matter-of-factly.

"At this point, it was just a few weeks before the bar exam. I guess Anil could tell that I was really starting to panic. I started to study all the time. I even asked him to leave the apartment so that I could study. I am sure it became abundantly clear that I was officially freaking out when I took a practice exam and failed it and I broke down in tears. I get annoyed when people cry, and I was annoyed with myself, but it happened anyway. I also wasn't sleeping or eating. The reality was starting to sink in that I officially had fucked up and not studied nearly enough. As I took practice test after practice test, my anxiety became worse and worse. I even walked around the apartment screaming '*Fuck*!' I had lost it, completely," Rose shared.

"The day finally came where I had to take the exam. Anil wasn't sitting for this bar. He was waiting until he found a job and was going to take the bar wherever he got a job. The exam was an hour away, so I spent the night at my friend Sam's apartment. He was also taking the bar. Sam had a fantastic apartment with every luxury. He was very clean, and his home always smelled wonderful. I loved sitting on his rooftop deck overlooking Boston. It amazed me that Sam always had trouble finding a nice boyfriend. He was tall and nice-looking. He dressed impeccably and always looked good. He drove a BMW 5 Series, and he had great taste in food and wine. Sam and I had planned to take the bar, then take a small vacation together in PTown," Rose explained.

"I found a parking spot in front of Sam's condo, which was usually nearly impossible, and I parked my car. He must have been waiting for me, because as soon as I pulled up, he opened the door with a big smile and ran out to open my car door. Sam was always the complete gentleman. It was sad sometimes to me that he was gay because he would be the perfect boyfriend," Rose said with a smirk.

"Hi Sam," Rose said with a huge smile as she popped out of the car and wrapped her arms around him and gave him a huge hug.

"Hello, beautiful. I have been waiting for you. I made us dinner. You look like you could use a dinner or two or three. Have you been eating at all?" He sounded so concerned. Rose just smiled and shrugged. They headed inside.

"I'm starving." Rose ignored his eating comment and stuffed a piece of bread in her mouth.

They sat down at his table and had a fantastic meal. Rose looked at Sam and started to laugh. "This is like the last supper before I fail the bar," Rose laughed.

Sam smiled, "Stop, Rose. You are going to be fine. We are going to bed early, and I have three alarms set. I have mapped out a place on our walk to the bar exam for us to grab a bagel and coffee," he explained with confidence. This was why Rose loved Sam. He was so put-together and attentive. He took care of everything, and she didn't have a single worry. The pair finished dinner, took a last look at their books, and finally went to bed.

It turned out, they didn't need three alarms because Sam's condo was under an airplane path; when the plane went by, it looked like it was going to come through the window of his room. They both popped up in bed screaming as the bright light of the plane entered the room and then they immediately looked at each other and began to laugh. He looked at Rose and said, "Sorry, Rose. I completely forgot to tell you about that." Rose just laughed.

"The two of us walked to the center where the bar was being held and checked into the exam. The check-in process was insane. They take everything away from you. We had to turn out our pockets. They have your fingerprints on file, and, well, it is overwhelming. Sam and I were seated far from each other, which sucked," Rose shared with Amy. "The tables were small and wooden, and there were about three thousand people stuffed in the room. The exam was two days of hell. My fingers were killing me from writing for hours on end. I think that my finger retained the shape of the pencil for days after the test." Rose looked exhausted just talking about it.

"When the exam was over, Sam and I drove to PTown in complete silence. It was as if we had both undergone electric shock treatment. We ate dinner that night in a restaurant in complete silence. I don't even remember where we ate" she explained.

"Anil texted me the entire time I was with Sam. He texted me so much that Sam took my phone away. I am pretty sure that Anil was drinking to the point of inebriation. His texts seemed different and disconnected," continued Rose.

"Sam and I spent what felt like three days at a restaurant drinking margaritas and staring at the ocean. I thought we were drinking, drink after drink. As it turns out we were so out of it that we each actually only had two Margaritas that entire day. I was completely convinced that I had just failed the bar exam. I was surprised when Sam looked over at me and with the saddest face said, 'I just failed the bar.' 'Me too,' I'd said with excitement or maybe relief that someone else had failed. Then we just started laughing. I think we had gone mad. We left the beach early in the morning. At least on the way home we laughed and joked. We listened to music and danced in our seats. We celebrated our failure. I adore my Sam," Rose said, shaking her head and smiling.

"When I got home, I thought that my apartment would be neat and clean like I had left it. I understand that I am a bit extreme. As I explained, all my personal items are organized. My clothes are color-coded and my shoes are all in clear containers, but Anil had made a total mess. There were dishes piled in the sink and all over the counters. Beer bottles were everywhere. The bed was unmade, and sheets weren't changed. My home was a frat house. He looked worn out and I was pissed," Rose said.

❧

"What the hell happened?!" Rose asked; she was so angry.

"I missed you. I got a job interview in Georgia." Anil had a huge smile on his face.

Rose could not focus. She was pissed about her apartment and about hearing the words "interview in Georgia" come out of his mouth. He came up and kissed her.

Rose instantly stopped being angry.

"Georgia? You mean the South?" Rose asked, shocked.

"Yea," he said. "I want you to come on the interview with me. We leave in two weeks."

"Okay," Rose said with a bit of fear in her voice. Everything was happening so fast. She had never been to the South before. But she figured, why not?

Anil explained his parents knew someone, and they had gotten him the interview with this boutique law firm. If only they knew this connection would cause a giant shit show.

Anil called his mother that night to tell her that he was going on the interview and that he was taking Rose. That is when all hell broke loose. Rose could hear her squawking into the phone like a pterodactyl taking flight on the hunt for food.

"Why does she have to come? This is your interview. She does not need to go with you. She is trying to manipulate you. Does she have a job? Who is paying for her trip there? It is you, I bet! That is how these women are when they meet professionals," she went on and on.

Rose thought, *If my mother had spoken to me like that, I would have lost my mind. I would have yelled at my mother, and then there would have been crying and more screaming and then more crying.*

For Anil, it seemed like just another normal conversation. It was like a conversation that he seemed to have every day, almost like he was discussing the weather. He calmly stated, "Mom, she is coming to help me. I asked her to come with me. She isn't manipulating me. She can iron my shirts and stuff," Anil explained. Rose could hear his mother, and it sounded as if she flew into a rage.

"Your father and I can come and help you! We can iron your shirts and help you prepare for the interview. How can this girl help you more than your parents?" she asked. Anil calmly said into the phone, "I already bought the plane tickets, Mom."

His mother screeched into the phone, "YOU PAID FOR HER TICKET!? Who is this girl that you would pay for her ticket? Are you getting married?"

Anil sighed, "No, Mom we are not getting married. She is just helping me on my interview. I will talk to you later. Love you." I could hear his mother continuing to screech as he hung up the phone.

Anil and Rose took a flight to Georgia. It wasn't a long flight, but he managed to have two scotches on the rocks. When they got to Georgia, they rented a small car and checked into a hotel. The hotel was nice and big, and the room was a suite with a sitting room. The company that was looking to hire Anil had rented the room and car. The hotel wasn't too far from his interview, which was a good thing.

That night, Rose ironed his shirt and helped him pick out a tie. They both didn't get much sleep that night. Rose could feel Anil tossing and turning in the bed. In the morning, Rose got up early and grabbed breakfast for him while he got ready. She gave him a kiss and wished him good luck. He looked nervous and a bit awkward as he walked out the door.

Rose was at the hotel all day. She just hung out, watched TV, and ordered food. It must have been around four when Anil walked into the hotel room with a big smile.

"How did it go?" Rose asked, but she could already tell it went well by the smile on his face. He kissed her and said, "They want to take us both to dinner tonight."

"Me?" Rose asked surprised.

"Yes," he said, and he gave her a huge kiss.

That night they went to a small restaurant near the city. All the partners and their wives were there. The wives all had a glass of white wine in front of them. *They were nice enough...for being carbon copies of one another*, Rose thought. Rose just watched them with morbid curiosity. They had their three-carat rings and didn't work. They talked about shopping and shoes. Rose wasn't paying attention. She was off on a beach watching dolphins play in the water in her mind. As you would suspect, Rose had nothing in common with these women. They had a nice dinner. Anil and Rose let them speak.

Weeks later, Rose was packing the house while Anil was checking his email. At this point, Rose knew she was moving, she just didn't know where or when. Anil looked up from his computer and said, "They made me an offer."

"Really? That is great. What did they say?" Rose was excited for him, but a bit nervous at the same time. She was nervous because she wanted to be with Anil, but she didn't want to leave New England.

She loved New England. She liked the people, the food, the smell of berries in the air and the ocean.

Anil started to read the offer. It was a good offer for someone fresh out of law school. He seemed to grow more excited as he read.

Rose looked at him and said, "Wow. Georgia. Are we sure that we want to go to Georgia?"

"This is a good opportunity for me, Rose. I am going, and you can come if you want, but I am going either way," he said with conviction.

Rose was stunned. *Seriously??? I can go if I want. Did he not want me to go? Why would I want to be with someone who could say that to me?* Rose thought. Sadness washed over her. She felt small inside, and, somehow, she was able to justify those words and make the decision to go with him.

After Rose finished her story, Amy looked up at her and asked, "Why did you decide to go Rose?"

Rose stared at her with this vacant expression and said, "I don't know why I would go with someone who could say that to me. I don't know why I would want to go when he said that. When he said I can go if I want…I realize now that it was at this point where I set the stage for what would come. I set the stage for being second, and I set the stage for this chapter in my life," Rose said with sadness in her eyes.

CHAPTER 2

"THE NEXT FEW WEEKS were filled with packing and spending time with the friends that remained behind after the bar exam," Rose explained. "I thought that Anil and I didn't have a lot of stuff, but I guess over the previous three years, we had really accumulated a lot of shit. We went through each room and began to pack..." Rose trailed off.

"Well, I went through each room and began to pack. Anil just watched me. He was confused, like he didn't know where to begin. I boxed all our law books and notebooks. In my head, I thought, *We need these for when we both have jobs.* I guess I figured we could use them for research. In reality, we would never look at them again," Rose said to Amy with a giggle. "I began to throw away any items that seemed unnecessary and kept only the necessities. I labeled all the boxes and cleaned each room. I never realized how big that apartment was until I had to pack up and leave it behind. I still look back on that old Victorian home with such fondness. I miss that place so much." Rose paused for a moment with a faraway look in her eyes.

"I was in the kitchen making dinner when I heard Anil talking on the phone in the living room to his parents. I could hear him tell his mother that I was going with him to Georgia. I could hear the whole conversation. The walls were bare, and without any furniture and high ceilings, his conversation with his mother echoed throughout the apartment. Plus, Anil does not know how to whisper. He is a loud talker," Rose explained.

"Hi Mom," said Anil. "Hi, Dad. We are moving in three weeks," Anil said with hesitation. "Yes, *we*, Mom." Anil sounded annoyed as he tried to quiet his voice.

"She isn't manipulating me. No, we are not getting married. Yes, you will meet her. No, she does not have a job yet, but she is looking for work. No, Mom. That would be great if you helped us, Dad. You could just help us load the truck. We are driving and towing one car. It is a fifteen-hour drive, and we are stopping at a hotel. Yes, Dad, if you came a few days before we leave that would be helpful. Yes, Mom, those are dogs. No, Mom she pays for them. Yes, animals are expensive. No, she is clean. You would never know there are dogs here. Yes, they are big dogs. Okay. Sounds good if Dad comes for a few days. Bye, guys. Love you." Anil hung up the phone and walked toward the kitchen.

Rose continued to make dinner and pretended that she didn't hear the conversation. When he walked in, she said, "Dinner is almost ready." He smiled at her and told her that his father could help them move, and he would be there in two weeks. Rose smiled politely at him and began to set the table. "That sounds great," she said. "We could use the extra help." Rose had a lump in her throat after hearing the conversation.

"My dad is excited to meet you," Anil said with a smile. Rose didn't believe him, but she thought, *I am going to try anyway and make this work.*

"Make things work. What a funny phrase," Rose said to Amy through a slight laugh. "I guess I thought that once they met me, things would change. In my head, I had convinced myself that they didn't have a daughter, and I could be like the daughter they never had. I had this vision of his mother and me cooking and doing our nails together. I swear I had this ridiculous play in my head. You know like you see in a movie where they show these scenes with music of happy families at the beach, dinner, and on vacation. We are all in the water splashing each other as the waves come to the shore. That is what I held onto, that vision. The vision of a big happy family. I never saw the wave coming that would suck me out to sea," Rose said flatly.

"So, were you excited to meet his dad?" Amy asked invitingly.

"I don't know," Rose said. "I wanted to be excited. I wanted to be happy. I guess I was excited and nervous. I really wanted his parents to like me. I was so tired of being the outsider. You know, in my family I am the outsider looking inside, and I guess I just wanted to fit in somewhere for once. I had an opportunity to create that experience. The experience of being wanted and to fit into a family and be normal. I have always felt out of place. My family takes family vacations, but they don't invite me. This was my opportunity to be invited. You know, to be part of something normal," Rose concluded.

Amy looked up. She smiled and said, "Normal? Your normal or someone else's normal?"

"I don't know what is 'normal.' I wanted it. I think I wanted to be Anil's normal, because that normal I could create. I could create that for us. That was an illusion. I see that now. There is no normal. You just have to make peace with yourself," Rose shared.

"I knew I was going to miss New England. It was the middle of September. The weather was warm, and the smell of apples was in the air. We were all packed, and I just wanted to enjoy my last two weeks of my sleepy New England town. Anil and I went on walks and hiked with the dogs through trails. The last week of September the huge trees began changing colors. The colors are some of the most beautiful I have ever seen. The reds, oranges, and purples are brilliant. The air feels crisp and smells fresh and clean. I wanted to savor it all because I didn't know when I would be back again. As it turns out, it has been years since I have been back to my sleepy New England town. Anil and I keep saying we are going to visit, but we never do anything to make a visit happen," Rose explained.

"We went out to eat almost every night and chatted at dinner for hours. It was nice and, for a moment, I felt good and safe. I felt like I had made a good choice, and this was real love," Rose said as she rolled her eyes. "I used to believe in love, but now I think that love is an illusion too, except the love for a child. That is true love," Rose explained with conviction.

"The morning Anil's father was to arrive, we woke up early and took the dogs for a walk. We had all our stuff packed, and we had just a few big items that we had to get into the moving truck. We drove to the airport to get Anil's dad. I remember looking out the window wondering if his father was going to like me. After thinking about what I'd heard on the phone, I started feeling that pit in my stomach. As we got closer to the airport, the pit in my stomach grew stronger and stronger," Rose said with a pained expression.

"I saw Anil's father, Vishwa, standing on the sidewalk with a small bag. Vishwa is a small man, maybe five-five with salt-and-pepper hair, bulging eyes like a giant bug, and a large nose. He was wearing a pair of jeans that were pulled high up on his waist and a long-sleeve collared shirt. He hugged Anil, and Anil took his bag and threw it in the back of his car. Vishwa got into the back seat and shook my hand.

"It's nice to meet you," Anil's dad said with a smile.

"How was the flight, Dad?" Anil asked.

"It was good, very smooth," he answered with a heavy accent.

"How is Mom?" Anil asked.

"She is good. She is going to dinner with some friends tonight," he stated matter-of-factly. "Do you have everything packed and ready?" he asked his son.

"Yes," Anil said with confidence. "We just need to put everything into the truck."

"We can do it together, and it will probably only take a few hours," Rose said softly. "Do you like Chinese food?" Rose asked Vishwa. "We were going to grab some for dinner."

"That sounds good," Vishwa said. "I am a little hungry."

When they got to the restaurant, Vishwa looked over the menu and seemed annoyed. He immediately began complaining about the prices. He complained for over an hour as Rose's mind drifted off. She had been silent for so long that it startled her when Anil finally bumped her and asked, "How is everything babe?"

"Oh, it is good," Rose said. "I am just so hungry. Wolfing it down." She smiled at him.

When they returned to the apartment after dinner, Anil took Vishwa's bag and opened the door. "Oh, what big dogs," Vishwa exclaimed when they opened to door. "They are nice," he stated. "Very friendly."

Vishwa took off his shoes and began to walk through the apartment. Rose thought, *Vishwa is a quiet man, probably because he cannot get a word in with the incessant talking of Amita. He never smiles, but instead always wears an angry face. I never know if he is angry or he is just wearing his angry face.*

"Can I get you something?" Rose asked through a gulp.

"No, I'm fine," Vishwa said. "Actually, can I have some tea?" he asked.

"Sure! What kind would you like?" Rose asked with excitement to break the awkward air.

"Lipton is fine," he answered.

"Oh, I'm sorry, but I don't have that one. I have green tea, blueberry, orange spice, mango peach, chamomile, black, chai, and peppermint," Rose said, feeling proud of her selection. *One of those must sound good to him*, she thought.

"That is okay. I only drink Lipton," he said frankly. "Do you have whole milk? I like warm whole milk at night. It helps me sleep."

"Ah, no. But I have some almond milk. I do not typically buy whole milk," Rose said to him with a half-smile. *Great. Could this go worse? I mean seriously. I have a dozen teas and none of them work. Then for fuck's sake, whole fucking milk?* she thought. *Okay, just breathe. I am not giving up. There must be something that I can offer that he will like.*

"The TV is still hooked up," Rose shared. "Would you like me to put on a movie?"

Anil cut through this awkward situation. "Dad, I have a bunch of movies, some good documentaries. Would you like me to put one on for you?" Anil asked with a smile.

"Sure, that sounds good," he responded.

Rose was relieved to just watch the movie and not make any more failed conversation. She sat on the couch in complete silence.

The next morning, Rose awoke to clanging in the kitchen. The cabinets were being opened and slammed shut, and it sounded like the dishes were being slammed on the counter. She looked at the time—it was 5:30 a.m. She looked at her dogs, and they looked back at her as if she had interrupted blissful dreams; they didn't look happy. She stayed in bed and stared at the ceiling, listening to the banging sounds in the kitchen. After a half hour of noise, she left the bedroom. Vishwa was seated at the table, eating some cereal. He had made himself some black tea. *Hmm. I thought he only liked Lipton.*

"Good morning," Rose said to him.

"Good morning," he said. "Is Anil still sleeping?"

"Yes," she said. Vishwa seemed to not realize how incredibly noisy he had been, at six in the morning no less.

"I am going to take the dogs out for a small walk," Rose announced to Vishwa as he crunched his cereal. *He even ate his cereal loud. How can one person be so noisy?*

"Okay, have a nice walk," he said.

When Rose came back, Vishwa had lined all the boxes by the front door. Anil was still asleep.

"Thank you. That must have been a lot of work," Rose said to him as she unleashed the dogs. After a few moments of awkward silence, Rose moved into the kitchen to finish packing the food and spices. It wasn't long before Anil woke up and came out of the bedroom; he looked around with an amazed look.

"Wow, he said you guys really made some progress," he said.

"It wasn't me," Rose said annoyed. "Your dad moved all the boxes while I walked the dogs. I just finished packing the kitchen. I left you a bowl so you can have cereal."

"Thanks," he said.

"When are you getting the truck?" Vishwa asked Anil.

"We can leave as soon as I am done eating," he said to his father.

Anil finished his cereal, and then he and his father left. When they returned, they had the truck. It was a medium-size truck, but it would do the job. They all started to load the truck with boxes and furniture. Vishwa kept commenting on items that the couple should leave behind. In his view, it seemed the bare necessities were all they should keep. He certainly had a lot to say when it came to throwing away personal items.

"You should leave the TV. Why do you need a TV? Cable is expensive, and there are only a few shows worth watching," Vishwa said with authority.

"I like my TV. I like to watch my movies, and we have a Blu-ray player," Rose said, trying to hide her irritation.

It didn't take long for the three of them to load the truck. After they were done, Rose jumped in the shower and offered to take everyone to lunch. Vishwa didn't think she should spend the money, so they finished the cold cuts in the refrigerator. *I was going to use those cold cuts to make sandwiches for the road, but whatever*, Rose thought. The apartment was bare, except for a few last items. Rose walked around the apartment and reminisced how she found that old place and how excited she had been to begin her new life in that old Victorian home. They were going to leave early in the morning. *At least I had one more night here in this old place*, Rose thought.

"The next morning, Anil and I packed up the rest of the truck and quickly walked the dogs. We dropped Vishwa off at the airport and headed south," Rose started. "We didn't have a home and were planning on staying at an extended stay until we could find a rental close to Anil's work. We didn't have any real plans at all. We were driving to Georgia without knowing where we were staying or what we were doing, and it felt kind of good," Rose said with a soft smile. "It was freeing not having a plan. That trip was fun. We laughed and listened to music. We were excited for the future. The trip was only fifteen hours, but we stopped at a hotel and snuck the dogs inside to sleep for the night. It was nice to take a break in the middle of the drive. It was fun to sneak two eighty-pound dogs into a nice hotel. We giggled every time they barked," she said.

"Once we got to Georgia, we had to find a kennel to board the dogs for a few days. We got lucky and one of the partner's at Anil's new firm had fur babies and gave us the name of a great kennel. Once the dogs were safe and sound, we began to look at homes for rent. It didn't take long for us to find an overpriced, small ranch-style home close to his work in Atlanta. We moved in quickly. Within four days we had driven from New England to Georgia, found our new home, and began living together. I was so excited and nervous," Rose explained.

"Everything was happening so fast. We moved the entire truck into the house and set up the bed. Anil went and dropped off the truck, and I picked up the dogs. There were boxes everywhere, and that night we decided to go down the street and grab takeout. We set up the boxes as a table and sat on the floor and ate our dinner. It was fun. We were drinking wine, laughing, and talking about our future, our dreams. Anil didn't start work until Monday, so I had a day to get his clothes together for him and make sure he didn't go to work all wrinkly. As we were laughing and kissing and just being silly, Anil's phone rang. He looked at his phone and went into the other room. Most women would assume that when their boyfriend goes into another room to speak it is another woman that is trying to take her place. My other woman was Anil's mother, and she wasn't trying to take my place—she wanted me *out* of the place," Rose explained, looking Amy right in the eye.

"Were you able to hear what their conversation was about?" Amy asked kindly.

"I could hear him talking, but I could not make out what he was saying. However, I could hear the tone in his voice, and that pit in my stomach grew. I could hear him pacing back and forth in the room. When he came out of the room, I could tell that he didn't know how to tell me what he was about to say. But then it came out of his mouth, and I felt ice water hit my face.

"In two days, my mom and dad will be here and stay for three days," Anil said, then he poured himself another glass of wine.

Rose looked around at the room in boxes and clothes strewn about the floor. "What? Everything is still in boxes. Why? I need time to clean and put the house together," Rose said. "We just moved into this house."

"They do not care how the house looks. They are going to the coast for a week, and they are going to stop here on the way," he said.

Rose could feel her face getting red and her voice shaking. "But I care what the house looks like. I want to make a good impression. I don't want your parents to be uncomfortable. Why don't they go to the coast and then come here? That gives me more time to put the house together," Rose said to him.

"You are being ridiculous. My mom wants to see the house and my new office! These are my parents; they are coming to see me," he said, sounding really annoyed.

"They can still see the house and the office. I just don't understand why it has to be before they go to the coast?" Rose said, staring at Anil like he had a third eye.

"Why are you so difficult, Rose!? Why does it always have to be your way? No one cares how the house looks, only you!" Anil snapped and stormed out of the room.

Rose just stood there like a deflated balloon and watched him leave.

"I remember being so upset," Rose said shaking her head, looking around at Amy's shelves absentmindedly. "We were not even in the house *one* day. I thought it was ridiculous. I could not believe that Anil didn't understand. I could not believe that he would not just suggest that they come and visit on the way back from the coast. What was the harm in that? What I didn't realize at the time was that they were not coming just to see Anil. They were coming to inspect, make suggestions, and take back control. I could feel my anxiety overpowering my body," Rose explained.

"The next two days were filled with me frantically unpacking and putting the house together. I was so frustrated. We had moved into the home so fast that the landlord didn't have time to clean the house. My first job was scrubbing the entire home. The renters that were there before us were clearly not the cleanest people. I spent hours scrubbing and unpacking. The home was so dirty, I had to scrub all the cabinets and line them with cabinet liner. I had to put the beds together and fix up the room where his parents were going to stay. I was so pissed as I was putting together their room. I wanted to scream. I did all this while he was at work! I was doing this for *him*," Rose explained.

Rose could see Amy making notes as her face became red with anger. She looked at her and took a deep breath. Rose began to worry she was overreacting. *Maybe I am not having a normal reaction*, Rose thought. She began to judge herself and what she was sharing with Amy.

Not being able to take it anymore, Rose finally asked, "Does it seem ridiculous to you that I wanted to put the house together before they came?" Rose was worried her reactions would seem childish to her therapist.

Amy merely smiled at Rose and gently said, "No. You wanted to make a good impression. You wanted them to like you. You wanted to make a home. I do not think you were being ridiculous. I think Anil was being selfish."

"Yes," Rose said with a nod of her head. "I did. I really wanted them to like me. I really wanted to show them that I was good for Anil. I wanted them to see how much I cared. Anil thought I was being 'crazy and dramatic,' as he called it, my reactions, dramatic. I guess he thinks that I am dramatic because I am so animated when I speak. I don't know, he just always calls me dramatic. He made fun of me because I like all the cans to face in one direction in the cabinets. He thought it was funny that I wanted the home perfect before they came. Does it matter that I wanted to have everything perfect? Is that crazy?" Rose asked again with complete frustration. "I didn't ask him to help; I did it all. I didn't ask him to clean, cook, shop, paint, or do laundry."

Amy laughed, "No, it isn't crazy or dramatic. It is a normal reaction. If you want the cans all in one direction, then he should support that and not make fun of you. He didn't meet you in the middle. Maybe he does not know how to meet you in the middle, but it is important to remember that he is a grown man and has the ability to learn. He chose not to learn," Amy explained.

Rose considered Amy's point for a moment, then began again.

"The morning on the day that his parents were to arrive, I slid out of bed. It was hard to get out of bed. I had not slept well the night before, and my eyes were burning from being so tired and being subjected to bleach fumes from all the scrubbing and cleaning. Anil had already left for work, and I was alone to finish up the house. I cleaned up the rest of the house and jumped in the shower. When I got out of the shower, Anil called to tell me that his parents had left and should be at our house by dinnertime.

"You do not have to cook," Anil said. "My mom made a bunch of food, and she is bringing it. So, you can just relax."

"Great," Rose said. *I think he really has no clue what it takes to put the entire house together by myself on such short notice*, Rose thought privately.

Anil came home about twenty minutes before his parents arrived. He opened the door, came in, and gave Rose a hug and some flowers. "My dad called and said that they are a few minutes away," Anil shared.

"Okay," Rose said through her nerves. *Sometimes when Anil speaks, he looks like a little boy*, Rose thought. *Maybe that is his way of getting what he wants, to throw an innocent little look. Maybe?*

There was a knock on the door, and Rose could feel that pit in her stomach. She put on her happy face, and Anil opened the door. His parents blew into their home and took off their shoes. His mom and dad gave him a hug. His father said hello to Rose with the emotional energy of sand. His mother introduced herself in a civil manner. It was as if Rose was being introduced to the ice queen and king.

In her mind, Rose saw all the walls freeze and ice run up the windows. She gulped, trying to breathe the last bit of air in the room. They immediately began bringing in bags and a cooler. His mother commented on Rose's dogs and went into the living room and let them out into the backyard. His mother said, "Wow, these are big dogs. I'll just let them in the backyard. That is what dogs like—they like to be outside."

Amita is a small woman; she looks as if she weighs around one hundred pounds. She has big brown eyes and a short bob haircut. She, like her husband, has lived in the United States for at least thirty-five years, but she still has a heavy Indian accent. For Rose, it is surprising that for her size she is such a force, almost a tornado. She moved like a woman on a mission, like a linebacker moving around the field in a football game. There was nothing soft and dainty about her.

Anil brought their suitcases into the guest bedroom. Amita, Anil's mother, started to unpack the cooler and put the food away in the refrigerator and the freezer. She started opening cabinets and finding the dishes to set the table.

"Where are your napkins?" Amita asked as she rummaged through the kitchen.

"Here", Rose handed her a bunch of napkins.

"These are expensive napkins," Amita said with what sounded like clear disapproval.

"I like them," Rose stated stubbornly. "They are nice and thick."

They all sat at the table. Amita made a plate for everyone but Rose. She said that she didn't know what Rose liked.

"Where is the microwave we bought you?" she asked Anil.

"It is in the spare room," he said. "We are using Rose's microwave. It is newer," he said.

"The microwave we bought you is very nice," Amita insisted. Rose could see her frustration; her spoon was slamming against her plate.

"So, how was your drive?" Rose asked, trying to break the rhythm of the spoon hitting the plate. *There is still hope for her to like me*, Rose thought. *After all, we just met. I need to try harder and put forth the olive branch. I just want her to see that I am good enough. I get it. She is a mom who loves her son and wants the best for him.*

"It was good," Vishwa said.

"Your salt does not have iodine in it," Amita said with a tone that sounded critical. "I read the label, and it does not say 'with iodine.' You need iodine in your diet," she continued.

"I see," Rose said, trying not to slap her indignant look off her face.

"Did you put the curtains up?" Amita asked.

"Yes, I hung them," Rose said proudly. Rose was excited for her to see what she did.

"Don't you think they are too close to the vent? You may be blocking the air vent," she said. "If you block the vent, then you may be spending more money on your heating bill."

Rose got up and began to clear the table. Amita was on her feet immediately, and she started to clear the dishes with Rose. The two were washing the dishes at the sink when Amita turned to Anil and said, "We have a realtor to start looking at a home for you. We can go tomorrow during the day and start searching. I have a few homes for us to look at tomorrow. I think I found a nice one for you. Our friend Zaina used this realtor and she liked her. She said that she is good."

Rose felt like a bucket of ice water hit her in the face. She was stunned. They had just moved into this home, and they didn't know the area or anything. *I don't want Amita to pick out my home,* Rose thought. Amita turned off the water and pushed Rose with her little body and said, "Now I am going to have a look at this house."

She said it in a low voice and turned and walked toward the living room. She began to go through the house. Rose could hear her opening the closets and doors. *This is unnerving*, Rose thought. It horrified Rose that Anil didn't see any issues with his mother's behavior.

That night, Rose went to bed with a massive headache. As she was slipping into bed, she turned and said to Anil, "Your mom was crazy today. She pushed me out of the way and in an almost evil voice said, 'Now I am going to have a look at this house.' Anil, it was unnerving."

Anil looked right at Rose and said, "Babe, I am sure she didn't mean it that way."

"What?" Rose popped up and her head began to pound. "She went through the house like a whirlwind. She pushed me out of the way! She was mean." Rose felt her eyes bulging from her head.

"Babe, I am tired," Anil said in a frustrated tone. "I am sure she didn't mean it the way you took it. It was probably her accent that made her seem angry to you."

"Whatever," Rose said, hurt and annoyed. *Is he kidding me? He really believed that her accent was the reason I thought she was being an asshole.* Rose pulled the covers up and tried to go to sleep.

Rose woke up to the sound of slamming and loud talking. It was one cabinet slamming after another. Amita spoke so loudly that Rose had to look to make sure she wasn't in the room. She took her pillow and put it over her head to drown out the noise, but she also darkly hoped she'd smother herself. *At least my head isn't pounding anymore*, Rose thought. But she hated what she saw in the mirror after not sleeping well. Rose turned on the hot water in the shower in the hopes that hot water would bring color to her pale skin. She stood in the shower for ten minutes, and she finally felt like she had peace. Unfortunately, Rose didn't know that her day was going to be anything but peaceful.

When she got out of the shower, she could smell food cooking and could hear Amita telling Anil that Rose was a manipulator. Anil's mother was saying that Rose wanted his money, and a good Indian girl would wait until they were married to have sex. When she spoke, it wasn't a conversation but more of a lecture. Ironically, these conversations would happen every time she spoke with Anil, and this would ensure some predictability in Rose's life.

Rose got dressed and walked down the hall. She turned into the kitchen, and Amita was at the stove cooking. Vishwa was showing Anil townhomes that were for sale, which he and Amita had chosen as candidates for his new home. It was understood that once Vishwa and Amita had found one that they liked for Anil, they would give Anil the money for the down payment for the home.

"Renting is throwing away money," Amita said. "Listen to your father. He knows how to make money grow. You spend too much money, Anil. You must focus on your job, family, and preparing for retirement."

Rose couldn't take it anymore, she finally broke into the conversation, saying, "I do not know if we want to buy a house on this side of town. I do not know where we want to live."

She turned around and looked Rose right in the eyes and said, stretching out the words, "*We*? Is it *your* money? I do not think so." Then she turned around and left the room leaving a path of ice behind her.

The rage that she created in Rose could have blown up a small island. *We will not go house hunting*, Rose thought. Rose pulled Anil into the bedroom to talk.

"Your mother is out of control!" Rose said. "Why do your parents think it is okay to pick out our home?" Rose could feel fire shooting from her eyes and face.

Anil whisper screamed back, "They are only trying to help me. They want me to have a good future. I am sure you misunderstood my mother, and besides, I didn't hear her say what you are accusing her of saying."

Rose wanted to choke him, but instead she screamed whispered back, "What? Because you didn't hear her, she didn't say it? Are you kidding me right now? I am not having your parents pick out my home! Your mom and dad can pick out their own home. We just moved here for fuck's sake! You fix this and make it stop or I will!" Rose stormed out of the room, shutting the door firmly behind her.

The next morning, Rose awoke to another symphony of clanging and banging. She walked into the kitchen to find Amita cooking and heating up Indian snacks she made for Anil's office.

His parents left around 11:00 a.m. to bring the snacks to his office. They came back around 3:00 p.m. talking about his office. Amita was so proud that everyone tried her snacks.

"When are you going to get a job?" Amita snarled at Rose.

"I am looking," Rose said to her.

"Well, you shouldn't be so picky. You do not have to practice law right away. You just need a job," she said to Rose, as if she had plans to live off her son.

Rose just looked at her and said, "Right." She walked into her bedroom and sat in there with her dogs until Anil came home from work.

Once he arrived, Amita and Vishwa immediately began critiquing Anil's employer. She voiced her opinion like it was gospel. She had an opinion for every person in his office. Then she and Vishwa began to talk about how good it was that his coworkers met his parents.

Was she serious? Rose thought. *He is a grown ass man, and his parents made snacks for his work like he was in kindergarten and they were bringing the cupcakes.*

Amita and Vishwa had made dinner plans for all of them at their friend's home. They had known the couple for years. Zaina and Abdel were from Lebanon and had met Amita and Vishwa when they first moved to the United States. Zaina and Abdel also had two boys, and their boys were close in age to Anil and his brother.

Rose got out of the shower and began to pull out something to wear. Anil looked over at her and said, "Make sure you wear something conservative."

Rose could not believe that had just come out of his mouth. She looked him dead in the eyes and said, "Oh, sorry. I will put my stripper outfit away. Did you really just say that to me? When have I ever dressed inappropriately?"

He looked like he felt bad. He hugged her and apologized. "I'm sorry. I am just stressed out." Rose hugged him back. She could understand how he would be stressed out. His parents were suffocating.

They all poured into Rose's car, and she drove to Zaina and Abdel's home. It was in a really nice neighborhood about thirty minutes away. The homes were big and lined with trees. Rose parked her car in the driveway, and they all walked up to the door. As soon as the door opened, she could smell the food cooking. She was starving and it smelled so good.

They were greeted at the door by a very attractive woman, who Rose learned was Zaina. She was dressed well. She looked like she had been dressed from a Talbot's magazine. Her hair was salt and pepper and looked whimsical. She had big almond-shaped eyes and high cheek bones. She welcomed everyone into her home with a big smile and excitement. Her husband was silent. He had a big smile and shook his head politely. He was tall with grey hair. He was dressed in gray dress pants and a white shirt. Rose would find out later that he had a stroke and lost his ability to speak.

They went inside and sat down in the living room for snacks. Another couple was seated on the coach. They were Anil's age. They didn't say much, but they seemed nice.

Zaina had some nuts and sweets set out on the coffee table. It was a very formal room, and she seriously liked pink and Ethan Allen furniture. The group was eating some snacks when Anil asked Rose if she would like a Coke.

"That would be great," Rose said. Zaina told Anil that there are cold drinks in the refrigerator, and that he could help himself. Anil came back with the Coke, opened it, and handed it to Rose. "Thank you," Rose said just before she kissed his cheek.

A little while later, the group sat down and had a nice dinner. Amita kept peppering the young guests with questions. She asked the young girl if she was going to get married. The young girl replied, "I am married. This is my husband." She asked when they were going to have children, what they did for a living, and where they lived. I really think Amita missed her calling as a world-renowned interrogator. After the meal, everyone helped clean up and then they were given a tour of the home before dessert.

Dessert was fun experience. Zaina asked Rose if she would like some dessert. "Sure," Rose said, excited to try something new. Amita looked at Rose as Zaina put a large piece of dessert on her plate.

"I will take a small piece," Amita said looking at Rose. "I do not want to get fat."

Rose immediately started thinking about how she had gained about ten pounds. *But Amita didn't know I had gained weight. She'd just met me!* she thought. *What a bitch thing to say.*

Rose took a huge mouthful of that cake.

After dessert, they all helped clean up, said their goodbyes, and left. Rose drove home in silence while Amita talked about the home and how well Zaina was doing. She went on and on and on. They pulled in the driveway, and Rose jumped out of the car and took a breath of air like it was her first one ever. She walked into the house.

It was only nine, but she looked at everyone and said, "I'm exhausted, and I am going to bed. Goodnight."

Once again, the next morning Rose was awoken by the sounds of pots and pans banging, doors slamming, and loud talking. Rose's dogs looked at her as if they blamed her for the intrusion and noise. Anil was out cold. *I guess he grew up with this loud ass family, so he was used to it*, Rose thought. She got up and let the dogs out. Then she made herself a cup of coffee and listened to Amita talk at her husband in the kitchen. Vishwa got up, and Rose could hear the sliding glass doors open.

"How old are you?" Amita asked abruptly.

Rose had been told to lie. Rose told her that she was Anil's age.

"How old is your sister?" she persisted. *Great, now I have to do math*, Rose thought. *I became a lawyer so that I didn't have to do math.* I made her sister six years younger than her actual age.

"How old is your brother?" Amita continued. Rose made her brother only two years younger than his age. All she kept thinking was that she was never going to remember all these lies.

"Oh, so you are the oldest child. What does your sister do for a living? Is she married?" she asked, as if she was taking a bright light and shining it in Rose's face. The interrogation had begun. *I mean why not? She has me alone,* Rose thought. *But I am going to remain positive. Maybe she just wants to get to know me.*

"No, she isn't married, and she is a counselor." Rose was trying to keep her answers simple.

"What about your brother? Is he married?" she asked.

"No, he isn't married. He is an accountant." Rose responded.

"Does your sister have a boyfriend?" Amita continued

"Yes."

"How long have they been together?" she asked.

"They have been together a while," Rose said.

"What about your brother?" she continued.

"He has been seeing someone for a while," Rose said through a tight smile.

It went on like that for over an hour. When Anil came into the kitchen, Rose gave him a kiss good morning. She stood up and walked into the bedroom for a hot shower. While she was in the bathroom, Anil and his mother got into a huge fight. She was upset because he got Rose a soda at her friend's house. She felt as though Rose should have gotten her own drink.

"Why did you get her a drink?" Amita asked Anil with annoyance.

"I was getting her a soda, Mom. She wanted something to drink," he explained.

"She can get her own soda. Can she not get up and get her own drink?" Amita yelled.

"Mom. I got her a soda! It wasn't a big deal, and I should not have to explain this to you," he yelled back.

"She is lazy. She does not have a job, and she is using you! She is a manipulator!" Amita yelled.

"She isn't a manipulator. If you don't like the way I act around my girlfriend, then you can leave," Anil said with conviction.

"You are choosing her over us?" She screamed and began to cry.

"No, Mom! You are making me choose. She didn't do anything," Anil said, a frustrated look creeping into his eyes.

"Fine! If you are choosing her over us then we are leaving! You are choosing some girl over your mother and father. Come on Vishwa.

Let's pack our things and go! Anil is choosing his girlfriend over his parents," she yelled.

Rose must have been in that shower for at least thirty minutes. Once the water turned cold, Rose got out of the shower and got dressed. She took a deep breath, opened the door to the bedroom, and walked into the hall. She saw Anil close the front door; his parents were leaving.

"What's going on?" she asked.

"They are leaving," he said.

Rose was confused. "But I thought that they were not leaving for another day or two."

"They decided to leave early," he said.

"Is everything okay?" Rose asked.

"Yes," he said.

Rose wouldn't learn about the fight that had occurred until a year later.

Anil did get a phone call from his parents when they arrived home. One of his family's childhood friends was getting married, and Anil was invited to the wedding in Washington, DC. His mom told Anil that Rose wasn't invited and that she felt uncomfortable to ask.

This didn't sound right to Rose, so she asked Anil, "You were invited to a wedding without a plus one? That does not make sense."

"My mom said that it is only going to be close friends and family, Rose," Anil said.

"Yes, but usually they have a plus one," Rose said.

"What are you saying, Rose? That my mom is lying? She doesn't lie!" he said sternly.

"I am not saying she is lying," Rose said. "I just think that maybe she didn't tell your friend you were living with me. I think your friend would have given you a plus one if she knew. I think your mom is up to something."

"Rose, seriously. Give it a rest. You always think the worst about my parents," Anil said, with what sounded like irritation.

"Fine, Anil. We shall see," Rose said as she walked away.

CHAPTER 3

Rose looked exhausted when she looked up at Amy. "When the fall holidays started, we had been in our home for about three weeks. The house was built in the early seventies, but the landlord had pumped some money into the home and updated the house. I was disappointed that it didn't have a garage, but it did have a large carport. The entire house had new hardwood floors, which I loved. I liked the small entryway because you didn't have to walk straight into the living room or stairs when you entered the house. It was cool there was an actual small foyer. The foyer was big enough where you could put a small seating area for guest to take off and put on their shoes or coats. The kitchen was through a small open doorway on the left. The countertops were a dark green granite, and the cabinets were painted white. To the right of the entryway was a long hall with a guest bathroom and two spare bedrooms on the left; the master bedroom was on the right. The master bedroom had a nice size bathroom with a large Jacuzzi tub that didn't work. Our living room was the largest room in the house, with the laundry room through a door at the back of the living room. The living room had two massive windows and a sliding glass door with a gap that let all the bugs into the home. I had to stuff the gap with this foam to prevent bees and other bugs from coming into the house. The best part of the home was opening the sliding door to this raised stone patio with this huge backyard. I loved that backyard. It was like a forest in a fairy tale. There were these huge trees and stone walkways with massive berry bushes that filled the backyard. The fence was hidden by bushes and shrubs whose flowers filled the air with a sweet aroma. This backyard made you feel like you were in the middle of the woods instead of the city," Rose said, her eyes growing misty.

"In between pumping out resumes, I was fixing up our home. Anil was making good money, and for the first time, we were both just breathing and having fun. Anil was at work, and I had spent the days cleaning and putting the house together. We didn't have real furniture in law school, so we had to buy almost everything for our little home. We went out on the weekends and purchased furniture. During the week, when the furniture was delivered, I arranged the new furniture. I put our bedroom together. I put our nightstands on either side of the bed, and I covered our bed with this pretty comforter. It was bright with flowers and lots of color. I put neutral curtains on the windows that let in the light. I put photos on the nightstands along with lamps. I was so excited. I walked into the living room and looked at our new leather couch and chair. I put two throw pillows on the couch and smiled. I even had time to hang the curtains in the living room before Anil came home," Rose shared.

❧

Anil was going to be home in forty-five minutes. Rose was a mess. She hadn't even showered. She finished picking up and ran into the bathroom. *Shit, I didn't even think of dinner, but I did see a pho place down the street that looked yummy*, Rose thought. When Anil got home, she took him on a tour of their home. She showed him all that she had accomplished. He seemed happy, and they ended up in bed having their crazy monkey sex. They got up and went to the pho place, which ended up being delicious. They drank wine and laughed at the people walking down the street. They made up a story for every person. Anil and her just clicked. They were both nerdy and quirky. They got each other, and it was nice.

"Okay," Rose said. "Look at that guy in his suit getting into his fancy car. What do you think?"

Anil smiled as he played the game. "I think he is getting into his car and meeting his friends at the gentleman's club because he has no life and he does not want to hear his six kids screaming."

"Ha!" Rose laughed.

On the way home, they picked up pumpkins for the front porch and candy to hand out to the kids on Halloween. Rose had wanted to get mini chocolates, but Anil insisted that the hard candies were the best. So naturally, they bought both. They had so much candy that they filled two huge bowls. They even carved the pumpkins and toasted the seeds. They decorated the house and snuggled on the couch and watched zombie movies. The dogs were in heaven when their popcorn hit the floor; they loved the popcorn.

On Halloween night, Rose made her traditional chili with all the toppings. They even had candied apples. Rose bought Anil his favorite beer and herself her favorite wine. They dressed the dogs as bumblebees, which they seemed to love. Anil and Rose had a blast handing candy to the kids with their bumblebees. The kids would giggle when they saw the dogs, and Anil was right—the hard candy was a success. Anil was great with the kids. They seemed to love him. He gave them handfuls of candy at a time. Trick or treating ended around nine, and they plopped themselves on the couch and relaxed. To Rose, it seemed like everything had gone back to normal between them. There was no stress or pressure. It was just Anil and Rose. All was good. But all good things must come to an end.

Anil gave Rose a kiss and asked, "Do you mind if we drive to my parents' house for Thanksgiving this year?"

Rose gulped. *How could I say no when I was going to ask him if we could spend Christmas and New Years with my family?* She smiled and said, "Of course. I don't mind. It will be fun." *Fun?* Rose was still hoping that his parents would like her and that all would be well. her stomach knew better, and the pit started forming.

"I am going to see if George wants to meet us there since he doesn't like spending time with his family," Anil laughed. "What do you think? Do you mind?"

"I don't mind. I think it is a good idea," Rose responded. "Poor guy. I mean he just can't catch a break, but he does have a pretty sweet job," Rose said. "Would you mind spending Christmas and New Years with my family?" Rose let out in almost a burst. "They haven't met you, and my mom's house is amazing. You don't have to buy the tickets," Rose continued. "My mom offered to buy our tickets."

Anil leaned over and kissed Rose. "It sounds fun. Maybe we will even have snow, and you can have that white Christmas that you always talk about," he said with a big smile.

The next day, the pair made breakfast and hung out. Rose made her morning call to her mother. Rose usually speaks to her at least once every day. Her mother was still living in Colorado; she had been since the whole family moved there from the East Coast when Rose was younger.

Rose's demeanor changed a bit when she started talking about her mother. "My mother is this little Sicilian lady. My mom is shorter than I am, but she looks young, like she's my sister. I know she looks young because she is about twenty years older than her current husband, and no one can tell the difference in their age. I mean I think she is pretty, but she is my mom."

Amy provided an encouraging smile.

"She always dresses very stylish," Rose continued. "She still picks out my clothes. My mom likes to look good, and she has these great legs that she loves to show off. She grew up in New York, but her parents were from Italy. My mom is a firecracker. Maybe that is why I am a firecracker. She always speaks her mind, which she calls 'her truth.' It is my opinion that her truth is just a green card for her to say nasty, bitchy things to me and get away with it. Then she can say, 'I was only speaking my truth.' I think that is the nature of a mother–daughter relationship. She has always helped me with my house and decorations. We have fun decorating and fixing things up. I have fond memories of us decorating together. My mom likes to have nice stuff. I mean she loves her stuff. She isn't a hoarder. She just really likes nice things. If my mom buys leather, then you can bet it is Italian leather. She is extremely talented and has this amazing eye. She decorates for a living, but she is extraordinary. She is one ambitious tiger lady," Rose continued. She was speaking almost in a state of stream of consciousness, not sure where the details would take her next.

Rose felt her throat tighten up. "My mom and I clearly had rough times. They were hard, but at the end of the day I truly believe she loves me, and I love her. She is my mom. She has been going to therapy to try and mend our relationship. I guess what I mean to say is that I think she tries and sometimes I feel that I am too hard on her."

"You know, my mother had me when she was young. I think when parents have their kids young, it can be tough because they are trying to figure shit out and then they have these little people who totally depend on them. Parenting is hard, but I think it was especially hard on my mother. She and my dad were so different…" Rose trailed off.

"I think I told you that my dad's family is from Naples. My father has dark hair and deep brown eyes. He is a thin man of average height. He and my mom met because of the war. My mom was friends with his sister and my dad's sister asked my mom to be my father's pen pal. He, on the other hand, does *not* care for material things. He is so very simple. He is a nice man. He does not speak much and likes to whistle. He was a talented painter and woodworker. My dad can do anything with his hands. He just doesn't have much ambition. My parents got divorced when I was seventeen. Did I tell you that already?" Rose asked Amy.

Amy leans forward and smiles, "Yes, some of that you told me, but it is fine. Maybe it resonates with you in some way."

Rose looks up and shifts again. "I usually spend holidays with my family, but this year was different. I would be spending the Thanksgiving holiday with Anil's family. Once it was decided, I picked up the phone and called my mom to explain," Rose began.

"Hello, queen," Rose said.

Hi, babe," Rose's mom said. Rose could tell her mom was happy to hear from her. "How's the house treating you?"

"Pretty good," Rose said, still trying to think of how she would tell her that she wasn't coming home for Thanksgiving that year. *I know she will be disappointed. Honestly so am I. I enjoy my loud Italian family. I mean yes, they drive me nuts, but I love them so very much*, Rose thought. *Also, my mom can cook like nobody's business. She can make a mud pie taste like chocolate cake. Her food is, well it is mouthwatering just thinking about it.*

"Did you have lots of kiddos for Halloween?" she asked.

"Yes. They were all so cute, and we dressed the dogs like bees. It was fun," Rose said.

"Did you take pictures?" she asked.

"Yes. I will send them to you," Rose told her. She could feel her throat tighten. "Mom, I am going to Anil's house for Thanksgiving,"

Rose said with hesitation.

"Oh, okay. I understand. You must do what makes you happy," she said. But Rose knew she was disappointed; the way she said it made it sound like she was disappointed. Then she said, "I mean, I'll miss you and I want to see you, but have a good time and we will talk every day. You must do what makes you happy." Rose felt guilt wash over her.

A few days later, Anil and Rose started getting ready to go to visit his family. Anil grabbed the last of the mail and looked at Rose. His face grew pale, and Rose knew instantly—they had received the results of her bar exam. *Holy shit, the results are here.*

"Okay, you open mine," Rose said.

Anil counted, "One, two, three!" He ripped the envelope and started to read the results. "The Board of Bar Overseers would like to congratulate you…" The most amazing feeling washed over Rose. *I passed the exam!* she repeated to herself. They both started to hug and kiss each other. They felt like they had conquered the world. *I passed the exam. Now, if I could only conquer Amita*, she thought.

This would be Anil and Rose's first Thanksgiving together, and Rose was excited and nervous to spend the entire time with Anil's family. She was looking forward to meeting his brother. She had heard a lot about him, and Anil said his brother was extremely smart and got an amazing scholarship to medical school.

They had to travel eight hours to Amita and Vishwa's home. They had to drive through the Appalachian Mountains. It wasn't a bad drive and the weather was great. It was a pretty drive through the mountains in Virginia. Rose had never driven through the Appalachians before. They listened to music, sang together, and talked while they drove along the windy roads. They packed snacks and a light lunch, which was a good idea because there weren't many places to stop. They ate in the car to save time, then they hit heavy traffic. It was terrible, but they laughed and had fun. In that moment, it seemed that Anil and Rose just clicked. They could make anything fun together.

They arrived at Amita and Vishwa's home around nine at night. They had been driving all day, and they were both tired and hungry when they arrived. They pulled up a long driveway to a large home—it was probably about six thousand square feet. To get to the home, you passed trailer homes and entered a development with all large homes. Every home sat on at least an acre of land. It made you feel as if you are crossing to the other side of the tracks, almost like a divider between the haves and the have-nots. They drove up the long driveway and parked outside the three-car garage.

They walked in through the garage and took off their shoes in a narrow hallway. Rose could see the kitchen straight ahead. The first floor of the home was all hardwood. It impressed her that there weren't curtains on a single window. The windows had the blinds on the inside of them instead. It was a very functional, clean home. The furniture was from all different decades and mismatched. The kitchen had an eighties table with that Santa Fe look. The office looked like Ethan Allen tried to have an Italian flare. The dining room had this large Victorian table and was all Ethan Allen, but there was art from Egypt and India. The living room had these oversized black leather couches with a reading lamp hanging over the couch. The coffee table was from the seventies, and the lamp was a brass lamp from India. The television sat in a corner on an IKEA table, and there was a Thomas Kinkade painting above the fireplace. There wasn't a lot of furniture, just the basics. There were family pictures on the walls and decorations from places they visited as a family. The basement was about three thousand square feet. The living area had a couch that was probably thirty years old, and the television was probably the same. *Maybe they kept it from their first home*, Rose thought. There was an old dining table next to the couch. Both bedrooms had a bed and dresser that were the same, and it looked as if they were bought from some furniture row type place. There was a storage room and a game room with a ping-pong table. Rose went to use the bathroom, and the home was so functional that the towel to dry your hands was pinned up so that it dried more efficiently.

George had beaten them to Anil's parents' home. George was sitting with Anil's brother, Arjun, and Arjun's girlfriend, Sarah. Arjun was tall, with jet black hair and dark skin. He had a pirate's smile. He clearly worked out, but obviously had no care for fashion; his clothing choices were purely functional. Sarah was a pretty girl. She was thin with a boyish body, pale skin, and blue eyes. Arjun gave a warm, friendly hug and his girlfriend followed suit. Vishwa and Amita offered a smile and a lazy hug to Rose.

"Was there a lot of traffic?" Vishwa asked them.

"It wasn't bad until the end," Anil said. "We sat for a long time, but it wasn't too bad." Anil plopped onto the couch.

They all sat on the couch and began catching up. George filled them all in on his latest crush, who is clearly giving him all the signals that she wasn't interested. Of course, George thought that she was really into him, and that she was the love of his life. Anil and Rose had been listening to this story for over a year; every time they hear it, the girl's name changes.

Amita began heating wonderful-smelling dishes. They were all starving. Rose's stomach was making all kinds of noises; she was actually excited to try some real Indian food, not some store-bought imitations.

Amita came over and handed Anil and George a dish. George just looked at Rose. Rose could tell he was debating handing her his plate. Rose thought maybe Amita just serves the men first. *Okay, whatever, when in Rome do as the Romans do*, Rose thought to herself.

But then Anil said, "Rose is hungry too, Mom. Did you heat something up for her to eat?"

Amita turned and said, "I do not know what she eats."

Rose looked over at Anil, and she saw the look on his face—confusion. She had spent time at their house. They all ate together.

It was clear Anil didn't know what to say, so he said, "Mom, she eats what we eat, food, remember?" Anil seemed annoyed, but it was clear he still didn't understand how mean and unhospitable she was being.

When Amita returned, she handed Rose a plate with yogurt and rice. Rose was shocked when she saw the food. She took it and ate it, but she knew the whole situation was weird and sad. She watched Rose eat the entire thing.

Rose felt like crawling into bed and disappearing under the covers. *I guess this is how she wanted me to feel, small and inadequate,* Rose thought. *It's not like I need help in this department, but thank you, Amita, for helping.*

Amy smiled, "Did you ever think that maybe she is jealous of you?"

"Jealous? Of what?" Rose asked with surprise. "I always thought that it was because I wasn't Indian. That she felt I wasn't good enough for her son."

"You think? Amy asked. "Did she make any of her own choices? You chose Anil. You chose your school and your life."

"I mean, Anil told me her marriage was arranged to his dad, but she got to choose from three suitors. She only met with Vishwa three times before she married him. Then he moved her to the United States away from her family. I guess Amita's mother was cruel to her, and she could never do anything right by her mother. I don't know. I think Amita is just the devil. I know she wanted to be a professor, but her husband wouldn't let her. I know she is amazing at her profession. She was an architect, but then she became a physical therapist after an accident. Now she runs the town's physical therapy center. I don't know...Now I feel bad for her, Amy. I feel bad." Rose stayed quiet for a moment.

"Anyway, I just wanted to get away, so I told Anil that I was tired, and he took me downstairs and showed me the bedroom where we were staying," she continued.

"I'll be down in a little bit," Anil said, and he gave Rose a kiss and went upstairs. Rose could hear his family upstairs. They were so loud, and the lack of furnishings, decorations, and curtains created an echo throughout the entire house. Rose jumped in the shower and stood there until she couldn't take the heat anymore. She got ready and went to bed. Surprisingly, she fell asleep with all the noise. She woke up at about three in the morning. She turned over and realized Anil wasn't in bed. She didn't hear anyone speaking upstairs, and the house seemed quiet and still. She got out of bed and put on her robe. She quietly went up the stairs. It was dark and the TV was turned off. Rose started to look around the house. She remembered that a bed had been set up in the storage room. *No, he wouldn't be in the storage room,* Rose thought. She quietly creeped toward the storage room. There was Anil, sleeping on the bed.

"Anil," Rose whispered. "What are you doing in here?"

"I was tired and I wanted to sleep," he said in a groggy voice.

"Why are you in this room, though?" Rose pushed.

"I don't know," Anil said.

"How can you not know? Do you not want to sleep with me?" Rose asked.

"No. I do. It's just my mom doesn't think we should be in the same bed because we are not married," he explained.

"Are you fucking kidding me right now? We live together! I am thirty-seven years old, and you are twenty-nine! Are you fucking kidding me? Get up and come to bed," Rose insisted. "I am not sleeping in this creepy ass house alone."

"Yes, but she doesn't know you are thirty-seven," Anil said.

"No, which is a whole other crazy, but she fucking knows you are twenty-nine, and you live with me," Rose said with serious irritation.

Surprisingly, Anil got up and came to bed. *I guess fucking her son's brains out in the bedroom is my way of retaliating*, Rose thought.

The next morning, Rose woke to loud talking and banging in the kitchen. Anil didn't wake, per usual. Rose got up and went upstairs and made coffee. It was Thanksgiving morning, and Rose was excited to make dinner for the family. Amita is a vegetarian, so Rose had planned several vegetable dishes to prepare.

"Good morning," Rose said.

"Good morning," Amita and Vishwa chimed.

"May I watch the parade?" Rose asked Amita.

"Yes," she said.

Rose sat on the couch, turned on the TV, and started watching the parade, like she did every year on Thanksgiving.

Amita sat next to her and began peppering her with questions. *She never stops talking, and I don't think she takes a breath when speaking*, Rose thought. Rose noticed she always started the conversation the same way. She was very sweet and seemed like she was really interested in getting to know you. She asked questions about you and your family. She wanted to know what you liked and about your childhood. Unfortunately, these weren't her true intentions. In reality, she was always judging and trying to manipulate. *For some fucking reason, I step into it every time*, Rose chastised herself. *I keep thinking if she gets to know me, she will really like me. A part of me feels sorry for her too. Another part of me wants to punch her in the face and it sucks. The whole thing sucks.*

"Do you watch every year?" Amita asked.

"Yes," Rose answered. "I have even been to the parade a few times. I really love it." Rose thought the conversation was going great, and she couldn't see there being anywhere for it to turn bad. They were chatting about a holiday parade, after all.

"Did you go with your mom?" Amita asked.

"Oh, yes, and her husband," Rose answered. "They came to visit, and we saw the parade and spent time together. We had so much fun. My mom is my best friend," Rose said. Rose could see her eyes get big.

"Do you speak to your mom *every day*?" she asked.

"Yes. I usually speak to her a few times a day. We talk about lots of stuff," Rose responded.

"Oh, wow. That is a lot. Anil does not call me *every day*," she said.

Rose felt that when a girl is close to her mother, then she listens to her mother. Eventually, she'd explained this to Anil. This is different than a mother who feels she has control and can control another relationship. *I guess that is because Amita tried to do that, and so did her mother. Maybe Amita wanted control. Maybe she wanted to control our relationship, and if my mom was in the way, then she felt like she could not control the relationship*, Rose thought.

"Well, guys are different with their mothers," Rose explained. "Guys usually don't call their moms every day. I think girls are closer to their moms."

"It is hard with sons," Amita said. "They bring home their girlfriends, and then their girlfriends act like this is *my* boyfriend." Amita's eyes doubled in size, then she said, "But he is *my* son, and if you are not nice to my son then you can just leave this house. I am the mother," she said with authority.

Every time this bitch is alone with me, she must pee on her territory. It's exhausting.

"Okay," Rose said. "Thank you for letting me know." She kept talking, but Rose didn't pay attention. She just wanted to enjoy the parade.

When the parade ended, Rose's phone rang. It was her mom. She just got up and walked into the kitchen to answer.

“Happy Thanksgiving, Mom.” Rose was so excited to hear her voice. It gave her a precious break from Amita.

“Happy Thanksgiving! How are you? How is the weather?” she asked.

“I am well. It is nice here. We don’t have any snow,” Rose said, knowing her mom will be able to tell by the sound of her voice that she wanted to cry. “When is everyone coming to the house, queen?”

“I think everyone will be her around three,” her mom said. “I have the two turkeys this year, and we have twenty people coming over,” she said with excitement. “I have been cooking all week.”

Rose and her mom have the same conversation every year, whether or not they’re together for Thanksgiving. Her mother loves the holidays. They both watch the parade, then when Santa comes at the end, they call the other and say “Santa’s here!” It is their *thing*. Rose’s mom also tells her that she has two turkeys, and that she has been cooking all week, every year, but Rose still loves to hear it, even though she knows it’s coming.

Anil finally woke up and came upstairs. Rose knew his mother being an asshole wasn’t his fault, but she still wanted to punch him in the face. Instead, Rose gave him a kiss on the cheek and said, “Good morning.”

“Good morning,” he returned. “Did you get to see the parade?” he asked.

“Yes,” Rose said. “I’m going to prep the turkey and get it started,” Rose said to him.

Rose started cleaning and basting the turkey. She put it in the pan and placed it in the oven. She started chopping the vegetables, and around the corner Amita came. She was fueled up and ready to go. She looked like a mini linebacker as she headed toward Rose.

"I watched *Rachael Ray*, and she said that when you make the turkey you should..." Amita's mouth was moving in slow motion, and Rose could hear sound and see her puppet face, but she really couldn't tell you what she was saying. She was just looking at her. She was going and going and going. She must have been going for at least ten minutes before Rose heard someone break in.

"Mom, leave her alone and stop interfering. You have never even made a turkey. You don't eat meat. Why don't you stay out of the kitchen?" Arjun snapped.

Rose turned toward the voice. "Hello. Happy Thanksgiving," she said to Arjun as she gave him a hug. Rose was so relieved to see him.

"Happy Thanksgiving. What are you making for dinner?" Arjun asked.

"Well, we are having butternut squash soup for the first course. Then we have mashed potatoes, stuffed mushrooms, stuffing, green beans in a butter almond sauce, broccoli, and salad. I made rolls. Oh yea, and macaroni and cheese. I am making it fresh," Rose said with a smile. "Anil and I brought all the ingredients with us, so I am prepared to cook." Rose's smile deepened.

"Sounds amazing," Arjun says.

Rose went into the dining room and began wiping the table and setting it for dinner. From there, she could hear Amita talking to her sons.

"Arjun, you have been with that girl for six years. You really need to marry her. You are not being fair to her," she said.

"Mom, she does not want to get married right now. I don't want to get married," Arjun said with what sounded like irritation.

"Every girl wants to get married," Amita insisted. "She has probably talked about it with her girlfriends, and she is probably wondering why you haven't asked her," Amita continued.

At that moment, George came up the stairs, and Amita began to bug George about when he was going to find a nice girl. *No one was safe from her.*

Dinner was ready around three in the afternoon. Anil's family had a nice tradition of sitting around the table and stating what they were grateful for before they started eating. They all sat down at the table and stated what they were thankful for this past year. Anil's mom is a cancer survivor. She had ovarian cancer, but she beat it. Almost every person at the table gave thanks that she was clear.

When it was Anil's turn, he said he was thankful that his mother's cancer being gone, then, as an afterthought, Anil said, "Oh, yes, I am thankful for my friend Rose." Amita shot Rose a sly smile, and Rose smiled back, imagining she punched her in the face.

They all started to dig into their meal. Rose served the soup first. Everyone was raving about it and she thought to herself, *This is a good start.*

"I love these stuffed mushrooms," Arjun said.

"This is good," George smiled while stuffing his mouth.

Everyone was eating Rose's food and enjoying the dinner. She looked over at Amita, and her plate had barely any food on it. She sat eating quietly like a bird, which wasn't typical of how she ate. She claimed that she was watching her weight, and that I used a lot of butter and cheese. *Oh I see how this is going to be!* Rose thought. There wasn't much conversation at the table. It was pretty quiet. They did talk about 401(k)s and IRAs.

After dinner, the guys watched football, and Rose got stuck cleaning with Amita. The only time that Anil got up was to get another beer, and his beers were adding up.

"Anil, that is enough drinking. It isn't good for you," Amita squawked.

"Okay," he said, but he didn't stop. By the time everyone was ready for bed, Anil was smashed and Rose was annoyed.

Rose woke up to banging and slamming. The music had begun. She looked over, and Anil was sound asleep, which irritated her. She debated on whether or not she should get up and grab coffee. After thirty minutes of debating, she got up and went upstairs to get coffee. She was pleasantly surprised to find Amita on the phone. She made her coffee and ran back downstairs to read in bed. Eventually, Anil woke up.

Anil looked up at her and smiled, "Good morning."

"Good morning," Rose said. "You really drank a lot last night."

"Yeah, I know. It was like a little party," he said.

"Well, you better hope your mom doesn't smell the weed," Rose said.

"True, but she doesn't know," he said. "Did you get me a coffee?"

"No. I didn't know when you were going to wake up. There is a whole pot up there," Rose said.

"Are you coming up?" he asked.

"Nope. I'm going to finish my coffee and then shower. I heard your mom on the phone, and it sounds like they want to take a hike and then get some coffee in town. Just let me know the plan," Rose said.

"Okay," he said, then he headed up the stairs.

About an hour later, Anil came down and said that they were

leaving in twenty minutes to go on a hike. While Anil jumped into the shower, Rose went upstairs and grabbed a banana to eat, then ran right back downstairs. Fortunately, Amita was getting ready, so Rose could avoid her.

It must have been seventy-five degrees outside. The sun was shining bright, and there wasn't a cloud in the sky. The trail was about a ten-minute drive away. When they got there, they all piled out of the SUV, and Anil and Rose walked ahead toward the trail. They were all talking and joking. Anil put his hand in Rose's as they walked. Amita came crashing between their hands and positioned herself between Anil and Rose. She said, "You are walking like a married couple."

Rose couldn't believe it. Arjun chuckled. George looked at Rose and Rose looked at Anil. Anil dropped back, grabbed Rose's hand, and said, "Mom what are you doing? We are holding hands." Then he gently pushed her out of the way. *He has to be embarrassed by her asinine behavior,* thought Rose.

"Well, you are not married!" she exclaimed.

"I am going to hold Rose's hand," he said, putting emphasis on squeezing it.

"You two walk around like a married couple," she said. "You are acting like a married couple. You are not married," she persisted.

Anil just ignored her and walked ahead. When she was out of sight, he lit a bowl and sucked so hard Rose thought he would suck in a tree. Arjun and George were right behind him. I guess that is how they deal with her. *Ya know, it isn't a bad idea*, Rose thought. She hit the bowl too.

As they walked through the woods, Rose could hear Amita going on and on, but she couldn't tell you what she said. Everything felt okay, Rose was relaxed. She just kept walking, and after a while, all Rose could hear was the sounds of nature. It was a great walk; this was the first nice time Rose could remember having with Anil's family. Before they went to the coffee shop, they all snuck ahead and hit the bowl again. Surprisingly, the car ride wasn't bad to the coffee shop, and when they got there, the conversation didn't annoy her. Rose was so happy having her coffee and eating a cookie. *Yup, all is well. Great, actually.*

When they got back to the house, Amita started cooking dinner. While she was cooking, Arjun and Anil's friends started coming over to the house. That night, they had a big fire going in a fire pit, and Anil and Arjun got shit faced. That is how the group would spend the next few days at the house—drinking and hitting the bong. What surprised Rose was that his parents didn't know. They didn't even seem to know that the boys were drunk. Although, Amita did run around telling Anil that he was drinking too much. Once she said, "Your eyes look funny." At the time, he was stoned out of his mind. *I guess ignorance is bliss.*

When Rose and Anil finally got to leave, the drive back was better. They didn't hit traffic because they had stayed an extra day. Anil hit the bowl a few times, and he seemed relaxed. Rose was quiet and just listened to music. When they got home, they unpacked the car and sat on the back porch and had some drinks. This would be the start of a ritual for them.

The next few weeks, Anil and Rose prepared for Christmas. They picked out a tree and decorated it together. They went shopping for their families and started sending packages. Rose did Christmas cards, and she started to bitch about Anil's mother.

Rose could hear Anil's phone ring. "Hi, Mom," Anil said.

"Hi, Anil," his parents said at the same time. "How are you doing?" they asked.

"I'm fine. We are getting ready for Christmas," said Anil.

"Are you alone?" Amita asked Anil. Rose saw Anil waiving for her to come over. Rose walked over to him, and he sat on the couch with her. He put his hands to his lips, signaling her to be quiet. "Yes, Mom, I am alone," he said as he put the phone on speaker.

"Dad and I have been talking," Amita started. "And we think that Rose is a manipulator. She is manipulating you. She acts like you two are a married couple," Amita continued, and Anil put his finger to his lips, reminding Rose to stay quiet.

"She isn't manipulating me, guys," Anil said.

"Well, she talks to her mother every day. That isn't normal behavior. Dad and I think that her mother is controlling her and running your relationship," Amita explained.

"Mom, they talk about stupid shit, like fashion and stuff," Anil said.

"Why doesn't she have a job yet?" Amita fired back. "Who is paying for everything? You? Women are manipulators. My friend buys all these clothes, and she does not tell her husband. He does not know, then she says they were gifts, but they weren't. That is how women are, and you are being manipulated," Amita squawked.

"Mom, she doesn't even like to shop. If you would just get to know her, you'd know that," Anil said.

"If she is so good, then why is she living with you? Why are you not married?" Amita screamed. "Even your dad thinks she is a manipulator."

Rose paused in telling her story. "I think the reason Amita uses Vishwa as the voice of reason is because the boys see him as more credible. Any time she wants the boys to think that she is right she will say, 'Even your dad thinks so.'"

Amy looked at Rose, "Do you think he is the voice or reason? He doesn't seem to say much."

I always thought he was just unhappy all the time because he never smiled. Maybe it was just because he didn't have a happy life, ya know? I know he didn't want to get married, but he made a promise to his mother on her death bed. He wanted to travel and do charity work all over the world, but instead he married Amita. After he made the promise, Vishwa put an ad in the paper looking for a good wife. He came from a very poor family, but he was educated, so Amita's father spoke to him. Amita came from a wealthy family, and as a result I think they gave Vishwa a hard time. The whole story seems so sad to me, but my husband's family speaks of it like this sweet love story," Rose shared.

"Okay, Mom. I have to go," Anil said. "I love you." He hung up the phone. Rose got up and went back to making dinner. Rose didn't know what she was supposed to say about what she'd just heard. Every time she heard Amita speak or she heard her name, Rose saw this miniature linebacker barreling through her life.

Rose didn't know why Anil started putting his mom and dad on speaker and letting her hear all the mean shit his mother was saying. She didn't know if he thought it would make things better, or maybe it was his way of telling her everything. All Rose knew was it caused some serious resentment toward them and ultimately him. It was hard hearing them say all this shit about her, and Anil didn't really fight for Rose. Rose wanted him to set boundaries and fight back, but he didn't, and it began to wear on her. When Rose thought about it, no one in that family ever really told that woman to step the fuck back. Everyone made excuses for her. If they weren't making excuses, then when they were drinking or smoking weed in excess when she was around. Rose also noticed that when she spoke, no one really listened. She could be in the middle of saying something, and her boys or husband simply walked away while she was speaking. They didn't even notice that they did that to her.

Rose finally had finished all the holiday shopping. She had shipped the last boxes to Colorado. Shipping boxes and sending gifts to other states wasn't cheap. Anil and Rose had one last task for their trip—packing. They were living in this nice state with warm weather, but they hadn't gotten rid of any of their winter gear. Anil and Rose packed like they were going to Alaska. They had two large suitcases each. Rose honestly didn't know why they packed so much. Anil called for a Lyft, and off they went to the airport with a month's worth of clothes.

The airport was a nightmare, and, as usual, they didn't allow enough time. The two of them had to run through the airport. Anil was annoyed because Rose's suitcase kept flipping over, and she kept running into people. They finally got to the gate, which was at the end of the terminal, and they were the last ones boarding.

"I hate flying," Rose said through a lump in her throat.

Anil smiled. "Why? You fly all the time? Aren't you used to it yet? It is relaxing, and you can read or just sleep."

"The turbulence freaks me out," Rose said. She knew the science behind it, but it scared her. "I can't sleep on the flight because I am freaked out, and I get motion sickness, so I don't read. I also always get the kid behind me who kicks the seat," Rose sighed.

Anil looked behind her; sure enough, Rose had a seat-kicker. She just looked at Anil and smiled.

"See," Rose said. Rose proceeded to ask the stewardess for a scotch. She needed the scotch for her nerves and to deal with the seat-kicker. "Um. Actually, I'll take two bottles, please," Rose said.

The flight wasn't long. It only took them three hours and fifteen minutes, which was about all Rose could stand, especially with the kid behind her. They got to Denver around six in the evening, so the ride to her mom's house took longer.

They pulled into her mom's driveway and were immediately greeted by her mother. She must have been waiting by the window and saw the car pull up. She always gets so happy when Rose visits; it was such a nice feeling for Rose.

"Hi, Mom," Rose gave her a big hug and a kiss on the cheek. "This is Anil," Rose said to her with a big smile. Her mom immediately gave him a big hug and said, "Hi, just call me Gia." My mother's husband, Daniel, gave Rose a huge hug and grabbed the bags and brought them into the house.

Daniel was a really nice guy. *He's so nice that it almost doesn't seem that he is for real,* thought Rose. He was smart and a top engineer. He was a tall, thin man with ice blue eyes and dark hair. He always wore a smile and could find the best in anyone. Rose had never seen anyone work harder than Daniel. He got up at five in the morning and didn't not stop until eight or nine at night. He did this almost every day of the week. Rose's mother didn't want for anything. He really loved her.

We walked into my mother's home and took off our shoes. Her house was impeccable; everything had a place. Sometimes, for fun, Rose would move an object a hair over just to see if her mother would notice. She always did.

Her mother's house was a two-story home with a basement. The entire house had hardwood flooring, and it shined like it had just been cleaned. Her walls had Italian scenes painted on them from a local artist. When you eat dinner there, it looks like you are looking out over Tuscany. Her house looked like it was out of a magazine. There was a loft that looked over the entryway, and a staircase that wound up to the loft. You could hear the water falling from a fountain on the wall; it was so peaceful. Rose's mom's house always had this fresh smell. The house was decorated for Christmas, and her mom had a tree in almost every room. The decorations looked like they had come straight out of a Hollywood movie.

"How was the flight?" her mom asked as they rounded the corner into the kitchen.

"Wow, Mom! It smells great! What did you make? I'm starving," Rose said to her as she gave her a squeeze.

"I didn't do much," her mother responded. It was clear that wasn't true. The table was set like Martha Stewart had been over; it looked beautiful. "I made spaghetti and meatballs, an antipasto dish, garlic bread, and a salad—nothing much," her mother explained.

"It smells wonderful," Anil said. "Thank you so much, Gia. This is great."

"Thanks, Mom. Everything looks amazing. The house looks great," Rose added.

After dinner, Daniel turned on his curved sixty-five-inch television and asked us what movie we wanted to watch. My mom began popping the popcorn, and Daniel poured some more wine.

This is great, Rose thought. They all just relaxed and watched a movie. After the movie, Anil and Rose went up to bed. Their room was decorated for Christmas; it even had its own tree. It was really nice and romantic with the Christmas lights filling the room. Anil and Rose slipped into bed and snuggled under the covers.

The next morning, Rose woke to the smell of coffee. She got up and went downstairs. Her mom and Daniel had music playing while they were making breakfast.

"Good morning," Rose said.

"Morning," they both said at the same time.

"How did you sleep?" Rose's mother asked.

"I had the best sleep ever," Rose said as she poured her coffee into a giant mug.

"Good. We just bought that bed and I put a topper on it," Rose's mom said as she put eggs and bacon on her plate. "Do you want to go shopping? I have to pick up the fish for dinner tonight," she continued.

"Sure, I'll take the ride with you," Rose said. Rose's mom makes the traditional seven fish dishes every Christmas Eve. She sets the table the night before, and they usually have about eighteen people for dinner. That year, they were only going to have twelve.

Around three in the afternoon, everyone started pouring into the house. Rose's sister and her boyfriend arrived first. Juliet looked like Rose, except she was skinner, shorter, and the pretty one. She had the biggest blue eyes that Rose had ever seen. She had a quick sense of humor and was always finding the bright side of every situation. She had this naivety about her that made her all the more charming. She had no idea that she was beautiful. Her boyfriend John was a nice guy. He was funny and fit into the family well. He liked to joke and tease. He was average height with jet black hair and brown eyes. They made a nice couple.

"Hey," Rose said to her sister and gave her a hug.

She smiled and gave her a huge hug in return. "I missed you. I'm so glad you came home for Christmas. I am going to get the gifts from the back of my car," she said with excitement. Before she left she said, "Hi, Anil, nice to meet you." She gave him a hug before shooting out the door. John greeted everyone and then walked out to help Juliet.

Rose's brother was right behind her with his best friend. Tony was so much fun. He was average height and slender with hazel eyes and brown hair. He had a passion for bike riding, so he could eat whatever he wanted and never gain weight because he was so active. His best friend was like a brother to Rose. They all grew up together. His name was Tray; he was a good-looking guy who was so vain that Rose was pretty sure that song was about him, but he had a heart of gold and would do anything for anyone.

As family and friends arrived, the noise level kept getting louder and louder. Like every good Italian family, all the action was in the kitchen. Rose's mom had a spread on the island in the kitchen. She had so much food, you'd think that one hundred people were invited. Every dish was placed on the island with care and decorated with trimmings. Daniel was running around helping her and making sure everyone had enough wine. Rose's brother came over and immediately started poking her in the arm like a child. Anil was talking to Juliet and trying to have a conversation, but Rose didn't know if he could hear what she was saying. Every time someone came to the door, everyone would scream "Hey!" Rose probably should have warned him that they all kind of talked over each other; it was very celebratory.

Dinner wasn't any quieter. Rose's mom kept bringing out the dishes, and everyone would cheer her on and say they were so full; they all kept stuffing their faces anyway.

Tony started sharing war stories from when the siblings were younger. He reminded Rose and Juliet how they made him eat ants when he was a kid. Everyone was laughing about how mean the sisters were. While they were giggling, Anil walked over to Rose and slipped a ring on her finger. He didn't say a word. He just put a ring on her finger, and the whole table went wild. *The best dinner ever*, thought Rose.

On Christmas morning, Rose could smell the coffee and breakfast. Her mom had this amazing French toast dish baking in the oven. Rose smelled bacon and pie. She was in heaven. Everyone started eating, then they started opening presents.

After opening up our gifts, Anil called his mother and father to wish them a Merry Christmas and to tell them that they were engaged.

"Merry Christmas, Mom and Dad," Anil said.

"Merry Christmas." Rose heard them return the greeting.

"Mom and Dad, I have something to tell you. Rose and I are engaged!" he shared with excitement.

"What? Engaged, you mean to be married?" Rose heard his mom say.

"Yes, Mom. We are going to get married," he explained.

"When are you guys going to get married?" she asked.

"I don't know, Mom. We have not picked a date yet," he said to her.

"Well we are doing the engagement party. Her parents are responsible for the wedding," Rose heard her say. "What is her mom's name and number?" Amita asked.

Anil gave his family my mom's information, then said, "Okay, guys. We are going to eat, so I will call you back later. Love you." Anil hung up the phone.

As soon as Anil got off the phone, Rose's mom's phone rang. Rose heard her mom on the phone. She could hear the annoyance. Her mom said, "Well, I will do whatever Anil and Rose want, so if Rose and Anil want to have an engagement party, then they can tell us what they want. It was nice speaking with you, but I have to go now. Thank you for calling." Rose's mother hung up the phone. She shot Rose a look. She came over and put her arms around Rose and said into her ear, "I know she was still talking when I hung up, but I just couldn't take it anymore. This is supposed to be happy," she said as she walked away.

Rose felt that pit in her stomach growing. She didn't want her mom to lose her shit and speak her truth.

"Knowing what I know now," Rose explained in Amy's office, "I wish my mother would have spoken her truth to Amita. Amita needed a little truth."

Amy looked up and said, "Didn't she tell you how she felt?"

"Yes. My mother told me multiple times how she felt, but I would not listen. I loved Anil. I never was like he is *the one*, but I knew I loved him," Rose explained.

"Why didn't your mother tell Amita?" Amy pushed.

"I think for the first time, my mom shut her mouth for me. She wanted me to be happy, and I think she knew it would have fueled Amita's fire. It didn't matter. Amita was fired up and ready to go. I remember that night, Anil called his parents to say goodnight and talk. I think he was looking for the reaction that my family had when he proposed. I think that he was looking for the approval and joy, but he wouldn't get it," started Rose.

"Hi, guys. How was your day? What did you get each other?" Anil asked his parents.

"Oh, we don't exchange gifts anymore. We are too old," Amita said. "When are you going home?"

"We are leaving after the New Year, on the third," he said.

Amita lost her mind. She just started screaming. "You are staying two weeks! Why are you staying so long? You didn't stay here for two weeks. She is already not letting you be with your family," Amita complained.

"Mom, we have seen you twice. We have to fly here, so Rose doesn't see her family as much," he explained.

Amita just started to rage out. Rose could hear her screaming into the phone. Anil ended up just cutting her off and saying goodbye to her.

Rose really resented her for taking her joy. She made her happy day all fucked up and Rose was pissed. Anil was upset and he proceeded to drink himself stupid. Rose really blamed Amita for all of it.

CHAPTER 4

"The time after the holidays is my least favorite of the year," Rose explained to Amy. "It is after the holidays. I have to fly home, and I know it will be a while before I will see my family again. The January sky is gray and gloomy most of the time where we live. I don't like gray and gloomy; it makes me feel blah and a little sad. January is also my birthday month, and it sucks because it is right after the holidays and everyone is broke. January was also Amita's birthday month, which means every year she wanted us to come to her house," Rose explained.

The flight home for Rose always sucked because she knew that she was going to be far away from her family again. But she was excited to see her dogs and play with them again. Anil and Rose picked up the dogs, got some pizza, and headed home. After they ate, Rose unpacked their bags and put all their stuff away. They took a quick shower, then went to bed.

Rose awoke the next morning to the smell of coffee and Anil talking on the phone. "Happy birthday, Mom. What are you going to do today?" she heard him say.

"Dad and I are going to Rushi's house for tea and cake later," she said.

"That sounds nice," Anil said.

"Why don't you try and come for a weekend this month? Maybe this weekend?" Amita asked.

"I don't know, Mom. It's Rose's birthday this weekend, and we just got home," Anil explained.

"What, she can't spend her birthday here? You can't come home?" Amita squawked.

"Mom we are going to take the bar next month, so we really need to study. Every state has different laws, and she must relearn everything. It is going to be hard on her to not confuse the two states," Anil said. He almost sounded exhausted. "Okay, Mom, I'll talk to you later. Love you." Anil hung up the phone.

"Good morning," Anil said to Rose, then gave her a kiss. "I made coffee."

"I know, it smells wonderful, and I could really use a cup this morning. How's your mom?" Rose asked.

"She is fine. Today is her birthday, so maybe you can text her," Anil said. "She wanted us to visit this weekend, but I told her that it was your birthday too, so we wouldn't be coming."

"I see. I don't really want to travel again so quickly, so thank you for telling her no," Rose said. "How old am I again?" Rose smirked. Anil leaned over and kissed her. "My sister and brother emailed me, and they are coming to our bar swearing in ceremony April if we pass. So, we will have a full house!" Rose exclaimed.

"Uh, do your sister and brother know that they will have to be different ages? I mean, your sister and you can't be the same age that you are now. Well, I guess your brother can be his age, but your sister needs to be at least a year or two younger," Anil said.

Rose looked at him and sighed, "I will tell them before they come. They are going to be irritated. My sister hates lying."

Anil smiled, "I know, but look on the positive side, everyone will be younger. That is good right?"

"Except, I am not younger. Maybe if you magically make me younger. I would like to be thirty again. I feel like that was a good look for me. Oh wait, before you magically pull that trigger can I have the knowledge that I have now?" Rose asked, trying to find the humor in the situation.

Over the next couple of weeks, Rose started to prepare for their guests. Rose didn't study for the exam much. She was over studying. Instead, Rose found a nice little bed and breakfast for Anil and her to stay at after the exam in South Carolina.

When their test day finally arrived, Anil and Rose were prepared, but not for the exam. They had a babysitter for the dogs, and they packed their bags the night before and put them in the car. They were prepared to get away for a weekend. They would be staying at a hotel close to the testing center. Neither one of them studied for the exam, but this time Rose wasn't anxious. Anil never studied nor does he have to study. He was just smart.

The bed and breakfast was relaxing. It was better than Rose expected. The house sat on a river, and their room overlooked the river. They had a king-size bed and this huge claw bathtub that Anil and Rose could sit in together and take a bath while looking at the river. They had the most amazing couples massage. They took a boat ride on the river and ate at a local restaurant that had the best seafood. They truly relaxed. When Anil and Rose were alone together, they enjoyed each other.

When their little trip was over, they drove back to Georgia. Anil began working, and Rose began looking for work. Anil was getting ready for his trip to DC for his friend's wedding that weekend.

"You know that wedding you are going to this weekend?" Rose asked.

"Yes," he said.

"Well, I was talking to Laurel. She lives in Maryland, and she thought that I could take the drive with you and stay at her house. It would be fun because I have not seen Laurel since law school. What do you think?" Rose asked.

"I think that is a great idea," Anil said.

So that weekend, Anil and Rose drove up to DC. It wasn't a long ride, and Rose was so excited to see Laurel. Rose missed her so much. Rose dropped Anil off at his parent's hotel, and she told him to give her a buzz when he was ready for her to come and get him.

Saturday night, Laurel and Rose went out to eat and met a few law school friends for a drink. So many of their classmates lived in DC. It must have been about ten when Anil called her. He sounded totally wasted.

"Rose, you were right! My mom lied. I told my friend about you, and she asked why I didn't bring you to the wedding. She didn't even know you existed," Anil said.

"Anil, where are you? You need to chill out." Rose could tell that he was really upset and that he was walking around DC. Rose could hear the wind over the phone.

"My mom didn't tell her about us. The whole night my mom tried to have me dance with some Indian girl. She has no respect for me. We went back to her hotel and got into a huge screaming fight. My mom kept screaming that you are a manipulator! Can you come pick me up, please?" he asked.

"Yes, I will come to the front of the hotel. Just wait there. Love you," Rose said.

Laurel and Rose drove to the hotel and picked up Anil. Then they drove to Laurel's place and gave Anil some water and food. He was going on and on about how his mother tried to set him up with someone else. How she manipulated the whole thing.

Rose knew she had done this the whole time. Rose told him, but he was too drunk to talk to about it. She wanted to scream, but Anil passed out and the next morning Rose drove them home in silence.

When they got home, Vishwa called Anil. Rose guessed he was worried Anil would not speak with him anymore.

He said, "Hi, Anil."

"Hi, Dad," Anil said.

"You mom does not know that I am calling, but we need to talk," Vishwa said in a desperate tone. "I don't want to lose you, beta. I never told you this, but your mom is very jealous, and she can overreact. One time she got jealous of the cat because she thought that

I gave the cat more attention than her. Your mom became furious when I gave Arjun's girlfriend a cough drop and blanket when she was sick. I cannot tell Rose that I like the way she decorates, because your mother becomes so jealous. That is why I do not talk to Rose or other women; your mom accuses me of hitting on these women if I so much as ask how they are doing. I love you beta, and I don't want to lose you, just ignore your mom. She loves you too."

"Okay, thank you for telling me this, Dad. Everything makes more sense now. I understand why you do not speak hardly ever," Anil said.

"Please don't tell anyone. It would hurt your mom," Vishwa said.

"Okay, Dad. I love you," Anil said.

"Bye, beta," Vishwa said.

Immediately after Anil hung up the phone, he began to tell Rose about the entire conversation. Anil kept going on and on and on about the phone call. It seemed like so many things began to make sense to him after that conversation with his father.

The very next day Anil came in from work with a handful of mail and a look on his face.

Rose looked at the envelope that he was gripping—it was their exam results. It was an envelope that seemed to have a single piece of paper, which is supposed to be a good sign. Getting the results of this bar exam didn't take as long as my other bar exam. The results came back about four weeks after we took the test. Anil and Rose both passed the exam. They called their families to tell them that they passed. Rose could hear Anil on the phone with his mother.

"Hi, Mom and Dad," Anil said.

"Hi, Anil. How are you doing?" his parents asked.

I am doing well. I got the results of the bar exam today, and Rose and I both passed," he said.

You could hear how proud he was of himself. Rose could tell that he was waiting for a reaction like what she received when she told her family. Her family acted like she had just won ten million dollars. The first time she told her family, they sent her gifts and they were screaming. This time they screamed too, and Rose was sure the gifts will follow. Anil's mother and father were different.

"Oh, good. Now you have to take the patent bar," they said. That was it.

Anil got off the phone. He looked completely deflated. It was as if someone had taken the air out of his sails. Rose knew what happened. He didn't have to tell her. He looked at her and, with the most defeated voice, he said, "Why can't they just be happy for me?"

Rose wanted to say because they are insensitive assholes, but instead Rose said, "They are happy for you. They just have a different way of showing their excitement. Why don't you and I go celebrate your success with some sushi? My treat."

"Okay," he said. They headed out the door and went to their favorite sushi place. Anil drank so much that night. Rose guessed what his parents said really affected him, because by ten o'clock he was sitting down crying and saying, "Why aren't they ever proud of me? Why can't they be happy for me?" He was totally wasted, and it was so sad. Rose never realized until that night how much what his parents said and did really affected him, but Rose guessed they were all affected by their parents.

The next few weeks, Rose prepared for a full house. Anil's parents and her sister and brother would be there soon for the bar ceremony.

They only had one extra bed, so Rose had to go shopping. Anil and Rose bought extra pillows and an air mattress. They went to the store and bought extra groceries. Rose was excited to see her brother and sister and have them at her house. This was their first time coming to Georgia, and they were going to experience it with her.

Before Rose knew it, they were going to be sworn into the Georgia State Bar. Her little sister and little brother caught an afternoon flight. The airport wasn't too far from their house, so Rose had time to pick up some fresh flowers for the house before she left for the airport. Rose pulled up to her siblings' smiling faces, and they got into the car.

"Hey guys, how was the flight?" Rose asked. Rose was so excited to see them, but she couldn't help thinking about how she was going to ask them to lie for her. It wasn't a little lie. Rose was asking them to make her seven years younger than she was. She was also asking them to lie about themselves. The messed-up thing is they had to remember the lie and keep track of the lie. Rose felt like shit about it.

"It was good," Juliet replied.

"Are you guys hungry? I have dinner going." Rose smiled at them.

"I can eat," her brother said. "There are so many trees here. It is so green."

"I know. That is one of the things that I love about this place. Here we are," Rose said as they pulled into the driveway. Rose could hear her dogs barking. She opened the door and helped her sister and brother into the house with their bags. The second they walked in the door, the dogs were circling around them with excitement.

"Welcome to my little house," Rose said, excited to see what they thought.

Her sister smiled a big bright smile. "Hi, doggies. I missed you little guys. This is great. I love how you decorated it. It is so nice." She went to the sliding glass doors and looked out the glass. "Wow, your back yard is amazing. It is like a forest back there. Oh my, is that a bee? That thing is huge!" she exclaimed.

Rose could hear the bee hitting the glass. It was huge. Its body was about the size of a quarter. Rose looked at her sister's face, and she looked horrified. Rose laughed and said, "Yes, our bugs get as big as jets."

"Rose, this is great. Wow, that yard is amazing. Was it hard to find this place?" her brother asked.

"No. We pretty much took the first place we could find. You guys want a glass of wine while the chicken finishes cooking? We can sit out back on the deck if you want," Rose said.

"Sure, sure," her brother said.

Rose got a bottle of red out and began pouring the glasses for everyone. They all walked outside and sat on her little iron table on the deck. Her sister and brother were looking around the yard, sipping their wine watching the dogs run around. Rose knew that she had to tell them, and she wanted to tell them before Anil came home. Finally, after ten minutes of idol chitchat, Rose blurted, "So Anil's parents are driving into town tomorrow. They should be here around four o'clock, and I need you to lie about my age…and yours."

"What?" her sister laughed. Rose could tell she thought she was joking, but when she saw that the expression on her face didn't change, she just looked at her like she had grown an extra eye in the middle of her head. "You are serious. Why are we doing this?"

Her brother just laughed at the idea. Surprisingly, her sister wasn't mad at her. Rose thought she was just baffled by the request. They both stared at her waiting for her response.

She chuckled and said, "Well, Anil's parents are old school. His mother and father have this idea that the girlfriend should be five years younger than the boyfriend. I am seven years older than Anil, so Anil thinks this will cause an uprising. He absolutely does not want his parents to know that I am older, because his mother will lose her mind and he will never hear the end of it. Anil and I both agree that making me five years younger than him is too much, but I can pass as his age easily. Juliet, you only need to be two years younger than I am, and Tony, you only have to be two years younger than Juliet. I'm sorry for having to ask you guys to do this for me. I know it is a lot to ask."

"What the fuck, dude. I get gipped on this deal. You and Juliet get to be way younger and I get a year younger than I am. You guys always get the better deal," her brother laughed. "I don't care Rose, I'll do it. I'm just giving you shit. You don't have to be sorry."

"Juliet, are you upset with me?" Rose asked. "I feel so bad asking you to do this, but I really don't want Anil to have to deal with the aftermath. His mom is already unsure of me. I just want her to get to know me without one more roadblock in her mind."

Her sister just smiled her angelic sweet smile. "I don't care. I'll do it. I just feel bad that you have to lie to his parents, and I don't think lying is a good way to start, but I will do it for you. One question, why do we all have to be two years apart? Doesn't that seem weird to you? A little made up? Are you going to tell Mom and Daniel?"

Rose just started laughing. "Anil's mother believes that each child should be two years apart. She has all these notions of how things should be in a family and with relationships. I figured since mom is so much older than Daniel, and she had three kids, that maybe we could get one thing right." Oh my God, when Rose heard herself say it out loud, it sounded really crazy. They all burst out laughing. "And yes, I am going to tell Mom and Daniel. I guess sooner rather than later."

"I'm still pissed. I only get to be about a year younger. I feel like you guys always get the better deal," Tony said laughing.

"Let it go, dude. Let it go." Juliet poked at Tony.

"Dude, so everyone knows how old you are except his parents?" Tony continued.

Rose looked at Tony and poured him and Juliet another glass of wine. "It is kinda messed up. Everyone knows our ages. You guys know and our friends know; it is just his family and his hometown friends who don't. Anil's brother won't lie to his parents, so Anil has chosen to lie to everyone in his family. Crazy, right?"

"Holy shit, dude. That is so messed up. But hey you get to go back in time. Just think you will get to do every birthday twice," Tony laughed. "Is dinner ready yet? I'm starving."

"Yup. It is done," Rose said. "Anil should be home any minute. We can get started."

Rose got up and went inside to take out the chicken. She didn't know if it was the wine or the fact that her brother and sister were so fucking cool about the whole situation, but Rose felt relaxed. Rose felt safe. It was nice having her siblings around for a few reasons. Rose missed them and they were so much fun to hang out with, and she wasn't alone with Amita. Rose knew that she could not act a fool in front of her own siblings. She knew she would not act like an asshole in front of her siblings. One thing about Amita is that she must look good to everyone she meets. She does not want anyone to see who she really is and how she really behaves. Rose's brother and sister would be her armor this weekend, and that thought made her smile like a Cheshire cat.

The next morning, Rose woke up early and started breakfast for her brother and sister. The coffee was brewing, and Rose made a huge vegetable frittata with a side of bacon. Her sister and brother love her frittatas, so it gave her joy to cook for them.

Anil had already left for work, and Rose was planning on hanging out with her siblings until Amita and Vishwa arrived that afternoon. Unfortunately, Amita and Vishwa left early so they would probably be arriving around three in the afternoon.

"Good morning," Tony smiled. "I see you made coffee." He poured himself a cup.

"I did and I also made breakfast," Rose said proudly, and she began to pull it out of the oven.

"That smells so good," he said as he started to grab a plate.

Rose grabbed his plate out of his hand. "You know that just came out of the oven, right? You'll burn the shit out of your mouth. Give it a second. Where is Juliet? Is she still asleep? I was thinking we could go to the city for a bit, maybe grab some food later and walk around. There are some cool shops and stuff. I don't know; it is up to you guys. What do you think?" Rose asked her little brother.

Tony took the plate back and smiled. "I might have lost a year or two, but I can decipher what is too hot to eat. I don't care what we do today. I'm here for five days. We can just chill out, or go to the city. It really doesn't matter. I came to see you."

"Okay. I was thinking the city because there is also a nice market, and I figured we could make pasta and sauce for dinner. Pick up some fresh Italian bread. Does that work? Hey, good morning, Juliet. How did you sleep?"

"I slept great knowing I was going to wake up years younger today," she poked. "Smells good. What are you making?"

"You two are never going to let me live this age issue down. Frittata, all vegetables," Rose said.

Tony and Juliet in unison said, "No!" and they both started to laugh.

"You really think we are ever going to let this go?" Juliet said with a smirk.

They all decided to go into the city. The day was nice and bright. It was around sixty degrees, and the air was starting to lose its crispness. They found a decent parking spot off a little street with all different types of shops. Rose parked the car and her sister and brother began bouncing in and out of the shops and enjoying the springlike weather. There was a small park that they walked in with beautiful trees and a small stream that ran through it. It seemed like lots of people had the same idea, because the park was full. It must have been all the walking because it didn't take long before they both were hungry wanted to try some "real" southern food. They stopped at this small restaurant off a side street. It was a little hole in the wall place, but the food was amazing. The inside has about six tables, and the walls are exposed brick. The smell of fried chicken filled the air. They sat at a table near the window, because like Rose, her siblings loved to people watch.

Her sister grabbed a menu off the table, and she smiled. "Mmmm, sweet tea and red velvet cake. I am trying it. Everyone always talks about the sweet tea. Do you like it, Rose?"

"I got sweet tea by mistake once. Apparently if you don't ask for your tea to be unsweetened, the default is sweet tea. It is pure sugar. I think it is gross," Rose said sticking out her tongue. What amazed her is that her sister was going to have sweet tea and red velvet cake, and she would not gain an ounce of weight. If Rose looked at that damn cake, Rose would have gained ten pounds. She sat there and watched her sister drink that sweet tea and eat that cake with shear amazement.

They all had such a nice time. They loved the city, the restaurant, and the market with all the fresh vegetables. They all enjoyed reminiscing about the old days.

When they got to the house, Amita and Vishwa had already arrived. Rose took a deep breath. She was disappointed they had arrived an hour earlier than they were supposed to arrive. Rose was hoping to have some relaxation time before they arrived. *Oh good, that awful pit in my stomach has returned. Well at least there is consistency*, Rose thought.

Rose looked at her brother and sister and smiled. Rose didn't want them to see her disappointment or stress level.

"Well, Amita and Vishwa are here. Remember your ages!" Rose was trying to make light of the situation, but inside Rose just wished Amita and Vishwa would go away. Rose wished she could just explain to them how silly and ridiculous this whole thing is, the ideas and notions. The battle for control. It is so hard having to be someone else and watch and weigh every word that is said. Rose really thought she could see Amita judging her when she looked at her. It was so hard having to watch Anil sneak small bottles of scotch when they were around. He kept them in his pockets and hid them in his backpack. He'd smoke before they'd come, and then he'd smoke in the morning during their visits right when he woke up.

They walked into the home and the introductions began. Amita and Vishwa shook Juliet's and Tony's hands. Rose noticed almost immediately that her dogs were not in the house. Rose saw them outside in the backyard; she became instantly annoyed. Rose noticed they had taken items that they intended to use and placed them on her counters. Rose noticed that her milk had been poured into a smaller container in the refrigerator, and a small bowl of sugar had been placed near a teapot on the stove. Two of her coffee mugs sat on the counter with masking tape with *Amita* and *Vishwa* written on the masking tape and placed on the mugs. Her almonds were in a bowl on the counter with a spoon to scoop them up into your hand. *They came into my home and took over! They put my dogs outside!* Rose could feel her blood boiling. Rose barely said hello. She marched like a lunatic to the sliding doors and let her dogs back into her home.

Tony must have read her thoughts, or maybe it was her face, because he offered to make dinner. "I can start dinner if you want. Rose? Rose? I can start dinner."

Rose was so immersed in thought, she barely heard her brother speaking to her. Rose snapped out of her fantasy world and said to her little brother, "Oh sure, that would be great. Thanks, Tony."

"Oh, you can cook?" Amita squawked.

"Yes. My mom taught all of us," said Tony. "I enjoy cooking."

"Oh, that is nice," she said. But you could hear the jealousy or at least what sounded like jealousy. The way she drew out the words. It was always a competition. "Arjun can cook, but Anil never learned. It is good that your mother taught you all how to cook. She must be a very good mother."

"She's the best," Rose said through a smile. Rose knew that would irritate her, and it did judging by the look on her face. Rose also knew that she would pay for that remark later, but at the moment it felt so good.

Amita watched Tony as he began to take out the ingredients. She stood by his side, asking him question after question about making the sauce. She gave suggestions on how to make the sauce. She offered to help make the sauce. She had to know how he learned to make the sauce, and where he learned to make the sauce. How long has he been making the sauce? Her poor brother had to endure her constant questions for over two hours. He handled it like a champ. He smiled the entire time and laughed. He answered her questions with patience. It also probably helped that he had hit Anil's stash of weed before he started cooking.

After dinner, they all sat down to watch a movie. Rose made popcorn and gave everyone their own bucket.

Rose noticed that Anil never asked what anybody wants to watch. He will ask if anyone has seen a specific movie, and if no one has seen that movie then Anil puts it on. Anil picked out the movie and started playing it.

Amita talked through the entire movie. It was two hours of nonstop questions about the movie. "Why is she saying that to her husband? I don't think you should say that to your husband. Is that another man? I thought she is married. Anil, is she married? Where are they going? Why are they leaving? Oh, she is very pretty. Don't you think she is very pretty? Well I think she is very pretty." She did this the *entire* movie. Rose could not believe that anyone could or would talk that much through a movie. To this day, Rose had no idea what that fucking movie was about. Rose knew her sister and brother didn't know what the movie was about either, because they told her they had to rewatch it. Rose didn't think anyone knew what the movie was about.

The next morning while Rose was making breakfast, Rose could hear the Amita interrogating her sister. "How old are you? Do you have a boyfriend? Why don't you get married? Do you live with your boyfriend? Does your brother want to get married? How long have your mom and Daniel been together?" While she was interrogating Juliet, Rose saw the funniest shit ever. Her sister got up and left in the middle of what Amita was asking, but that didn't stop Amita. Amita didn't even notice. She just began to follow Juliet around the house talking. Her sister was walking from room to room. She looked like she was gliding along the floor as Amita was on her heals. Rose knew it was mean, but her sister was doing this for her and Rose was laughing. Juliet was a quiet person, so this must have been maddening to her.

When Juliet finally broke away, she walked over to Rose and whispered in her ear, "Oh my God. She does not even take a breath."

"I know, dude, I know," Rose said, relieved that her sister understood. Her sister always saw the best in people, so if she was getting annoyed, then Rose know she was not being ridiculous.

After breakfast, they all rested. The swearing ceremony was that afternoon, and Rose knew it would be a little hectic. Amita and Vishwa started laying out the plan. They decided that Juliet, Tony, and Rose would ride together. Amita, Vishwa, and Anil would follow behind them. Rose let her dogs out one last time and locked the sliding glass doors. Her landlord had mentioned that he was having someone come and trim the bushes, so it would be best to keep the dogs inside the home. Rose sat in the car and waited for Amita, Vishwa, and Anil to get into the car so that they could follow her to the event center.

The ceremony was in an event center, and the room could fit about one hundred people. The planners had set up the room so the new lawyers were sitting in the front and all friends and family were sitting toward the back. They swore them in all at the same time. After the ceremony, there were cocktails and hors d'oeuvres. It was a small spread, but Anil and his parents managed to gorge themselves on the food. Vishwa kept insisting that the food was free, and we should eat more, except Rose didn't care for what was being served.

They went home directly after the ceremony. Rose went into the bedroom to get changed, and while she was changing, it occurred to her that her dogs didn't greet her at the door. Rose ran into the living room and said to Anil, "Where are the dogs?"

He looked at her puzzled, then his mother said, "I let them outside before we left. Animals like to be outside."

Rose ran out the sliding door. The gate was open, and her dogs were gone. Rose completely lost her mind. Anil and Rose immediately jumped into the car and began looking for their fur babies. They were screaming out their names as they drove through the neighborhood, "Maxie! Soukie!" It didn't take long for one of their neighbors to bring their sweet girl over in the back of her truck. She was bleeding and had just been struck by a car. Soukie looked dazed and confused. Rose found out later that she was going into shock. The neighbor, Aly, told her to get in her truck. Rose hopped in the back and held Soukie as Aly drove them to the emergency veterinarian. Anil kept looking for their little boy, calling out on the streets.

When Rose got to the vet, they took Soukie out of her arms and carried her away. Rose didn't even get to say goodbye. She just stood there with blood all over her and cried. Rose went inside and filled out the necessary forms. Rose handed the assistant her credit card and said, "Please do whatever needs to be done; just charge my card. Thank you." Rose left.

Rose got home to sullen faces. Her little boy was still missing. He was out there all alone. Her brother and sister held her as she cried. Anil was sitting with his hands in his face.

Tony looked at Rose and said in the sincerest voice, "I don't know how, but we will bring Maxie home. He is a smart dog. Why don't we put his food and water out front? You take him for a walk every day, maybe he will find his way home." Tony got her up and helped her put food and water outside. "It will be okay. We will bring them home."

Amita and Vishwa didn't say anything. Rose didn't think they knew how to comfort or express much emotion. They just sat on the couch eating snacks. You would think that Rose hated Amita or blamed her, but Rose didn't. Rose blamed herself for not saying to her from the beginning, "These are *my* dogs, and you will not put them outside without asking me first." Rose didn't stand up for what she believed and now Rose was paying that price. Lesson learned.

Rose was getting up to shower when her phone rang. It was the vet and she had news about Soukie. "Hello, is this Rose Vella?" the vet said.

"Yes," Rose said. Rose could hear her voice crack.

"Soukie is out of surgery. She did well, and she didn't lose her leg. We are going to keep her for the next few days. I think she has a very good chance of pulling through."

"Thank you. Thank you so much," Rose said, and she hung up the phone. Rose looked at everyone and said, "The vet said that Soukie did well, and there is a very good chance that she will come home." Tony looked up and smiled at her and said, "Now let's get Maxie."

Rose didn't eat that night, and she didn't sleep at all that night either. She tossed and turned, worrying about Maxie. Every worst-case scenario ran through her head. Rose finally fell asleep just when she heard Amita rapping on her bedroom door.

"I saw Maxie!" Rose heard her scream.

She jumped out of bed and opened the door. "Where?" Rose said.

"Well, I thought I heard something outside and when I looked it was Maxie. I tried to call him into the house, but he took off down the street," she exclaimed.

Rose ran out of the house screaming Maxie's name. Vishwa and Amita ran out behind her also screaming. Anil pulled up beside Rose and told her to get in the car, and they whipped around the corner. They saw Maxie and followed him. They finally caught up to Maxie because someone had heard all the commotion and grabbed Maxie by the collar. Rose thanked the guy for grabbing him and put Maxie in the car. He looked fine. There wasn't a scratch on him. Rose was so relieved.

When we got back to the house, Tony and Juliet had woken up and made coffee for everyone. Rose's little sister, who is an excellent baker, had made banana muffins. The smell hit Rose in the face as soon as she walked in the door.

Tony looked at Rose, smiled, and said, "I told you Maxie is a smart dog. I knew he would come home."

"Thank you, little brother," Rose said with clear relief in her voice. Rose picked up the phone and called the vet to see how Soukie was doing. The vet said that Soukie was doing well, and if she keeps this up that she may be able to come home in three days. Rose picked up one of the muffins and ate it in two bites; her sister just laughed at her.

It was sad to see her sister and brother leave. Rose missed them so much; she was lonely. Anil worked all day while Rose pumped out resumes. Rose didn't have any friends or family. She was at home with the dogs all day, then with Anil at night, but he started to drink more and more. When he wasn't drinking, he was going over the patent bar packets. He had to take that test. So, he wasn't present either.

Spring was in the air, and Anil and Rose had picked a date to get married. They had decided on a winter wedding. Rose didn't want a big wedding, and she thought a destination wedding where they could spend time with friends and family would do the trick. Rose also wanted a nice wedding, but she didn't want a wedding where she had to do a lot of work putting it together. Ultimately, they decided on a cruise ship with the wedding on the beach.

"Babe, what do you want? Is there anything that you want?" Rose asked.

"I like the idea of taking a trip with everyone," Anil said as he kissed her head. "Plus, I think it would be fun to share our honeymoon with our families."

"I figured we could do it during Christmas. I know Christmas isn't a big deal to your family, and that would be a good way for us to spend the holiday with both families," Rose smiled.

"Sounds great. You plan it and let me know," he smiled.

They picked a December 21. Rose was so excited; she called her mom immediately.

"Hello, queenie," Rose said.

"Hi, babe. How are you doing?" her mom asked; as usual, she was excited to hear her voice.

"I'm doing well. We picked a date. We are going to do a cruise wedding in December. I am going to send you all the information. I figure that way we can take a big trip together as well." Rose was excited to go away with her family, and Rose thought they would have fun.

"Okay. That sounds good. I really want to buy the dress for you," she said.

"Sounds good. We can get it when you come to visit in August. I love you."

"Love you. I will talk to you later," her mom said.

While her mom and Rose were speaking, Anil had gotten on the phone with his mother. Apparently, she had picked a date for the engagement party.

"Hi, Mom," Anil said.

"Hello, Anil," both his parents chimed.

"Rose and I have picked a date for the wedding. We are doing a cruise in December. Rose will send you all the details."

"We are having the engagement party on June 30. Please send us a list of all the people that you both want invited. I also need everyone's measurements. I need Rose's whole family so that I can have the Indian clothes made. I will need Rose's measurements for the sari. What is her favorite color? We can go over everything when you come for Memorial Day weekend," his mother stated.

"Mom, we weren't planning on coming for Memorial Day weekend," Anil stated.

"What? Is she taking all the holidays? Why? We need to prepare for the engagement party!" she squawked.

"Okay, Mom. I'll talk to you later. I love you. Bye," and he hung up the phone.

Anil came into the room and grabbed a beer from the fridge. He sat down on the coach next to Rose and put his arm around her. "Do you mind if we go to my house for the holiday weekend?" he asked.

"They were just here," Rose said.

"I know, but my whole family will be there and my friends. Also, my mom wants to show you some of the work she has done for the party and go over some stuff with you. She is excited about this, Rose. Please don't start in, okay? We spent two weeks with your family," he said.

"Right, but we have seen your parents every month and they are mean," Rose said.

"Rose, I think you are just mistaking the way they say things. Remember, English isn't their first language. Sometimes they don't even understand the meanings of the words," Anil said with agitation.

"Are you kidding me right now? I am pretty sure your mom understands when she says that she will kick me out of the house! Your dad is a professor at one of the top universities, and you want me to believe that they do not understand the language? You are kidding, right Anil?"

"Rose, I don't want to fight. I think that you just don't understand when they are joking, and now you just don't like them, so everything they do is wrong in your eyes," he said.

Rose was so annoyed. *He is fucking blaming me!* "Whatever, Anil. Yes, your mom is a comedian, a regular fucking Bill Maher!" Rose got up and left the room. Rose felt like throwing herself on the floor like a child and pounding her fists on the ground. She was so frustrated.

The next day, Rose sent Amita a list of friends to invite to the engagement party. What was super fucking annoying was that Rose had asked for the engagement party to be on the Fourth of July weekend. Her mom's husband has a hard time getting off work because he has some classified job. Fourth of July weekend would have been perfect for everyone. However, Amita said that didn't work for Arjun, so we had to have the party on June 30.

Rose began to work on the invitations for the wedding. She found this cute website that allowed her to make her own invitations. She had picked the colors red and gold, since it was a Christmas wedding. The front of the invite had a palm tree in the sand and a nice little saying. It was simple and perfect. Rose began to fill out all the forms for the wedding, and to her surprise, she was done within a day or two. The only thing that she had left to do was buy the dress, and her mom was going to help with that part and finalize the number of guests two weeks before departure. This wedding is exactly what Rose wanted: simple, easy, and small.

Unfortunately, Memorial Day weekend had arrived faster than Rose wanted. They left early on the Thursday before in order to miss traffic, and they were going to stay until Tuesday to avoid traffic. They arrived at his family's house around dinnertime, so the table was set. Arjun and his new girlfriend, Samantha, had arrived before them. He had broken up with is old girlfriend around Christmas, and Samantha had filled Sarah's spot quickly. Apparently, Sarah and Arjun were having some issues because Sarah wanted to get married. Samantha was the friend who gave an ear, and Rose was told by Amita that she had written Arjun a letter that had really upset Sarah. Amita snarled when she recanted the story.

Rose redirected her attention to Amy. "Amy, I know this is so wrong of me, but when I found out that Amita disliked Samantha more than me, I was so fucking overjoyed. I felt like a deer being hunted by a lion and then out of the blue comes a weaker deer. The slower deer. The deer that interrupted the relationship with Arjun and Sarah. Sarah, the one Amita liked. How fortunate that while I'm running from the jaws of the Amita lion, she turns and grabs Samantha, I mean the deer, by the throat and I am free. It was totally refreshing and a bit of a relief," Rose explained.

Samantha was different than Sarah. She was more talkative. She was a plain girl with a boyish body and wasn't as pretty as Sarah. She didn't wear makeup, and her hair was a stringy, dirty blonde. She seemed nice enough. According to Arjun, she wasn't as smart as Sarah and couldn't cook like Sarah, but she would experiment more in bed."

Rose rolled her eyes. "Amita wanted to know all about my wedding, but the truth is that wedding was the easiest to plan. The cruise sent me a checklist. All I had to do was look at pictures and read descriptions," Rose laughed.

They all ate dinner and Rose tried to get to know Samantha. Rose told her if she wanted to come to the wedding that she was more than welcome. "I can't," she said sadly.

"I'm sorry," Rose said, "but you are always welcome." Rose got up and began clearing the table. Samantha and Rose did the dishes and when they were done, she asked, "Would you like a glass of wine?"

"That would be great," Rose said. Rose was so happy to have a woman other than Amita to talk with.

They sat down and Samantha looked Rose straight in the eyes and said, "Is the wedding in December the real wedding, because Amita says it is just the licensing ceremony. She said the real wedding is in June. I mean, at least that is what she is telling everyone."

Rose could feel her blood boil. *Holy shit, she is turning the engagement party into a fucking wedding.* Rose looked at Samantha and through her teeth, Rose said, "No, the party in June is just an engagement party."

The rest of the night, Rose brewed over the statement. When Anil and Rose went to bed, Rose blurted out what Samantha had said. Rose was furious.

"Babe, Samantha isn't that smart. I am sure that isn't what my mom said," he smiled.

"She may not be the brightest star in the sky, but I heard what she said, and it was very clear," Rose said. Rose was so over the excuses.

It was such bullshit.

The next morning, Rose awoke to Amita preparing for the party. She had already sent the invitations, and she began to show them to me. She was excited that almost everyone had responded. "They look like wedding invitations," Rose said.

"I didn't mean for them to look like wedding invitations. I picked the color purple because I know that is your favorite color," she said with a smile. "If you do not like them, I can send out some other ones."

How is she supposed to send out other ones when she already fucking sent these? Rose snapped out of it and said, "Thank you. Yes, that is my favorite color."

Anil came in the room. "What are you guys doing?"

"We are going over the engagement party," Amita said.

"Oh, nice. What have you guys decided? Can we do that walk around the fire at the party?" Anil asked.

Amita smiled and said, "Yes, that should not be hard to do for you both. Are you okay with that Rose?"

"Yes. That is fine."

What Rose didn't know, and what she would come to find out, is that required a Hindu priest. What Amita didn't tell her or Anil was that little request to walk around the fire was about to seal the deal on that day being my Indian wedding day. Conveniently she didn't tell her that was going to happen, she just made the plans. Rose didn't know what the fuck was going on, and by the time she figured it out, it would be too late.

Rose sat on the couch and began to start her wedding registry. "What are you doing?" Amita asked.

"Oh, I am setting up my wedding registry," Rose responded.

"I do not think that is a good idea," she said. "Then people won't give you money. You don't need stuff. You have enough stuff," she said.

"I agree," Anil chimed in with his mother. "Wouldn't we just want the money?"

"I am doing a registry. What if some people don't want to give money, and then they buy me what I don't want? I would rather have a registry. I am doing a registry." Rose could hear her voice shake.

"Well, I am just making the suggestion. I think it is a good idea not to have too much stuff," Amita persisted.

"And you don't," Rose said with a smile. Rose flipped her off in her head.

After lunch, they all went for a ride, and Amita showed them where she was planning on having the party. It was a nice local hotel, and it would work for their guests because they could stay at the hotel and go to the party. The hotel wasn't big, but it had a nice courtyard for the ceremony.

Rose was thrilled when they finally got to leave and go home. She walked through the door of their house and took a deep breath. She didn't have to deal with asshole behavior until the party. *Fantastic.*

That week, Rose was checking her email, and she had received an invite for a job interview. She was excited, and she ran out to tell Anil. He was on the phone with his mother.

"Wow, that is a lot of people," he said. "Yes, she likes henna," he said. "That sounds fun."

When he got off the phone, he proceeded to tell Rose that the party was going to be huge. "Babe, 150 people responded. My family from India is flying into the States for our party. Oh, and my mom has these cool events planned. The first night everyone is going to get together and have snacks and music. The second day, we are getting together and having a henna party. The cousins have games that they want to play, and one of my cousins is going to dance and another is going to sing for us. Then the third day will be the engagement party."

"Wow, a three-day party. That is a lot," Rose said. "I mean…it seems like a lot."

"Why do you always have to shit on everything?" he asked. "Can't you just be happy? My parents are really working hard for us," Anil screeched.

"It sounds like a wedding, Anil. It sounds like she planned a wedding. That is how I feel. I don't want the priest. This is total bullshit," Rose screamed. "This is supposed to be *our* day, *our* wedding, and she is taking control over everything."

"Fine. I will tell her no priest." He picked up the phone and called Amita.

"Hi , Mom, Rose and I were talking, and she does not want the priest," he said.

"What do you mean? I thought you wanted the priest? You asked her when she was here," she responded.

"I know, Mom, but it feels like a wedding, and that isn't what we wanted."

"What about you?" she screamed. "What about what you want? Don't you get a day to celebrate? You don't get to have your culture, your wedding?"

"Mom, that isn't what I want. We were not going to do anything like this on either end," he said.

Vishwa started to talk, "Anil, what are we supposed to do? All these people are coming."

"Fine!" Amita screams into the phone. "We will tell everyone it is off. We are not doing anything!"

"Mom, if you would just listen," he said.

"No, that is fine! We will call it off!" She hung up the phone. All Rose could picture was Amita's and Vishwa's faces on toddlers who were laying on the floor throwing a temper tantrum.

"She hung up on me," Anil said defeated. "You know, any other girl would be grateful. My parents are spending the money on this, and you never considered what I want. Maybe I want a little Indian ceremony. Any other girl would do it. You always have to be so difficult," he said.

"Are you serious? We talked about this," Rose said. "If you wanted an Indian ceremony, you might have said so. Instead, you speak to your mother and all of a sudden, I am taking something from you. Seriously?"

"You never consider what I want," Anil screamed.

"Anil, do you not see what she did? She made an engagement party into a wedding. She lied to both of us. Doesn't that bother you?" Rose asked. She was feeling defeated. Maybe she was being unreasonable. Rose felt like Amita was ruining what was supposed to be a happy day. She was starting to feel like Amita was a complete and total joy killer. It was like she and Vishwa have this bow and arrow and wherever they see happiness and joy, *wham*, they shoot it dead.

"Why can't you just be grateful? Does it matter if we have fun and get money? Any other girl would do this happily for the person she loves!" he said with such force.

"So the means justify the ends," Rose said. "Her lying is okay? Whatever. I am so over you always taking their side and never defending me. I don't know what the fuck is in her cooch juice that you just can't see how controlling and underhanded this is. Do whatever you want. I will never consider it my wedding, just know that!"

CHAPTER 5

ANIL AND ROSE were lying in bed. It was a beautiful Sunday morning. They had about two weeks before the party, and they were both tired. Rose was in his arms as he kissed her. It felt so nice and reminded her why she loved him so very much. He smiled and kissed her head and said, "My parents were wondering if your parents wouldn't mind giving my parents gifts for marrying me."

"Gifts? I don't understand," Rose said.

"Well, you know, like gifts, gold jewelry. I told them no, but I thought I would ask you," he said.

"You mean a dowry? They want a fucking dowry?" Rose said in shock.

"They said it isn't a dowry, and I said no to them anyway, but I thought it might be a nice gesture from you," he said.

"If you said no, then why are you asking? I don't care what your parents are saying—it is a dowry. A dowry, Anil. That is exactly what it is."

Rose felt like she was losing her mind. This was when Rose started saying to herself, *What is in this bitch's cooch juice that no one can see how she manipulates?* Rose started to notice it with other mothers too. She would listen to her friends, and after their husbands or boyfriends would be around their mothers, it was like they changed and were tweaked.

"No. It isn't a dowry. They swore it wasn't," he tried to reassure her.

"Anil, if my mom and her husband are giving your parents gold for marrying me, that is a dowry, and I do not care what they fucking want you to believe. The answer is no. No, I am not insulting my family in that manner, and no I am not being bought or sold or whatever words you would like to use for it."

"I knew you were going to take it wrong," he said. "That is why I said no."

"Good. Because I am not even asking," Rose said. Honestly, Rose wanted to take a dictionary and smack the word *dowry* into his brain.

Amy looked up at Rose. "Why didn't you tell him how it made you feel? How did it make you feel?"

"I didn't know how to feel. I guess I thought maybe I was being difficult, I mean this is his day too. I should be more accommodating, but I felt bowled over and disrespected. Looking back, I should have called off the whole thing, but I thought to myself, *Weddings are stressful, and families can be difficult.* I was really upset about the dowry, but at the same time I felt that I had to respect his family. In the end, I just couldn't do it. I couldn't have my mom and her husband give a dowry for me. I didn't want it. I thought that had been done away with years ago, but I guess not everyone had done away with it," Rose finished.

"It is insulting, and it is disrespecting you," Amy said. "It is saying that you are property."

"That is exactly how I felt," Rose said. "I felt like everyone saw me as property."

"Well, they did," Amy said matter-of-factly. Amy saying that to Rose made her feel better. It validated her feelings, and Rose told her that.

The week of June 30 arrived quickly. Anil went to his parents' house a week before Rose was supposed to arrive. He was planning on hanging out with friends and family members who were arriving early to spend time with him.

Rose's friends Amanda and Jessica had decided to come to Rose's home after Anil left. They thought it would be fun to have some one-on-one girl time before they all drove out to Anil's house for the engagement party. They were also concerned about Rose taking that long drive alone.

When Amanda and Jessica knocked on the door, Rose could feel the joy burst right out of her. She gave them both huge hugs. It felt so good for her to see their smiling faces.

"This is my abode," Rose said as she began to show the girls around.

"This is great," Amanda and Jessica both said.

Jessica looked Rose in the face and said, "Where is that wine and cheese we really came for? Because I know there is a stash," she smiled.

"Yes, ma'am," Rose said in her best southern drawl. "You guys look great. I missed you both so much. It has been too long."

It had actually been about six years since Rose had seen the two of them. Rose had known Jessica the longest. They met when she lived in New York City. She was at a bar, and Jessica bought her a drink. She was looking for a girlfriend, and Rose was looking for a good friend. They had been friends ever since. Jessica was a speak-her-mind kind of a girl. You always knew what she was thinking, which could make her seem rough around the edges, but inside she was a softy. Jessica was really beautiful. She had jet black hair and green eyes. She was medium build, but she thought she was fat and dressed in baggy clothes. She knew that she was beautiful and used that with her girlfriends. She had a revolving door of women in her life.

Amanda and Rose became friends during an LSAT study course. She was a super chill girl, a hippie. She had long, curly blondish hair and blue eyes. She, like Jessica, considered herself to be fat because she was a size 8 and not a 2. She looked great to Rose, but of course, she wouldn't listen to what she had to say on the subject. She was an activist and loved to work in the public sector. She was always desperately looking for the "one." Rose knew that the real reason she had come to this engagement party was so she could meet a mate. *I just happen to be a side benefit to that agenda*, Rose thought.

They were all sitting on the back porch when Jessica blurted out, "Rose, what are you doing? Are you sure you want to do this?"

"What? Yes. Of course," Rose said, surprised that she would even ask such a question.

"Really? Rose, come on. Look who you are talking to here. You are living in the South. You don't go out anymore. Neither one of us hear from you for months at a time. This isn't you. Look at this place. It is nice, domestic, country, and 100 percent not Rose," Jessica said with certainty. "None of this is you, Rose. Not the clothes, the food, nothing. Look at you, you are wearing *pink*! When the fuck do you where pink? You wear black, always. You love life and the city cars put you to sleep. You used to call your friends every fucking day whether or not you were in a relationship. You love the big city. You have passion and a love for the arts. Where is the art, Rose? And to be frank, you have gained ten pounds. You never gain weight. You are not happy."

Amanda just looked over at Rose but didn't say a word. "I am happy," Rose said, digging her heals in. "And so what if I gained ten pounds! That is bullshit, Jessica. You are an ass. You are lucky I love you, or I'd punch you in the face, right now!"

"I know, but I love you and someone needs to say, 'Rose, please don't do this,'" she said in a begging voice. "You have done nothing but cry about his family. You are marrying them too. Don't you get that?"

Rose was just looking at her thinking, *I can do this. Anil and I love each other and that is all that matters. His family will come around.* It must have read all over her face, because Jessica abruptly stopped.

"Okay, Amanda and I have said our peace. We both know you are stubborn and that you are going to do this. We love you and support you, but we needed to tell you how we felt because we adore you. Now enough with the heavy, we have a present for you, so close your eyes and put out your hands." Rose did as she was told. She felt a piece of jewelry drop into her hands. "Okay," Jessica said. "Open."

Rose opened her eyes and saw a necklace in her hands. The necklace had this small little frame, and in the frame was a picture of the three of them on vacation. They were so happy on that vacation. Rose jumped out of her chair and gave Amanda and Jessica a huge hug. "Thank you so much. This is the best present ever. I love you both."

The next morning, they packed up the car and headed to Anil's house. Jessica talked about this new girl she was dating. "Rose, she is so amazing. Not like the other girls. She has a career and a house. I can't wait for you to meet her. The only thing that bothers me is she is still married."

"What?" Amanda and Rose both exclaimed.

"Are you kidding me right now? You gave me that big ass speech, and you are in a relationship with a *married* woman? Okay you are forbidden from giving anyone relationship advice," Rose said laughing. This was pretty typical of Jessica's relationship behavior. Her aversion to commitment was incredible.

Amanda looked over at Rose and said, "Do you think that there are any single men there that will be interested in dating me?"

"I'm sure there will be single men there, Amanda. But seriously, shouldn't you take a break?" Rose asked.

Amita and Vishwa had paid for the girls and Rose to stay at the hotel where the party was going to be held. Anil and his brother were staying at their parent's rental property about ten minutes away. Some friends and family were staying at the hotel, but most of Anil's family were staying with Amita in her home.

The girls arrived at the hotel around three in the afternoon. Their room was a suite, which meant that they had two king beds and a sofa. Jessica and Amanda plopped themselves on the bed, and Rose went out on the balcony to call Anil.

"Hey, babe. We are here." It was nice for Rose to hear his voice; he sounded happy.

"How was the drive?" he asked.

"It was fine. You know I had hours on end of hearing about Jessica's love life and Amanda's lack of love life. It was a very interesting ride."

"I bet. We are having snacks and dinner at Samantha's tonight. My mom says everyone should be there around five. I guess Samantha's mom made a whole bunch of pizzas for everyone. I think it will be fun. Her dad is cool and plays guitar with Arjun and me," Anil sounded excited about it.

"Okay," Rose said. "Can you text me the address and so I can get directions? Love you."

"Love you." Anil hung up.

"Okay, ladies. We have about an hour before we have to get ready for my pizza party tonight," Rose laughed.

"Pizza's cool," Jessica said as she picked up the phone and ordered a bottle of wine for the room. "First we have a glass here."

"Cheers," Amanda said.

The girls got to Samantha's house on time. Samantha's parents, Mary and Tom, were friendly. They both enjoyed having guests and often had Amita and Vishwa over. The house was in the country and sat on a few acres of property. It had a barn-style home with different colored rooms and plants throughout the home. Samantha's mother is a painter, and her pictures hung on the walls. When they walked through the door, they could smell the pizzas cooking in the oven. There were about twenty people in the house; the rest of the guests would be arriving the next day.

"Hi, babe," Anil came over and gave Rose a hug and a kiss.

"Hi," Rose said. Rose could tell that the guys had already started smoking, and she was a little annoyed by this.

"We are all outside around a fire playing if you want to come hang out with us," Anil said.

Rose went outside and the guys had a huge fire going. They were singing and playing the guitar. Amita came over.

"Here are the clothes for the party tomorrow," Amita said.

"Okay, thank you," Rose said.

"I have put your whole family's outfits in the bag. Their outfits are only for the engagement party. I will have your saris at the house tomorrow. There are two of them, so that you can pick which one you want to wear. After all, this is your day," she said, as if Rose was really supposed to believe that all this was for Anil and her.

"Thank you. So there are three days of this engagement party?" Rose asked her.

"Well, all our family came from India, so we decided to have an event every day," she replied.

"Every day? Rose asked. "I don't understand. I thought we were just having a party on Saturday? Rose said as her head started to spin.

"Anil said you like henna. So I hired a henna artist, and I thought we would have a henna party before the engagement party," she said.

"A henna party? So there are three parties?" I asked.

"Well, this is just a get-together so the families can start meeting. The parties start tomorrow," she said while she walked away.

Samantha walked over to Rose and smiled. "Thank you for having this at your family's house," Rose said.

"Did you have anything to eat?" she asked.

"No. My stomach doesn't feel so well," Rose said. "How many people do you think are here?" Rose asked Samantha.

"Oh. There are about twenty people here," she said.

Rose could feel Jessica come up next to her. She handed Rose a slice of pizza and some wine. "You really need to eat something, Rose. It isn't good to drink on an empty stomach, besides the pizza is good. Here try a bite." She shoved the pizza in Rose's face.

"You are right," Rose said taking a bite. "It is good. Thank you."

"Amita said tomorrow the real wedding ceremony starts," Samantha said innocently. "I guess big Indian weddings last five days, but Amita and Vishwa had to shorten this one."

"I see," Rose said and she drank the rest of the wine like it was fruit juice. "Jessica, please get me another glass of wine."

"Maybe you should have more pizza," Jessica said as she shoved a bite into Rose's mouth.

"Seriously, Jessica, get me another fucking glass."

"Okay," she said, then she looked at Samantha and said, "Samantha is it?" Samantha just nodded her head. "This isn't Rose's wedding, okay? Rose is having her wedding in December. She is really excited about it. This shindig is just a party. Okay? Please don't say wedding again." Jessica walked off to get me a glass of wine.

"I'm sorry," Samantha said. "I didn't mean to say something to upset you."

Rose smiled at her and said, "No, it is fine. I am fine. This is great," she said through her teeth. One of Amita's friends came over and interrupted Samantha and Rose.

"Amita really wants Anil to wear the turban, but he won't wear it. Amita is heartbroken over it. Maybe you can convince Anil to wear the turban? He will look so nice with it on, and it is traditional." Rose seriously wanted to choke this woman she had never met. Rose looked at her, and before fire could spew from her mouth, Jessica appeared and said, "Hey, here is your drink, have a sip. Really, have a sip now," Jessica said.

"Thank you for sharing that with me," Rose said politely. "But Anil is a grown man, and he can decide what he would like to wear, because no one else is getting a choice, and—"

Before Rose could say another word, Jessica grabbed her and said, "Rose, Amanda is getting herself into trouble, look." Rose could see Amanda hitting on Arjun, and I looked at Jessica and we walked off to pull her away.

Luckily, they got to Amanda before Samantha noticed. "What are you doing? Amanda this is so stupid."

"*He* was hitting on *me*," she said.

"I don't care," Rose said to her. "Samantha is over there. I mean *seriously*!"

"Well, he said that he and Samantha aren't that serious. She isn't even coming on the cruise," Amanda snapped.

"Does it look like they are not serious? We are at her house! Come on, let's go back to the hotel," Rose said.

She walked over to Anil and gave him a kiss. "I'm leaving. I will see you tomorrow." He didn't really notice. He had been drinking and smoking. He was playing his guitar and singing. Rose didn't think he even noticed that she was still at the party, let alone leaving the party.

When they got back to the hotel, the girls went out to the hot tub. After Rose got in, she put her head back and looked at the stars above. She was just trying not to cry. Jessica looked over at her and said, "Holy shit, this is a full-blown fucking wedding."

"Jessica, I don't want to talk about it, okay?" Rose said.

"Okay, Rose. Well it doesn't have to be for you. It can just be a big party, right? I mean you aren't signing a papers."

Rose woke up around ten in the morning with a big headache. She looked over at the other bed and Amanda and Jessica were missing. Rose picked up her phone, and there were no messages from Anil. He was probably sleeping off his hangover. She got up and took three ibuprofens, then crawled back into bed and stared at the ceiling. When the door opened, and Jessica and Amanda came through the door, Jessica was holding a tray full of food and Amanda had a pot of coffee.

Jessica was wearing a big smile on her face. "Hello, sunshine. We got you breakfast. I got you a bagel with cream cheese."

Amanda chimed in with, "An everything bagel, of course."

Jessica continued, "Eggs benedict with turkey sausage and fruit. How are you feeling?"

"I'm fine. I just took something for a headache. Thanks for getting me breakfast. Did you guys eat already?" Rose asked.

"Yes. We both got up early, and we decided to walk around and grab something to eat," Amanda said softly. "This place is charming," she said with a smile. "Anyway, Rose you should eat something. What time are we supposed to arrive at your henna party?"

"We are supposed to be there at three," Rose said as she stuffed some bagel in her mouth. "Hey, this is pretty good. The coffee is good. Amanda, can you pull out that purple outfit. I am supposed to wear that tonight."

"This long dress thing with pants?" Amanda said.

"Yes, it is a kurta. Amita got one for everyone in my family, but I am supposed to wear it tonight."

"Wow, look at these pants. This is crazy. These really skinny legs and huge waste. Is this right?" Jessica asked.

"I think that is correct," Rose said. "Well at least it has a drawstring. The color is pretty. I like purple," Rose said with a smile.

Amanda smiled, "You will look beautiful in whatever you wear, jellybean. This color will look great on you."

"Thanks, Manda," Rose said. "So, what are we doing until we have to leave? It only takes ten minutes to get there. So we pretty much have the whole afternoon. What is the weather like?"

"It is nice and warm. Let's go for a walk and see the town and grab lunch before the party," Jessica said.

"Sounds good. I'll take a quick shower and then we can head out. Give me twenty minutes," Rose said.

It was a beautiful day. The sky was clear, bright, and sunny. It was about ninety-five degrees, and Rose tried to stay cool by wearing her hair in a braid, a skirt, and a tank top.

"This is a great town," Amanda said as she eyed a young guy who smiled at her.

"Seriously? Amanda, you really need to just chill out," Rose said.

"I want babies," she smiled. "My uterus hurts," she proclaimed.

"Gross," Rose said. "Sorry, I don't get that."

"You don't want kids?" Amanda asked in shock. "You say that because you are getting married. You found your person."

"No," Jessica chimed in before I could say a word. "Rose has never said anything about kids or marriage. Rose is all business, career, career, career for as long as I have known her."

"Thanks, Jessica. Now I officially sound like an ice queen. To answer your question, no, I do not want children. Anil and I already discussed it," Rose said matter-of-factly.

"What does Anil want?" Amanda asked.

"He says he wants kids," Rose said. "I told him that I do not want to have children. He knows I want to get my career started and travel the world. He seems fine with that. He thinks that I am selfish for not wanting children. You know, passing on good genes, blah blah blah. I just don't think passing good genes is a reason."

"I don't think everyone needs to have a kid," Jessica agreed.

"Sounds weird," Amanda corrected her.

"I'm just saying, maybe you shouldn't lead with, 'Hi, I am Amanda, and I want to get married and have your babies," Rose laughed. Amanda smacked Rose's arm. "Ouch!"

"Yes, well it was deserved," Amanda said. "I just want to be honest when I meet someone. When they ask what I want, I do not want to lie."

Jessica could not take it anymore, because she looked at Amanda and said, "It makes you sound desperate. No one likes desperate, not men, not woman, no one. So just fucking take a break and have fun. Dating should be fun."

Amanda didn't say anything; she looked hurt. Rose agreed with Jessica, but she felt bad for Amanda. She really did come off as desperate; she *is* desperate. She just didn't get it.

"I think what Jessica is saying...is that maybe you should just get to know the guy first before you start telling him your deepest desires. You know? Take your time." Rose could see Jessica roll her eyes, but it seemed to make Amanda feel better. "Okay, ladies, we should get back to the hotel and get ready."

While they got ready, Amanda was silent and Jessica was talking about her new girl and some clothes that she had bought. Rose put on her kurta and fixed her hair.

"You look cute in that," Jessica proclaimed.

"Thank you," Rose said. Her phone started ringing, and she could see her mom's number pop up on the screen.

"Hello. How are you guys?" asked Rose.

"Good," she said. "I have your sister and brother with us. We should be there in twenty minutes. I'm so excited to see you."

"I'm excited to see you guys," Rose said. "I will text you the address of the hotel and Amita's house. I'll see you soon. I love you."

"I love you too, honey. See you soon."

When Rose arrived at Anil's parents' home, she was instantly swarmed with cousins and family. There must have been one hundred people in the home. Everyone was nice and trying to be helpful. Anil's young cousins were all so beautiful. He had such a beautiful family. It was like a bunch of ken and barbie dolls from India. Rose had never seen so many good-looking people in one place. She could see Amanda's sullen look disappear as she eyed the male guests. There were all these beautiful statuesque men walking around the house. Amanda was like a lioness on the prowl.

A young girl came over to Rose. She was maybe twenty-three.

She had jet black hair and big almond brown eyes. Her skin was milky brown, and she didn't have a single blemish on her face. She looked like a movie star that had been airbrushed in a magazine, except she was standing in front of Rose. She had the face of an angel, and her smile lit up the room.

"Hi," she said in a heavy Indian accent. "I am Anil's cousin, Rashna, I am going to help you get ready." She had a shyness about her, but she was clearly excited to meet Rose. She had a huge smile and she was so pretty that it was hard to stop looking at her. "Would you like something to drink or eat?" she asked.

"Thank you. I am okay," Rose said to her. "It is nice to meet you." Rose followed her to a woman who was sitting in the living room waiting to apply henna.

"The henna is going to take a few hours," she said with a smile, "but don't worry, I will make sure that you have whatever you want. I can get you food or drinks," she said with such excitement. Then she looked at me and said, "You are more beautiful than Anil described." She was completely serious. *Has she not looked in the mirror?* Rose thought. She could feel the awkwardness creep up in her because she didn't feel beautiful. *She feel awkward. Rashna is so sweet and kind,* Rose thought.

"A few hours?" Rose asked. "Hours?" she repeated, as if she didn't understand the definition of hours.

She smiled. "Yes, maybe three or four hours. That is why you need someone to help you. You will need someone to bring you food and drinks."

"So I sit down for hours? Three or four hours?" Rose asked again, trying not to panic. She could barely sit still through a good movie, let alone *hours* while someone painted her body. "Can't we just do a few nice designs?" she gulped.

She smiled and said, "It will be fun, and everyone treats you like a princess. We will take care of your needs."

"Jessica, where are you? Jess?" Rose could see her running over. She could feel the panic. There were all these people she didn't know, and she had to sit in one spot and not move. Rose didn't want to be a princess. She just wanted pizza, wine, and beer. She could feel the blood drain to her feet.

"What?" Jessica asked.

"Please hang out with me," Rose said. "Oh, and please keep Amanda away from Arjun."

"So I am a magician now," she said sarcastically. "It's either hang with you or keep Amanda in check."

"Okay, well just check in with me, please," Rose said desperately.

Rose sat down and the woman began applying the henna on her feet. Rose didn't know it was going to take that long. Rose thought maybe she was exaggerating, but the henna on her feet and hands took over three hours to complete. It was these intricate designs that covered her feet, ankles, and hands. The woman was truly talented. She did a beautiful job. Jessica kept her promise and checked in on Rose in case she had to pee or eat. Amanda was herself and was all over every single guy at the party; she was making Jessica crazy, but at least she was staying away from Arjun.

Rose looked up and saw her family walking through the door. "Hi, guys!" she waved.

"Hey," Tony said, smiling. He came over with everyone and gave her a hug. "So what's all this?"

"Henna," Rose said. "I am getting painted for tomorrow. Are you guys hungry? There is food downstairs. You should go and help yourselves. I'll be down in a bit."

"Okay," my mom squeezed me. "Are you sure you don't want us to stay here with you?"

"No. I am fine, and Jessica keeps checking in on me. Go eat and have fun," Rose said. She watched her family walk down the stairs. Her brother looked back at her and gave her a thumbs-up sign. Rose smiled back at him.

When the designs were completed, two of Anil's cousins asked Rose to try on the saris and pick one for the ceremony the next morning. She followed the girls into the bedroom, and on the bed there were two saris, one was red and the other was purple. The girls were so excited for Rose to try on the sari and take part in this cultural experience. They made her feel welcome, and it was very nice.

Rose looked at the girls, smiled, and said, "I really like the purple one the best. They are both beautiful, but the purple one is my favorite. Purple is my favorite color." The girls suggested that Rose try them both on in order to make the best decision. They told her that they really liked the red sari. While Rose was trying on the dresses, she could hear the girls outside the door speaking with Amita.

"Sorry, we are really trying to get her to wear the red sari, but she likes the purple one," one of the young girls said. Rose heard Amita whisper, "Okay, okay, well keep trying. I want her in the red sari."

Rose took off the dresses and folded them. She was so mad at Amita. She needed to have control over everything. Rose got dressed and opened the door. "I am going to wear the purple sari," she said. "Thank you for helping me."

Rose went downstairs to a room full of guests. There was a wine bar and Indian food being handed out by a caterer. There were so many people. The downstairs had over a dozen tables with white tablecloths. Big paper balloons were hung on the walls, and colorful material was draped over the tables. The cousins had decorated, and it looked really nice. Rose saw her family standing by the French doors talking to some of Anil's cousins. They were smiling, and it looked like they were having a nice time.

As Rose looked out the French doors, she saw these gigantic black clouds rolling in toward them. She could see the large oak trees sway back and forth like they were little blades of grass in a strong wind. She gulped as she looked over the tree line. The sky filled with streaks of lightening and then instantly the thunder crashed. The clouds opened, and a torrential downpour ensued. It was raining so hard that the guests who were outside were soaked in seconds. They were laughing and joking, but Rose was really concerned. *The trees in the back of the property are so large. What if one of the trees came crashing down? What if the electricity goes out?* Rose thought. Then it happened: all the electricity failed, and they were all standing in the dark. It was so dark that it was frightening. Rose saw a flashlight go on, and she could see Amita try to remain calm. She began lighting tea lights and placing them on the tables. Anil's cousins began to help out and light the tea lights until the room was glowing.

Amita gained control of the crowd, then announced that Anil and Rose were going to play a game. The couple sat on chairs with their backs to each other. Both Anil and Rose held paddles with *yes* and *no* on either side. The crowd gathered around them, and everyone got silent and the game began. They were asked a series of yes/

no questions to show how compatible they were, and remarkably, they answered all the questions the same way.

Then one of Anil's cousins performed a dance for the guests and another cousin sang. Rose could tell the cousins worked hard on all the performances, and she thought it was so kind and sweet. It was late when the performances ended, and the party started to break up. The storm had passed, but the electricity was still out. Rose walked over to her family and gave them hugs and kisses.

"Do you guys want to follow us back to the hotel?" Rose asked.

"Sounds good," Rose's mom said as she squeezed and hugged her. "You feeling okay?" she asked.

"I'm fine. I am just tired. Come on and follow us back to the hotel. We can all have breakfast together in the morning," Rose said.

"How were you feeling?" Amy asked Rose, prompting her to pause her story.

"I was overwhelmed. The party was nice, and the henna was beautiful. At this point, I was resigned to the fact that I had been duped into a Hindu wedding. I knew that I could either make the best of it or be miserable. I tried to make the best of it. Anil's cousins were all so nice and kind. They had put a lot of effort into the party and really went out of their way to make me feel comfortable. I couldn't help but think that maybe I was just being difficult. Maybe Anil was right, and any normal girl would be happy to do all this for their spouse. I was just so resentful that Amita lied to me and tricked me. I was angry that she took over as if I didn't matter. It was just eating at me and clouded my wedding. She stole my day. I thought she was a selfish, manipulative liar."

Amy grew serious and had the tiger gaze. "She did manipulate the situation. However, I do not think she is trying to be mean or evil. I believe part of this is cultural. This is what is done. Did she plan her wedding?"

Rose shrugged. "I know and I agree, but it does not hurt any less. It does not make it easier, and it pisses me off. This was my day and she stole it! I hear you, Amy. No, she did not plan her wedding. Her mother-in-law took over too. So my question is if she did not like it done to her, which she clearly did not because she bitched so much, then why do it to me?"

Amy laughed. "Maybe she thinks she is doing the right thing. Maybe she just thinks that this is the way 'things' are done. Whatever it was, I think it is good that you tried to enjoy the experience."

Amanda, Jessica, and Rose went back to the hotel. They all sat on the bed and started talking.

"The henna is beautiful," Rose said looking at her hands.

Amanda smiled. "I love it and you look beautiful."

Rose started to put on her pajamas, which consisted of boxers and a T-shirt. Rose could see Amanda watching her.

"I think you are lucky to have great boobs. Maybe if I had great boobs, I could be a guy magnet too," said Amanda.

"Thank you?" Rose said, unsure of what to say. She continued getting ready for bed and then she slipped under the covers. "You think it is my boobs?" Rose asked after some time.

"I don't know," Amanda said. "Not like that, but you know it gets guys' attention."

"It got my attention," Jessica said, laughing.

"Every skirt gets your attention," Rose said with a smirk. Jessica hit her head with a pillow.

"Are you excited?" Jessica asked.

"I am happy," Rose said. "I'm not nervous because I don't really feel like it is my wedding day. I feel like this is a ceremony for Amita. You know, it is her time to show off. She can bounce around and say her son is married. I think it is a huge deal for her kids to be married. Hopefully, she will back off a little bit now that she got her way."

"No, then she will probably bug you for grandkids," Jessica corrected.

"Great," Rose said as she put the pillow over her face.

The next morning, they all got up around the same time. Rose threw on a skirt and a tank top and pulled her hair back into a ponytail. She could feel the humidity pouring into the room already. She turned on the TV to see what the weather would be like. The weatherman promised clear skies. He also said that it would hit a high of ninety-five degrees, which Rose wasn't thrilled about. The ceremony was to be outside on gravel, and she knew they would all feel like they were melting. The guests were not going to be under tents during the ceremony, and the tent the couple would be under would have this fire going the entire time. All Rose could picture was everyone melting in their places.

The girls walked downstairs for breakfast. Rose's mom, Daniel, Juliet, and Tony had already had gotten a table. They had ordered coffee and were waiting on them before they went to the buffet. The buffet was nice. It wasn't a typical buffet where you placed the food on your plate; it was a made-to-order buffet. So, Rose ordered a vegetarian omelet, light on the cheese.

"What's the deal for today?" Tony asked.

"After breakfast, I am going to take a nap and then get ready. The ceremony does not start until three," Rose said. "I guess you guys should get ready too."

"Dude, what is the deal with the pants? The waist and ass are huge with little tiny legs," Tony said as he laughed.

"I think that is just the way they are made. My pants last night were the same way. It made me look pregnant," Rose said. "For the dress that I have to wear today, three women need to help me put it on, and I am worried that I am going to fall when I walk. How am I going to pee? Do I have to take everyone to the bathroom?"

"You will be fine. Juliet, Amanda, and I will stay next to you. We won't let you fall," Jessica said. Rose still felt nervous that she was going to make a fool out of herself.

"It will be fine," Rose's mom said. "You always do just fine, Rose."

Rose finished up her breakfast and went back to the room with her friends. She jumped in the shower and let the warm water hit her body. She just needed to relax. She hadn't heard from Anil, but she guessed he was busy with his cousins and friends. Rose got out of the shower, wrapped herself in a towel, and went to lay on the bed. Jessica and Amanda were watching a show. An hour had passed when there was a knock on their door. Jessica got up to answer, and Rose could see a young girl at the door.

"I came to help Rose with her hair," she said.

"Hi," Rose smiled. "I'm sorry, but I don't know your name."

"I am Aahna," she said with a huge smile. "I am Anil's first cousin. I thought you might like some help with your makeup and hair."

"That's great," Rose said. Like all of Anil's family, she was a very pretty girl. She, like Anil, didn't have an accent.

"How do you like your hair?" she asked.

"Anil likes my hair curly," Rose said. "Besides, with this humidity, I don't think we will have much luck trying to get it straight." Rose watched as she took out a bag and began to heat a curling iron. She pulled out a chair, and Rose sat down. Aahna started to put makeup on Rose's face. She could see Amanda and Jessica getting ready.

"Close your eyes, I will make you look like a bride," she said with what sounded like excitement, but it made Rose's stomach get a big pit in it. Rose could see Jessica's face as she looked at her. It looked like Jessica was worried about Rose's reaction, but she just sat there.

"Thank you," Rose said. She was trying to be gracious, but really all she could think about was how terrible Amita was. Rose knew this girl had nothing to do with it; she was trying to be kind.

As Aahna left, Amita, Gitamami (Aahna's mom), and Nishamami walked in to help Rose into her sari. They took out the sari and began speaking in Hindi. It sounded like they were giving each other directions on how to wrap Rose up. They didn't say much. They took putting the sari on Rose seriously, and they wanted to make sure it was perfect. When they were finished, they each gave Rose a hug and told her how beautiful she looked and off they went to get ready.

Jessica smiled. "You look really beautiful, Rose. You really do."

"Thank you. I feel like a sausage stuffed into a casing," Rose said with a giggle.

"Well, you definitely do not look like a sausage. You are so beautiful. You have no idea." She gave Rose a hug. "Come on, we will all walk downstairs together," Jessica said softly.

Amanda and Jessica helped Rose down the stairs. Rose turned the corner, and she could see everyone sitting outside on white chairs.

"Jessica," Rose whispered into her ear. "Please hold me. Oh my god, there must be over a hundred people here," Rose gasped. She could feel her legs getting weak and the blood drain into her feet. Rose must have gone pale, because she felt Amanda push a seat under her and hand her water.

"We have you," Amanda said.

"Just breathe," Jessica said. "It will be fine. All you have to do is walk to that raised tent. We will be with you the whole way. I promise we won't let go."

"Jessica, there are so many people. Why are there so many people?" Rose asked as her throat began to dry up. She could see her family sitting under the tent. Her sister walked up next to Jessica.

"Is she okay?" Juliet asked.

"Yes, she is just hot. She is fine," Jessica said as she put the bottle of water up to Rose's mouth for her to drink. The music started. Rose could feel Jessica and Amanda bring her to her feet. She felt like they were moving her down the aisle through to the crowd. She could see Anil waiting for her. Her family looked hot…not in a sexy way. They were cooking in front of that fire. Rose could see the beads of sweat rolling down their faces. The girls walked her under the tent, then Jessica and Amanda took a seat and Juliet went into the roaster with Rose. She sat next to their mom.

The Hindu priest began speaking, and the ceremony began. It was about an hour long. The priest wrapped ropes around the couples' wrists, walked them around the fire, and made them exchange leis around each other's necks. It was a beautiful ceremony, but it was clouded by lies for Rose.

When the ceremony ended, they went to the banquet room. There were so many people. Samantha said that one hundred and fifty guests had come to the party. It was all Anil's family and friends. So many family members had flown in from India. The room was filled with cousins and friends putting food on their plates. It was a huge southern Indian buffet. Anil and Rose walked to the table to eat. It was a long table with immediate family members only. Samantha wasn't at the table, and Rose could not even see where she was sitting. It looked like Amita had stuffed her away in a corner. It seemed like Samantha was always stuffed aside.

As Rose took a sip of wine, Gitamami walked over to her and put a beautiful diamond necklace around her neck. She smiled and said, "This is the aunties' gift to you. I hope you like it."

How could I not like it? It is a beautiful eyelet necklace. I could use it to help boats find the shoreline it shined so brightly and is so large. "Thank you," Rose said.

When dinner was finished, the music started to play. Everyone began dancing and talking. Anil's family members could really party. They were dancing nonstop, song after song, and they were all pretty good dancers. They were all wearing such colorful dresses, it was like a sea of material floating around. It was lovely to watch.

Anil and Rose danced with everyone. Gitamami danced with Rose the most. She was born in India and married to Amita's brother.

She was very fashionable. Every time Rose saw her, she looked like she'd just stepped out of a magazine. She was very attractive. Her daughters looked like her, and it was no surprise that they had her sense of fashion. Gitamami had a great sense of humor, and she kept Rose laughing all night.

Amita must have been watching, because she came over and whispered in Rose's ear, "You cannot trust Gitamami. She is just a showoff and bragger." Rose didn't know why Amita said that to her, or why she felt that way. Rose suspected that it was out of jealously.

The party went for four hours and by the time it was over, Rose had so much gold hanging from her neck from cousins placing jewelry on it that it was completely covered.

Around that time, Tony and Juliet walked over to Rose. "What are you guys doing tonight?" Juliet asked.

"We were planning on putting on swimsuits and heading to the pool to swim," Rose said. "Do you and Tony want to join? I think Arjun and some of Anil's friends will be there. I know Jessica and Amanda plan on it."

"Okay, that sounds good," Juliet said with a smile.

Just as Rose went to turn and leave, one of Anil's cousins came to say bye and she said with a smile, "So do you feel married now?"

At that moment, Rose wanted to run up and punch Amita in the face. She could feel Jessica hold her arm like she knew what she was thinking. Rose smiled politely and said, "I feel the same." She gave her a hug, and they all walked off to get ready for a swim.

Anil and Rose got back to the room. They had been moved to their own room while the party was in progress. Rose slipped into her navy blue bikini, and Anil put on his trunks. The navy blue against

Rose's skin made her look paler than she was. Rose looked around the room that Anil's parents had arranged for them. *I guess we are sanctioned and allowed to be in the same bed now*, Rose thought.

"Amy, I started to realize that even the nice gestures that they did were starting to lose meaning," Rose reflected, while looking at the floor in front of the couch she was perched on. "I mean, it was nice that they gave us the room, but I could not help but be irritated by it. I was irritated that it always had to be their way. Like now that we are married, we can be in the same room. But we were not married! I didn't sign one paper! It was all just starting to become a joke to me. All the bullshit. I think this is where I really started to become resentful," Rose explained.

"Why do you think that you became resentful of the nice gestures?" Amy asked.

"In part, I think that I did not believe the nice gestures were real. I started to think that it was a way to manipulate or exercise control," Rose said through a cracked voice. "I don't want to sound ungrateful. I'm not ungrateful, but I felt like every time they did something nice then I would let my guard down and they would be mean."

Amy crossed her legs and leaned forward. "Do you think this was purposeful? I don't. I don't think they dislike you. It seems like they are unhappy. It is almost like they have to pick so they feel like they are in control because they probably never have been in control of their lives."

When the couple got outside, there was a fire going in the fire pit. Juliet and Tony had brought out some wine. Rose sunk herself into the hot tub, and Anil sat by the fire with his friends. After about an hour, Rose began to realize that Amanda wasn't out yet. That was when Rose heard her brother laughing.

"Look who is making out in the pool with Arjun," Tony said, laughing.

"I give up," Rose said. "Jessica, you were supposed to watch her."

"Really?" Jessica said. "She is a nightmare on wheels. Besides, I am tired of babysitting her! Why are we babysitting her anyway? She is a grown ass woman. Let her throw herself at whomever she wants!"

Rose realized Jessica had a point. *Why are we babysitting her?* They all watched as the two of them sucked face in the pool. Rose was so annoyed with Amanda. *Whatever*, she thought, *this isn't my problem.* Rose sat back and drank her wine. After all, Rose had her wedding to prepare for in the winter, and that was what she was going to focus on—her *real* wedding day.

CHAPTER 6

Rose paused for a moment. "Amy, I was so relieved to be home with my dogs after that. We got back on a Sunday afternoon, and I could feel the relief as I opened my door. I did miss my family, but the serenity and thought of having some time with Anil alone was a nice thought. I kept thinking maybe we should go on a trip, just the two of us. It had been so hectic, and Anil's birthday was coming up in August. We could go away for his birthday. I began looking for little mountain places that would be fun, and I found this nice little place on a lake and I booked it. I was excited to tell Anil," Rose explained.

Amy smiled. "What did you hope for by taking the trip?"

Rose smiled as her face became red. "I thought it would bring back the fun and lightness. Maybe the sex would feel like it used to feel. You know, where I would lay in his arms and feel safe. It would be our time alone. Just us being us, no filter."

"Sometimes it is good for couples to recharge together," Amy said.

As the pair crawled into bed, Rose told Anil that she had booked a nice place for them to celebrate his birthday. He seemed excited. "Where?" he asked.

"Lake Blue Ridge," Rose said with a big smile. "What do you think? Here, look at these pictures."

"It looks amazing. Thank you, babe. That is sweet of you," he said.

Anil was gone when Rose woke up the next day. She got up and made some coffee. *I love this backyard of ours*, Rose thought to herself as she drank her coffee. They had just gotten back from the party, and she was enjoying the silence. Fourth of July was in two days, and Rose could not help but think that they should go to a park and have a cookout. She could make chicken with potato salad or even an egg salad. Rose's phone rang suddenly.

"Hello?" Rose answered.

"Is Rose there?" a lady's voice asked.

"This is she," Rose said.

"Hi Rose, this is Charlotte from, Piper and McCall Law. I received your resume and would like to interview tomorrow if that is okay?" the woman said.

"That would be great," Rose said. "What time?"

"Can you do the afternoon?" Charlotte asked.

"Yes," Rose said, then she proceeded to take down the directions. She was so excited. *Finally!*

When Anil walked through the door, Rose could barely contain her excitement. She came whipping around the corner and practically ran him over. "I have a job interview tomorrow at this boutique criminal law firm!" Rose said. She was popping with excitement.

"That is great. Rose, I am so excited for you. Let's grab something to eat and go over some practice questions," he said.

Anil and Rose went out to eat and rehearsed for the interview. Rose was really happy. Anil was really into the question-asking, and he had good questions to prepare her. Anil was so smart.

"Rose, you are going to do great," he said. "Just remember to think about what they are asking you before you blurt something from nerves like you usually do. It will be fine."

Rose smiled. "Thank you. I'm not nervous. I have been waiting for this," she said. "I think I will wait to tell anyone until we know what happens. So let's just keep it to ourselves."

"Sounds good," Anil said before kissing her nose. "Come on, let's go home."

As soon as they walked in the door, Anil's phone went off.

"Hi, Mom and Dad," he said.

"Hi, Anil. How is married life?" his parents asked.

"Fine," he said. "It is the same as before."

"We are driving to you for the Fourth of July holiday," his mother said.

"Oh. Okay. When?" Anil asked.

"Tomorrow," his mother responded. "We should be there by four of five."

"Okay. Well, I will let Rose know. I love you guys. See you tomorrow," Anil said.

"Tomorrow?" Rose squealed. "Anil, we were just with them. I

mean we have only been home for a day. I was going to start on the wedding this weekend," Rose said through her teeth.

"They just want to be a part of our lives, Rose. They are my family," he said.

"I understand, but this is crazy. We were just with them, and I wanted to prep for the wedding, and I have an interview tomorrow," Rose said.

Anil looked over at her and said, "My mom can help you with the wedding. This is a good thing, Rose."

"I do not want her help!" Rose screamed, then she walked into the bedroom and went to bed.

The next morning, Rose awoke with big bags under her eyes. She didn't sleep much, and she felt like shit, but she got up and focused on her interview. She wasn't going to let this upset her and mess up the interview. She prepared that morning and tried to stay positive. *Maybe now that I was part of the family, Amita would be better to be around, and she would be more accepting of my relationship with Anil,* Rose thought.

The interview went well. It didn't take long, and it seemed like they were interviewing based on how well Rose would get along with the staff and not necessarily her skill level. Rose was pretty sure that she did fine, and honestly, all she could think of was how she was dreading going home. Home was her sanctuary, her haven, and now she was going to be judged and bugged in her peaceful place. She took a deep breath and thought to herself, *Rose you are being so negative. Maybe things will be different now.* She stopped at the grocery store on the way home to buy milk and some other items that she didn't keep in the house that her "in-laws" liked.

Rose walked through the door and took a deep breath. She could smell Amita's food being heated in the kitchen. Her dogs didn't greet her because they were put out back. Rose said hello to Amita and Vishwa and walked to the sliding door and let the dogs inside. *I guess this will be my new routine.* Rose rounded the corner to change her clothes, and she heard the door open. She could hear Anil coming in and his parents greeting him.

Rose was happy to see Anil home early, and his parents were better behaved when he was around. The table had been set, and Amita was putting the food on the table. Rose started to walk over to Anil to give him a hug when he asked, "How was the interview?"

Rose shot him a look as if daggers were coming out of her eyes. Rose had told him she didn't want anyone knowing about the interview yet.

Anil responded, "It is okay to tell my parents; they will be happy for you."

Rose couldn't believe he went against her wishes. They had just talked about it. She shook off the shock and said, "The interview went well. It seems that they want someone for just a few months, but at least I will learn the court system."

"That is very good," Amita said. "It will make you feel better if you are working. It will make you feel good that you are contributing. Samantha is a very hard worker," she said.

Rose knew *exactly* what she was doing. She was comparing her to Samantha, so Rose stepped up the pace. Amita didn't know that Rose knew how she *really* felt about Samantha. Amita told Anil that Samantha is lazy. She said that Samantha does not work hard, and she is always complaining.

"Well, Samantha is a good person," Rose said to Amita. "Everyone really likes her." Rose could tell her comments irritated Amita.

After dinner, they decided to watch a movie. As soon as the movie began, Amita started with her incessant questions. Rose finally couldn't take it anymore. "I am going to work on wedding stuff. I think I found a cruise, and I need to book it and set aside some rooms."

"I can help you," Amita said.

"Thanks, but there really isn't anything much to do. From the looks of it they send me a checklist, and I just check boxes. It is super easy. Goodnight, I am going to check boxes and then get some sleep." Rose walked away before she could respond.

She sat in bed for a few hours and booked a cruise. It left from South Carolina and made its way to the Grand Turks and the Bahamas. Rose could have this amazing beach wedding on a budget that she could afford. She sent out emails to all her family and friends. She told them to reserve a cabin and that formal invitations would be coming.

The next morning, Rose awoke to the sound of banging and clanging. She got up and pulled her hair back into a ponytail. Amita was in the kitchen drinking her morning tea.

"Good morning," Rose said.

"Good morning," Amita said as she drank her tea.

"Did you eat?" Rose asked.

"No, not yet," she said.

"Okay. I will make a vegetarian frittata," said Rose.

"Oh, you don't have to do that for us," she said.

"I know," Rose said with a smile, "but I think you will enjoy it."

Rose started chopping vegetables and whisking the eggs. By the time everyone was awake, breakfast was on the table. It must have been good, because Vishwa wolfed it down and Amita said, "I never noticed, but you have a forehead like mine. I don't like mine either."

Rose wanted to pick up that cast iron pan and bean her in the forehead. Instead, Rose said, "Amita, I do not know what you are talking about; you are beautiful." *That shut the bitch right up*, thought Rose.

Rose was thrilled that Fourth of July weekend seemed to pass by fast. Amita and Vishwa left on that Sunday, and Rose was free to resume her wedding plans. Juliet had found this cool place that did the invitations, and she helped Rose with the design. They came out well, and Rose was thrilled that the company even mailed them.

Rose ended up getting the job she interviewed for, but it was only for a few months. She started that job and made a friend, Dara. She seemed nice, and she was helping the firm out for only a few months as well. Dara and Rose actually ended up starting their own firm within about eight weeks of knowing each other.

Dara was also from the East Coast. She had lived in Florida for some years and had recently moved to Georgia. She was married and had a little girl. She only wore black and referred to herself as "dark and twisty," which Rose was pretty sure she got from a TV show. Dara was a few years younger than Rose. She had long, black wavy hair and hazel eyes. She and Rose ate lunch every day and hung out. All she did was talk about how sad she was because she could not get pregnant with another child.

As Rose was working at her new job and planning the wedding, her mom flew out around the second week of August for four days to help her pick out a dress. She had court early on a Friday morning, and she took her mom with her. She hung out while Rose worked a simple plea. When Rose was finished, they walked across the street from the courthouse where there was a boutique wedding shop; they ended up buying a dress there. Rose's mom bought it for her as a wedding gift.

The dress was cream colored. It was sleeveless and had French lace. The train took nine bustles to hold up, and it came with directions. That train was so long, the detail was amazing. It had these designs in the lace that when the light caught the train the dress shimmered as the material flowed behind Rose. The dress was really meant for a fancy church wedding and not the beach, but Rose didn't care—it was so beautiful. Rose's mom picked out sandals that went perfect with the dress.

"Thank you, Mom," Rose said.

"You look beautiful in that dress. Your dad would be so proud of you," she said.

Rose choked back my tears. "I hope so."

"He was proud of all of you. He just didn't know how to show it," she said. Rose thought she was trying to convince her of this. It was just hard because she felt like he didn't fight to stay. Rose knew that it wasn't fair. She knew he didn't have a choice, but that little kid part of her felt like, *Why didn't you fight to stay?*

Amy had a sympathetic look on her face. "How did your dad pass away?"

"He was making coffee, and he fell and never got up. I don't know. His wife didn't have the doctors perform an autopsy. Maybe a heart attack," Rose said. "That happened when Anil and I were first together. It was difficult. I was alone, and Anil, well, he was doing Anil and he had his own stuff to deal with, so I really just had to suck it up."

"Suck it up?" Amy said.

Rose's eyes teared up. "I was alone. My family was away, and Anil wasn't mean about it, but he was not present. I saw a grief counselor because I did not know how to deal with the rush of emotions. I cried all the time, and I missed my dad's hugs. I knew I would never have those warm, strong heartfelt hugs again."

"How long did you do the grief counseling for? What did you learn?" Amy asked.

Rose focused on a picture of Amy with her boys and smiled. "I was in counseling for about a year. My dad and I had repaired our relationship right before he died. We were finally at a place where we could talk about our dreams and feelings. Then suddenly in a snap, it was gone. His death changed my life. I realized that I needed to be present again in my life, and I started to enjoy the arts again. I even took up pottery."

Amy smiled warmly. "I did not know you did any pottery. It is important to be present."

Rose cocked her head to the side. "I started to appreciate the way my mom tried to make our relationship right again. It made me appreciate what I had rather than what I lacked."

Rose's mom continued in the bridal shop, "I am proud of you too."

"I know, Mom," Rose said. "I know." But the truth is, Rose didn't really know, and she always felt out of step.

Her mom could not stay for long this trip because she had to work. Rose was sad to see her leave that Sunday, but she knew that she would see her for the wedding close to Christmas, and that thought made her happy.

Rose got to the office on Monday morning and started to complain to Dara about her period.

"Can you believe that it has been two weeks, and it will not go away?" Rose asked, not giving it much thought. "It is so annoying, and I have never had this happen. Must be the stress," she said with a smile.

"I don't know," Dara said. "I think you should go to the doctor. I mean, what if it is more than stress?" she prompted.

"You think? I don't feel sick," Rose said to her.

"I really do think you should see a doctor," she said firmly.

"Okay, I'll call and make an appointment," Rose said.

That night, Rose told Anil about what Dara had said.

"I am sure you are fine," he said. "Why don't you give it a few more days?"

"I guess, but the doctor does not have an appointment until next week," Rose said. "So that is a few more days."

Anil always thought everything was going to be fine. He thought Rose worried too much. For the most part, he was right, but having your period for over two weeks is irritating at best, and Rose just wanted it to go away.

By the time Rose went to the doctor, her period had gone away. The doctor asked all the usual questions, then he said, "You have two cysts on your ovaries and a polyp on your uterus. I do not recommend surgery for the cysts, but you may want the polyp removed. More than likely, you will not be able to have children," he said. "We can schedule the procedure whenever you like. You can wait, especially if it isn't bothering you."

"Okay. I think I will wait just a bit," Rose said. "Maybe after my wedding." Rose smiled.

Rose left the office thinking about what he said. She felt weird, because most women would be upset to receive that news, but Rose wasn't upset. She thought to herself, *Well, I guess it is just not meant to be. I didn't want children anyway. All is well that ends well.*

Rose drove home and walked through the door. Anil was home before her. He had already ordered pizza and started eating. "How did it go?" he asked.

"Fine. The doctor said I will make it." Rose smiled. "He said I have some cysts and a polyp that I should remove. Not a big deal. Oh, and that I more than likely I will never get pregnant."

"So, we can stop using condoms?" he asked.

"I guess. Maybe I'll ask him when I have the surgery," Rose said.

"See, I told you. It wasn't serious," he said.

"You were right." Rose smiled and gave him a kiss, then his phone rang.

"Hi, Mom. Hi, Dad," he said as he got up to pace the room. "Oh, hang on, I will ask Rose." He looked over at her. "Do you mind if my mom and dad come for my birthday?"

"I bought us that weekend away. It is non-refundable," Rose said.

"Guys, Rose got me a weekend away for my birthday," he said. "Of course, I want to see you, but she already purchased trip. I don't think she is trying to keep me away from you, Mom. This is her birthday present to me. It is just this year. I know you want to spend every birthday with me, but it is just this time," he said. "Bye, guys, I love you."

Anil looked at me. "My mom was upset. They like to spend my birthday with me. Are you sure it cannot be refunded?" he asked.

"I am sure," Rose said. It annoyed Rose that Anil's parents interfered in every aspect of their life, and she always felt like she was on defense.

Anil and Rose went away on their trip to the mountains the following weekend. Anil's birthday falls around Labor Day weekend, so they always get a nice long weekend to celebrate. Rose did all the driving. Anil didn't like to drive, and she loved driving; it was therapeutic for her.

When they arrived, they drove to the main house and checked in with the front desk. Rose got the key to their private cabin and went back to the car. They pulled in front of their cabin, and they were shocked to see they were right on the lake. The cabin was amazing. It had huge windows that faced the lake and sliding doors that led to a patio. The patio had an outdoor couch that was so comfortable you didn't want to get off it. The cabin was cozy with wonderful handmade furniture that you could sink into and just relax in. There was a fresh tray of snacks and drinks. After they had moved inside, Rose looked at Anil and gave him a kiss.

"Babe, isn't this nice?" she asked.

"This is great," he said.

"They are having hors d'oeuvres and wine at the main house. Do you want to take a walk and go for a bit?" Rose asked.

Anil smiled and said yes, and they walked over to the main house. Rose wasn't sure if she was just being sensitive, but it didn't seem like Anil was excited. It is like every time his parents interfered, it flipped a switch in him. He drank more and acted different toward Rose. He lost joy. Rose was a pleaser, and this put pressure on her to make it better. She put pressure on herself to make him feel better in these situations.

"Anil, do you want me to get you a plate?" Rose asked.

"Sure. I will go grab us some wine," he said. "Do you want to sit outside on the patio?"

"Sounds great. They have a fire going and it looks wonderful," Rose said and smiled. Rose knew how much Anil liked sitting outside by the fire, and she was hoping that he would start to feel at ease and enjoy himself. She went outside and found them a spot by the fire. Anil came out and sat next to her. He took a sip of his wine and said, "I am really impressed with this place. This is beautiful."

Rose smiled and said, "Yeah. It is relaxing, just what we needed." They both sat back and enjoyed the view.

The next morning, Anil and Rose decided to go rowing on the lake. They got up early and went to the main cabin for breakfast. There was a huge spread. Anil and Rose gorged themselves so that they could have the maximum rowing time and not need to take a break to eat. Rose filled her plate with eggs, sausage, and fruit. It was good they ate so much, because they ended up being gone for five hours. Luckily, they had the foresight to bring water with them.

When they got back, they were so tired that they just ordered pizza and wine to their room. They took a shower and passed out.

Rose kept texting pictures to Anil's parents throughout the stay on the lake, but only his dad responded. His father's responses were short. He would say "nice" or "pretty," but at least he responded. Rose found out later that his mother would not even look at the pictures, she was so mad that Rose took him away on his birthday.

The weekend went by too fast; before they knew it they were back to their regular lives. On her way to work, Rose stopped to grab coffee and ended up getting caught by a road detour. While driving, she was taken through a development that was adding homes. Rose was so enamored by them that she I stopped to look at one of the models. She walked in the home and was greeted by a realtor named James.

She started to walk through the model home. It was an open concept with high ceilings. Rose liked that you walked into a large entryway before entering the home. To her left there was a space that could be a dining room or office. There was also a large entry closet. There were high tray ceilings with molding. The kitchen faced the family room. A sunroom was placed off the kitchen. The stairs rounded up to a loft with four bedrooms. The home was three thousand square feet, but with the high ceilings and hardwood floors it seemed much bigger. All three bathrooms were large. The laundry room was like a small bedroom. Rose fell in love.

She could not wait for work to end; on her lunch break, she took Dara through the home. Dara didn't like the open concept, and she didn't like that the laundry room was on the first floor, but she thought it was a nice home. However, Rose knew this was *their* home. Anil and Rose had gotten enough gift money to place a down payment on the house. All she wanted to do was get home to Anil to tell him about the home.

Once work ended, she raced home. She walked in the door and started dinner. She kept peeking out the window waiting for Anil. *Ugh, when is he going to come home?* Then she saw his car pull up and her stomach grew with butterflies. She was going to open the door, but then she decided to just sit on the couch and wait for the door to open. Anil walked in and said, "What?" He wasn't used to her sitting and waiting for him to come inside.

"I found a home for us!" Rose leaped up and kissed him. "It is amazing and in our price range. Do you want to look this weekend?"

"Sure, let's see," Anil said.

"Okay, but I really know you will like it. Please?" Rose begged.

This situation made Rose realize one of the biggest differences between Anil and herself. He was always content. She was like a mountain goat; she always wanted to climb higher.

That weekend, they went to look at the model home. "Okay," Rose said to Anil, "let's take a drive and grab something to eat."

They went to eat, and Rose drove by the models and pulled up to the home. She knew that once he saw it, he would love the home. "Let's take a look. This is the house I was telling you about."

They walked into the home, and James said with a big smile, "Hi. You're back."

"Hello," Rose said. "I brought my fiancé."

James smiled. "Take him around. Let me know if you need help with anything or if you have any questions."

"Thank you," Anil and Rose said together. They started their tour.

"Isn't it perfect?" Rose asked.

"I really like this place," he said.

When they finished their tour, they went back to speak to James. James took them around the lots that were left. Rose was surprised when Anil said, "We'll take this lot. I like all the trees."

They gave James their earnest money to hold the land. "See, if we didn't have the Indian wedding, we would not have our earnest money," Anil said. As soon as it came out of his mouth, Rose felt annoyed.

Late in September, Dara and Rose started their own firm. They opened up a small office. Rose was so excited, but Dara didn't even crack a smile. "Aren't you excited," Rose asked her.

"I hate being a lawyer," she responded.

"But we have a chance to really create something," Rose said. She didn't say anything. Rose realized that Dara was just usually negative. Rose was happy to be working and helping people though. Besides, Dara seemed nice enough. *So what if she is having some weird identity crisis? I mean, aren't we all having a crisis?* Rose thought. Dara was also unhappy because she could not have another child; all she ever wanted was to be a stay-at-home mom. She was funny and would say things like, "I hate women's rights. I just want to sit on my ass and have some man take care of me."

Rose paused for a bit, took a deep breath, then said, "I don't know, Amy. It was hard. I was attracting people into my life who just were not excited about life. I kept trying to be excited for everyone, but it was exhausting. I just wanted to be happy, but I also thought that I could make everyone around me want to be happy too. I could show Dara that our practice was fun, and she could make her own money, but that didn't work. She just resented me."

"Why do you think it is your job to make everyone happy?" Amy asked.

"I just like to be happy," Rose told her. "I love living, celebrating, and eating. I love sex. I want that for everyone, but the truth is, I just want someone to share that with. Someone to get excited over the stupid shit. For example, I love Disney, and I don't care that I am a grown ass woman. That is my place. When I go there, I feel like a kid again. I take pictures with every character. The lines do not bother me. I want to hang out with people that love that shit too. Just enjoy living. Life is so short, I want to enjoy the process," Rose said with an almost sad smile.

Amy smiled. "Then find those people. They are out there. Find likeminded people who respect you and your values."

"I know I can do that." Rose smiled. "Right now, I finally have a best friend who really loves life. When we hang out, I laugh so much with her. I just don't laugh with Anil anymore," Rose shared. "It is like the air has been sucked right out of our relationship."

September and October were filled with Rose working and picking out materials for their new home build. Anil didn't partake in any of the home-building experience. Rose was in their bedroom putting away laundry when she heard Anil come home from work. She walked over to him and could immediately see that something was wrong.

"You okay?" Rose asked.

He made a face and said, "I was laid off." He looked so deflated, and Rose wasn't about to make him feel worse.

"Okay," Rose said. "You didn't really like that job anyway." Rose wrapped her arms around him and said, "So, congratulations! Now you can focus on working somewhere that you enjoy. Let's go get something to eat and celebrate." Rose gave him a big kiss.

Anil told his parents, and they immediately began looking for jobs for him in the DC area. Apparently, they had heard that would be a good job market for Anil. It was so annoying, because they didn't even consider Rose and her life. She had just started a firm, and they put a down payment on their new home. She was doing well in court, and people were beginning to know her name. Rose put Anil in touch with a friend of hers who did contract work, and Anil began contracting. It wasn't a bad gig; at least the pay was steady.

Rose was busy at work. She started to notice a pattern with Dara. Every day, Rose would walk into work with a smile, and every day Dara would be sad. Every day, Dara would say, "We are going out of business," or "We have no money," or "We are bankrupt." She said things like this every day. Rose soon came to realize that she was just a very sad person in an abusive marriage. *It's weird*, Rose thought. *You have two woman who have careers, and by all accounts are successful, yet they allow the people in their lives to abuse them.*

Dara was an attractive girl with a pear-shaped body. She didn't like her legs, because they had a tree-trunk shape to them. She was short, about five-three. She was educated. Her husband, Brad, was tall. He looked like one of those jock types. Dara thought that he was good-looking. Rose thought he looked like a frog. He called her and screamed into the phone at least once a week, and Rose watched her shake. Dara told her that they had a bond, and that was why she didn't leave him. She also told her that he had never been faithful to her. *She can do so much better*, Rose thought. *But some people would say so could I.*

That night, Anil and Rose were sitting on the couch watching TV. Because it was October, Anil and Rose began their zombie, witch, and vampire movie marathons. They loved sitting on the couch and spooking each other out. Anil's phone rang, and Rose jumped. Anil laughed and answered his brother's call.

"Hey, brother," Anil said as he put the phone on speaker. Arjun sounded upset and he began to tell Anil that their parents were driving him crazy. Apparently, Amita and Vishwa could not stomach Samantha. Amita wanted Arjun to marry Sarah. Amita and Vishwa made a list comparing Sarah and Samantha, and at the top of the list was that Samantha was ugly. They listed Samantha as lazy, not smart, unappreciative, and a manipulator. Arjun was telling Anil how furious he was with his parents, and he was hurt that they made this list and called her ugly. Arjun made them promise not to tell Samantha, because he didn't want her to hate his parents. Then Arjun said, "So, Mom and Dad said you were coming home for Thanksgiving. Mom said that since Rose's family has Christmas, we get Thanksgiving."

"Yes, I was planning on seeing if Rose would mind coming," Anil said.

Rose was pissed. *How unfair. I know that I will not be able to see my family every Christmas because I had to fly and it was too expensive.* They just had to drive a bit to see Anil's parents. Plus Anil's family came to visit all the fucking time.

Then Arjun said, "Don't tell Mom and Dad that I told you, but they are planning on surprising you for Halloween." Rose felt like fire was shooting out of her ass. Anil didn't say a word. He just ended the phone call.

Rose looked at Anil and said, "I am going to fly home for the weekend and see my family. I think I need a break. Your mom and dad can come spend time with you." Anil didn't argue. Judging by the way she felt on the inside, the way she looked on the outside was probably not much better, because Anil even offered to pay for her airfare.

A couple weeks later, Rose got off the plane in Denver and was greeted by her sister. She had a big smile on her face. Rose gave her a huge hug and kiss on the cheek.

"I hope you didn't make any plans for tomorrow," Juliet said with a smile.

"Are you kidding?" Rose said. "I just want to relax for a moment. I planned nothing."

"Good," she said with a smile. "I planned something for you. It is a good surprise," she said. Rose knew Juliet; she probably did plan a very good surprise. She always gave the best presents.

The next morning, Juliet came to their mom's and picked Rose up for a day out. She had planned a shower/bachelorette party. It was Rose's kind of party, because it was just Rose and Juliet.

The pair arrived at a fancy spa called Anya. They walked into the spa and Rose gasped. It was amazing. The floor was marble, and the sound of mellow, calming music was dancing in the air. The walls were marble and rock. The colors were a calming sage accented with other earth colors.

They were immediately greeted and asked if they wanted tea or anything to eat as they were ushered into their room. The room was large and had a fire going. They were given white robes to put on and told to wait in a couple of oversized chairs nearby. As soon as they sat down, there was a knock on the door and a woman came in with tea and tiny sandwiches. She placed the tray on a table between them. Rose and Juliet enjoyed some of the tea before two women came into the room carrying oversized copper bowls. The ladies filled the bowls with warm water and oils and began washing the girls' feet.

Once their feet were cleaned, they were brought to another room with large massage beds. Two women came into the room and started giving the girls facials. Rose could smell cucumber and orange being rubbed on her face. *I'm in heaven,* Rose thought. When their facials were over, they were told that they could take off their robes and slip under the sheets. Rose slid out of her robe and under the sheet. Just as Juliet slid under her sheet, two beautiful men walked into the room. They began to give the girls their massages, and Rose literally felt like she was floating on a cloud. When the massage was over, the beautiful men left the room; Rose and Juliet put their robes back on. They were escorted to the fireplace room where they were treated to champagne and chocolate-covered strawberries. Juliet was the queen of best surprises.

Over the course of her visit, Rose's family treated her to lunches and dinners. They wanted her to relax and enjoy some family time. They watched movies and drank wine. It was a wonderful trip.

When Rose got home, the house was a mess. She had to clean up after everyone. She scrubbed the house and resumed her work schedule. She was dreading Thanksgiving, which was only two weeks away. *I would rather have a root canal,* thought Rose. *But maybe this time they will cool off.*

Two weeks went by fast, and Anil and Rose headed to his parents' house for the holiday. As they drove up the driveway, Rose could feel a pit in her stomach. They walked into the house, and to Rose's surprise, Amita had the table set and dinner for everyone was ready. *Maybe this would be a good trip. Maybe I am finally part of the family.*

In reality, this holiday trip would be a repeat of the year before with one exception—Anil and Rose could sleep in the same room. The entire time Amita tried to convince them that DC was the perfect job market for Anil. She even got a few interviews for him through friends. She gave them a down payment for the home that they were having built and then told Rose, "Well, there can be no divorce because that would be a waste of our money." Rose felt so defeated and so frustrated.

When they returned home, Rose had two weeks to put the finishing touches on the wedding. It was easy. The cruise members were always available, and all Rose had to do was email any changes. She sent in the number of confirmed guests; their total was twenty-five. Rose had to admit, having a small wedding was a benefit to Amita's shindig. Rose got to have the small, intimate wedding with close friends and family that she always wanted. It was also within the budget. Rose had to pay for her own wedding, and this trip fit the bill.

Two weeks later, Anil and Rose boarded the cruise ship. It was their first cruise, and they were so excited. The ship was a miniature city. As they boarded, Rose looked out at the ocean and felt a calm in her body. The ocean always soothed her soul. She was staring at the water, watching a pod of dolphins play when she heard Jessica and Amanda behind her. She turned around and gave them both huge hugs. They headed through security and toward the pool area to sit and hang out until they were allowed in their rooms.

Anil and Rose had booked a luxury suite. Rose was told that for a cruise ship, their room was massive. But it didn't look that big to her. It had a large bathroom with a walk-in closet. They had a sitting area with a bar and oversized couches. The bed was next to the couches. They had a large balcony that Anil and Rose fell in love with immediately.

"Babe, this is amazing," Rose said as she was texting their guests with their room number. Her phone started to ding with return messages almost immediately.

"This is great," Anil said. He started texting his friends and family too.

The first guest to arrive at their room was Rose's friend Jacob; he brought his girlfriend too. Jacob and Rose were close and spent a ton of time together in law school. He was Rose's cuddle buddy. Whenever Rose needed to feel safe, she would head to Jacob's and watch movies and cuddle. Jacob was tall and looked like a better-looking Tom Cruise. He had a great sense of humor, and Rose was so happy that he joined them that she jumped into his arms.

"Hi, Jacob!" Rose giggled. "It is so good to see you." She turned and immediately hugged his beautiful girlfriend, Megan. Megan was a soft-spoken girl with long blonde hair.

Anil poured them both a drink as other guests began to pour into the room. Every guest was told as they entered our suite that Anil's parents didn't know Rose was older than Anil, and to please not make jokes or mention their age difference to them. Juliet and Tony had already briefed Rose's mom and Daniel.

All the usual suspects were there; even Rose's old law school roommate, Laurel. She came with her husband. Laurel was a fellow Capricorn and the master at dressing exceptionally well. She had jet black hair and hazel eyes. Her cheekbones were high, and she had a tiny nose, which Rose always admired. Laurel was a solid friend, and Rose was excited to see her face. Her husband, Greg, was tall with glasses. He had a great sense of humor, and Rose enjoyed speaking with him.

Laurel looked at Rose and said, "Did you make an appointment to have your hair done for your wedding day?"

"Uh, no. Was I supposed to do that?" Rose asked her.

Laurel just shook her head and said, "Yes. That is why I booked it for you. I knew that you would never think of that. I bet you didn't hire anyone to do your makeup either."

"No." Rose smiled.

Laurel smiled. "I will be coming to your cabin to help you. I am proud of you. You did a nice job dressing for your first day of the cruise."

Rose gave her a huge hug and said, "I don't know what I would do without you; these are the clothes that you picked out for me in law school." Laurel looked at Rose and laughed. Laurel picked out every outfit that Rose wore, and she was damn good at it.

At that moment, a huge horn went off and the captain came

over a speaker. He informed all the passengers to meet at the deck on the top of the boat. When they arrived, they were broken into groups and given instructions in case of an emergency. Rose was so glad that there wasn't an emergency, because the process for disembarking was so complicated that Rose was sure she would end up going down with the ship in a real emergency.

After the demonstration was over, all the passengers waved to the people on the shore. Anil and Rose went back to the cabin to take a shower and relax before lunch. They went up to the deck and grabbed some sushi. It was so fresh and yummy that they could not stop eating. Rose began to realize she had to wait a week for her wedding ceremony, and if she ate like this the entire time she would not fit into her dress. With tears in her eyes, Rose put the chocolate cake down and watched Anil scarf the entire piece. *Now I know why some women push these men overboard,* Rose thought.

Anil and Rose started to explore their miniature city at sea. She could not believe how much there was to do on the ship. They had a seven-day cruise, and only three of them were at sea. Their wedding would be on the second to last day of the trip. It was going to be on a beach in the Bahamas. Rose didn't think they would be able to do everything the cruise had to offer, but she would have fun trying.

They arrived at their first destination a day after the cruise started—Grand Turks. A few of them had charted a boat for a snorkeling adventure. Anil's mom and dad and Rose's mom and Daniel didn't join the adventure. They met the guide right outside where the boat had docked. A young man, maybe in his mid-thirties with blonde locks and ice blue eyes, greeted them. He explained he had taken a vacation there about six years ago and never returned to

Boston. Rose could see why. Something about this island seemed magical.

They all got on his boat and he started passing out drinks while he took them to the first diving destination. Juliet and Rose jumped into the water first. Rose popped up out of the water and Juliet looked at her and said, "I think we are going to die." Rose looked around and saw thousands of tiny little jelly fish in the water. Their guide laughed and said, "Don't worry, they don't sting." The water was warm, clear, and filled with all different kinds of beautiful fish. They snorkeled all morning, and by the afternoon, they were all famished. At the request of Anil and some of his friends, their guide took them to a local pub where they could purchase weed and lunch. *Great, we are all going to get kicked off the cruise ship and end up in jail*, Rose thought.

As they headed back to the ship, a pit grew in Rose's stomach. She was freaking out about the group bringing weed back onto the ship. She was annoyed that Anil would risk their trip and the wedding for fucking weed. She thought it was ridiculous, but this wasn't the first time Anil was stupid about weed. Rose remembered one time he made her drive all the way to his hometown a few minutes from his mom and dad, and they had to stay in a hotel, all so that he could buy "good" weed from a friend.

It made no sense to Rose at that time, and it made no sense to her on their wedding trip. The panic must have not registered on her face, because they passed through security with ease. I watched as the others walked through security and made it through without issue. A part of Rose wanted Anil to get caught, because then maybe he would think before he did stupid shit. But he got through, and after dinner, everyone came back to their cabin and went on the balcony and got stoned.

As a huge gust of weed scent came in the room, Rose's mom asked, "Did they bring weed onto the ship?"

"Yes," Rose said to her annoyed.

"Where did they get it?" she asked.

"You don't want to know," Rose answered.

Anil's parents walked into the room. They stayed in the room until two in the morning and had no idea that all the guys kept going to the balcony to toke up, even though it was coming into the room.

The next day, they all hung out on the ship. During the day, Anil and Rose went swimming with their guests. They met up with everyone by one of the pools. Jessica and Amanda were already there sunbathing. Rose could see her sister and aunt making their way up the stairs with her mom and Daniel. They were at some sort of adventure pool with slides that shot you over the ocean. Rose was surprised to find more adults jetting over the ocean than kids. Daniel and Rose raced each other down the slides like two little kids. All of their guests had dinner every night together, afterwards the girls and Rose went dancing or swimming, and Anil went with the guys to the casinos.

The morning of their wedding arrived. Rose got out of the shower and opened the door to find Laurel sitting on her bed with breakfast and coffee. Anil had gone to meet his father and brother. Rose had tuxes sent to the male family members for the wedding. They didn't have a wedding party. They just had his brother as best man and Juliet as the maid of honor.

"Good morning," Laurel said with a smile.

"Good morning," Rose said to her. "Thank you for grabbing me breakfast. You always think of everything."

"I was worried that you would not get a chance to eat until tonight," she said. "Your mom should be here any minute. Then we can go and get your hair done." I gave Laurel and hug and a kiss on the cheek.

After their hair was done, Rose went back to her room and got dressed. Laurel began to put on her makeup, but her mom was freaking out.

"I am so nervous," Rose's mom said. "I am shaking. I can't even put this necklace on my neck."

"Laurel, can you please help my mom?" Rose asked. Laurel helped her with the clasp and did her makeup before they had to leave.

All their guests were on the island enjoying themselves. The wedding wasn't until two in the afternoon, and it took Rose all morning to get ready. Rose had trollies meet the guests in town and take them to the wedding site on the beach. They left the ship and met their ride for the wedding site. As they drove to the destination, Rose kept thinking to herself, *Shouldn't I be nervous?* But she wasn't nervous. She was having a blast with all her friends and family. She was excited to have them all together on a private beach. She was excited to marry Anil.

When they arrived at the beach, Rose could see all her guests sitting in chairs in front of the arbor. The arbor was filled with native flowers; it was so beautiful. The chairs were covered with white covers. The wedding coordinator came over to introduce herself.

"Hello," she said with a smile. "I am Penny. I have your bouquet here for you." She handed Rose the most beautiful bouquet that she had ever seen. It was full of local flowers, and Rose could smell the sweet aroma coming from the bouquet. She could see the orange hibiscus, yellow elder, and pink plumeria pulled together with a beautiful bow.

Tony and Daniel came up behind her and walked her down the aisle. She had her two favorite men at her side. Anil was already under the arbor waiting, and when Rose came to the arbor, he put his hand in hers. Juliet stood by her side, and Arjun was by Anil's side. The officiant was standing under the alter with them, and he had their vows, which Rose wrote for them.

Rose looked out at their guests; Laurel gave her a thumbs-up and mouthed how beautiful she looked. She saw Anil's parents sitting down. Rose noticed that there was no one sitting next to them. Rose found out later that it was because Amita would not stop talking. In fact, she kept telling all the guests that there would be no divorce.

Rose turned to Anil and smiled; she wasn't going to let Amita distract her from this moment. They said their vows, and Anil kissed Rose. The officiant laughed and said, "Hey, not yet. Okay," the officiant smiled. "I now pronounce you husband and wife, you may now kiss the bride." Everyone laughed, and Anil gave Rose another kiss.

They walked over to cut their cake and toast for pictures. Then it happened; the license was brought to the table, and it had their birthdays on it. Anil and Rose had to strategically cover the license as they signed their names. It was like they were doing this peacock dance. As soon as they signed the license, it was scooped up and taken away. They took more pictures on the beach, then Anil and Rose headed back to the cruise ship where their photographer took more pictures on the ship.

By the time the couple arrived at their reception on the boat, Rose was starving. Laurel was right, had she not brought her breakfast, Rose would have gone all day without eating. Anil and Rose walked into a large room. It was amazing. Rose never expected what she saw that night. She had only checked off boxes on a list, yet the ship had turned her checkmarks into a magical moment.

The tables had ice sculptures placed on them. Every food item on the table was made into a sculpture of some sort. Even the fruit dishes had these twigs made of sugar rising from the fruit that was placed into martini glasses. There were servers walking around handing out hors d'oeuvres. They had another wedding cake that was placed on a table decorated in local flowers. The wedding cake was all white with three tiers and a silver sculpture of hearts intertwined on top. The bar was full service with all top-shelf liquor and a friendly bartender who served the drinks.

The DJ announced their first dance. It was to the song "Our Love Is Here to Stay." It started playing, and Anil and Rose began to dance. It wasn't new and popular; it was an older song, but it was special because Anil used to sing the song to Rose. When their dance ended, the music changed and the guests began to dance.

Amita walked over to Rose and said, "You are wearing a white dress. I thought you were not going to wear white."

Rose smiled and said, "It is cream." Rose walked away from her and started dancing with her friends. This was her celebration, and she was going to enjoy her friends and family. She was going to celebrate with her husband. She would not let Amita steal another moment.

CHAPTER 7

When they got back from their wedding, it was a few days before Christmas. They were still in boxes in the new house, and Amita was torturing them to come see the new home. Rose put her foot down and told her new husband that she would not have Amita over right now; she could wait until they were unpacked. Amita claimed she "wanted to help her new daughter." *Honestly, what a load of shit. She just always has to control and dominate*, thought Rose.

"No. I am unpacking my own home," Rose said with authority. "I do not want anyone's help." Rose didn't want Amita to take over her home and go through her belongings. This time Rose would put her home together before Amita came to her house.

January was upon them, and of course, Amita wanted them home for her birthday on January 2.

Rose looked at Anil and said, "No, babe. I am not going across those mountains in the dead of winter. My birthday is in two weeks, and I just want to relax. We just got married and moved. Our house is still in boxes. Please, let's just enjoy some quiet," Rose said as they headed upstairs to turn in for the night.

"Okay," Anil said. Rose could see he was tired of bouncing around too. "Babe?" Anil said as she was slipping into bed. "Do you remember how the doctor said you can't get pregnant?"

"Yes. Why? Are you upset now or something?" Rose asked.

"No," Anil smiled. "Why are we still using condoms? I hate them, and you hate them. We don't need them. We aren't sleeping with anyone else, and you cannot get pregnant."

"True," Rose said. "I guess you are right. I mean the doctor was 100 percent sure. Okay," Rose agreed, but something in her stomach said, *Don't do this Rose, unless you are ready to be a mom*. Rose didn't know why, but she never listened to her gut; it had a pretty good track record of being right. It was always her brain that fucked everything up, and yet, for some reason, the brain always won. Every time she started to think and overrule her gut, things got messy for her.

Immediately upon returning to work, Dara began the "our business is failing routine." Rose wasn't sure why, but it seemed like she just loved being miserable. It became stressful working with negative Dara. Rose was beginning to think that she just could not be happy or positive. Rose secretly hoped that she would find another job and just leave the firm. Rose honestly felt like her negative energy was paralyzing their business.

Rose noticed every time she said something positive to Dara, she would find the negative. It was exhausting. She was so miserable all the time. She was so unhappy in her marriage, but she wanted a baby so badly. She was so unhappy being a lawyer, but she still practiced law. It was hard to work in such a negative black hole, then come home and deal with Anil's drinking and Amita's interference. Rose felt so tired all the time.

Around the second week of January, Rose was so tired that she could not lift her head off her pillow. She had a migraine and just stayed in bed. Anil came in and gave her some ibuprofen.

"You okay?" he asked.

"I feel so tired," Rose said. "I don't know what is wrong. I feel like I felt when I had mono as a teenager. I cannot lift my head off the pillow."

"Maybe we were out too late last night," Anil said. "I mean we were at Jackie and Matt's pretty late."

Jackie and Matt lived a few houses down from them. They had just moved into the neighborhood, and Rose and Anil became friends with them. They started to spend almost every weekend with them. They were also recently married, so they all had something in common—none of them knew what we were doing.

"Maybe," Rose said to Anil, but she knew something was wrong. She felt *bad,* and it wasn't like her to feel like she could not get out of bed. She also didn't get headaches, and she had a massive one almost every day that week.

Anil kissed my head and said, "My mom wants to come and see the house. She has called every day asking when they can come."

"Anil, I really don't feel well. Please tell your mom that I just can't right now. I don't think you understand how shitty I feel," Rose said.

"Okay," he said. "But are you ever going to let them come?"

"Anil, are you serious right now? Look at me, I cannot get my head off this pillow. I do not know why I have the energy level of an eighty-year-old."

"Maybe you should take a break from going to Jackie and Matt's," Anil said. He sounded annoyed with her.

Rose got out of bed and called her mom. She just need some reassurance that she didn't have a brain tumor, because according to every website, she had a tumor.

"Hey, Mom," Rose said.

"Hi, babe. You okay? Your voice does not sound the same," she said. Rose could hear the concern in her voice.

"I'm okay. I just feel so tired, Mom. Remember when I had mono?"

"Yes," she said.

"Well, I feel like that again, minus the sore throat," Rose said. "I am scared. What if I am sick again?" Rose said.

"Rose, you are fine. You just had a big year. You had two weddings, two jobs, Anil lost his job, and you had a move. You are probably just exhausted. I am sure you are fine," she said.

"You are right," Rose said, but she was still worried.

"Look, if you don't feel better soon, then go to the doctor," she said.

"Okay, Mom. I will. I am going to make lunch and head to the office. I love you."

"I love you too," she said.

Rose went to the office, and Dara was at her desk. "Hey, sorry" Rose said. "I just don't know why I feel so sick lately."

"You need to take a vitamin," she said. "I take my kids' vitamin every day, and I am fine," she said.

"Right."

The next few weeks would prove to be worse. Rose could still not find the energy. She had headaches, and she wasn't hungry. She lost about ten pounds. From searches online, it was very clear that she had some horrible form of cancer, which worsened her anxiety.

"Babe," Anil said at dinner. "My mom really wants to see us. When can she come?"

"Have you not noticed? I don't feel well," Rose said. "Look at me. I am sunken in, and I can't get my energy back no matter what," she said with irritation.

"I think that we have been partying too much with Jackie and Matt," Anil said. "We have been drinking and hanging out late," he said.

"No, Anil, you have been drinking too much. I am not feeling well," Rose said. "I did some research and there are like several cancers it could be. I am worried," Rose said.

"Look, I am not doubting that you do not feel well. Maybe you are stressed or maybe you are pregnant. Did you think of that?" he said.

"No. The doctor said it is impossible," Rose said.

Anil got online and ordered eight tests. Rose got home from work early a few days later, and there was a box of tests on her front porch. She went inside and stared at them for a while. She didn't know what she was afraid of; being pregnant would rule out her cancer theory, which was a better option.

She finally found the courage to take a test; within seconds it read positive. So, she took two more, which showed two more positives. Rose could feel her heart pounding in her chest. She never wanted children, but maybe she had just been afraid this whole time. The truth was, Rose was happy when she saw the results. She had always been afraid of having children. Rose was really afraid of failing as a parent.

Then it happened—complete and total panic. Rose had been taking ibuprofen. She had been drinking. She had lost weight. What if she had done something terrible to the baby? Just as her thoughts began to spiral, Anil walked in the door.

"Hi, babe," he said.

"Hey," she said, with a scared look.

"You okay?" he asked. "Babe? What happened?"

Rose looked at him and said, "The pregnancy tests came. I took some. They all say that I am pregnant."

"Really?" he said. "The doctor said that you could not get pregnant. Maybe these tests don't work well. They were cheap. I'll take some, and we can see. I mean, if I come up pregnant then we know the test is wrong."

"Okay," Rose agreed.

Anil took a few tests, but his were all negative. He looked at Rose and asked, "What do we do?"

"Well, I don't know. I have never been pregnant," Rose said. "I guess we are having a baby."

He looked up at her and said, "Call your mom. Ask her what we should do."

"Okay." Rose called her mom right away. She was still in shock over the positive tests. Her gut had told her this would happen, but she didn't listen. She shouldn't be surprised.

"Hey, Mom," Rose said. "So, remember when I told you I wasn't feeling well?"

"Yes," she said.

"I think I am fine, because I took a pregnancy test. I am pregnant," Rose told her.

"What? Oh, thank God. You had me worried the way you started. Don't ever do that again. I mean it," she said, sounding relieved.

"Okay, sorry. I just didn't know how to tell you," Rose said. "I am really happy mom, but I don't know what we are supposed to do."

"You make an appointment with the doctor," she said through a giggle. "I am so excited. I am going to have a grandchild!"

"Mom, please don't say anything. I want to make sure everything is okay. I am worried because I have had wine and ibuprofen."

"Rose, don't research. Go to the doctor. You are fine. Now go give Anil a hug and kiss for me. I love you both. No research, Rose," she repeated.

"Okay, Mom. I will call the doctor in the morning. I love you. Night." Rose walked over and gave Anil a hug and a kiss.

She got an appointment at the doctor almost immediately. Anil had to work, so Rose went by herself. She walked into the office and took a deep breath and signed her name on the sign-in sheet. Before she knew it, a nurse named Joanie came out and called her name.

"Rose?" Joanie called.

"Yes," Rose said, and she took her in a back room and handed her a small cup to pee into. When Rose came out, she ushered her into the mini lab and dipped a stick into the cup.

"Well, you are pregnant," she said with a smile after Rose had waiting in an exam room for a while.

"Yes," Rose said.

"Okay, well let's go into this other room for your sonogram." Joanie smiled.

"Okay. Sonogram?" Rose was confused.

"Yes," Joanie said. "The doctor is going to want a picture."

"Oh…okay," Rose said. Rose was confused and a bit nervous. She didn't know what to expect, and she was frightened because she never thought she would be pregnant. This was new territory for her. She laid down on the table, and another nurse came into the room. She smiled and said hello. She rubbed this cold gel on Rose's stomach, then began rubbing what looked like a microphone on her abdomen.

"Ah. There it is," she said. "Look, do you see that?" she asked.

"Yes," Rose said. But it just looked like a seed to her on the screen.

She looked down at Rose and said, "That is the baby. Do you want to hear its heartbeat?"

"It has a heartbeat?" Rose asked. She had no idea that it had a heartbeat already.

"Yes, silly. You are about seven weeks pregnant. Listen." She turned up the volume, and Rose heard the baby's heartbeat for the first time. She heard that heartbeat, and her heart melted. This was the first time in her life she felt love, *real* love. She was overwhelmed with joy, and she looked at the nurse and just giggled. Then she realized that the heartbeat was so fast, and she got nervous. "Is that normal?" Rose asked softly. "The fast heartbeat…is that okay?"

"Yes," she said. "Your baby has a wonderfully perfect heartbeat."

"Thank you," Rose said as she watched her print the picture of the baby. She then wiped off her stomach and said, "You can get dressed and go into the room next to us. The doctor will speak with you in there."

"Okay, thank you." Rose got dressed. She went into the next room where she met Dr. Ambrogio. He smiled and gave her a hug.

"Everything looks just as it should," he said with a smile. "Now we just need to set you up with some tests, and Joanie will give you a packet of information."

"I am worried," Rose said. "I have been drinking and have taken ibuprofen. I have had terrible headaches, and I have felt so tired."

"You are fine," he said. "The headaches and tiredness are normal. I do not believe you have caused any harm, but you do not want to do any of those things anymore. If you can push through the headaches that would be best, but if you need to take anything, try acetaminophen. The first three months are the most critical. Your due date looks to be the last week in September. Congratulations, Rose. You are going to be a mom."

Rose left the office feeling so excited. She kept replaying that heartbeat repeatedly in her mind. She started to talk to that little person in her belly.

Rose waited for Anil to come home; he was late. He had gone out drinking with some work buddies. When he walked in the door, Rose was so excited to tell him all about her visit at the doctor, but he didn't seem to be as excited as she was. She chalked it up to the beers, but the reality seemed to be that he didn't know how to show his emotions about their baby.

"I spoke with my mom today, and she really wants to see us," Anil said.

"Anil, I am exhausted. I know she wants to run through this house and pee in the corners to mark her territory, but she will have to wait. I am pregnant, and it isn't about her anymore. It is now about this little life inside me. Why don't we go see her? That would be less stressful on me. Why don't we go the last week of February?" Rose proposed.

"Okay," Anil agreed. "I will call her and tell her that we are visiting at the end of February."

"Great," Rose said. It didn't feel great. Rose felt annoyed. She could not understand why she and her husband could not have a second alone. It bothered her that she *just* found out she was pregnant, and they had to drop everything to go see Amita. On top of all that, Rose was working with the queen of darkness. Her husband was coming home late every night drunk. It was a lot.

The pair arrived at Amita's house around seven in the evening a few weeks later. Anil and Rose brought in the bags, while Amita began to put the food she had been keeping warm on the table. It was the usual. Rose was received with a half hug and the usual coldness that made Siberia seem warm.

As they began to eat, Vishwa looked at Anil and said, "Wow, you are putting on some weight."

"Yes, Dad. I have gained a little weight," Anil replied curtly.

"I think it is more than a little," said Vishwa. "Go downstairs and get the scale and bring it up. We will weigh you," Vishwa said.

"Dad, I am eating. I am not going downstairs to get the scale." Anil sounded annoyed, but he must have been embarrassed as well. Rose was surprised that Amita had not started in her. Usually, if Anil is drinking it was Rose's fault. If Anil is unhappy, it was Rose's fault. Any of Anil's shortcomings were Rose's fault.

"Well, I think it is all that olive oil and pasta that Rose makes," Amita said. "Italian food is very fattening, you know," she commented.

"It is well known that Indian food is the healthiest food and has the most healing properties."

It took all Rose had to keep her from taking the rice shoving it down her tiny little throat. "The Mediterranean diet is supposed to be the healthiest diet, and that is how I cook," Rose replied. "Here, let me google it for you so you can read all about it."

The next morning, Rose awoke to the sound of banging and the smell of coffee. The smell of coffee meant Arjun had arrived. She got up, jumped in the shower, got dressed, and went upstairs to greet Arjun.

"Hey," Rose said with a smile as Arjun greeted her with a big hug.

"Hey, hey. How's it going?" Arjun said with a smile.

"Good," Rose said. "How is your new job?" Arjun had moved to DC. He had decided to practice medicine there. It seemed like he was really enjoying it.

"I like it, and Sam has a great job there too," he said. "Samantha went for a quick run. She needed to stretch after the drive."

"I bet," said Rose. She stuffed blueberries in her face. Rose poured herself a cup of coffee and sat down to talk with Arjun. Anil came up the stairs.

"Hey, babe, is that coffee? You sure you should be drinking coffee?" he asked.

"Yes, it is fine. Just one cup," Rose said in almost a whisper, but she saw Amita look over.

"What are you eating?" Anil asked.

"I had some blueberries," Rose said.

"Don't you think that you should have something more to eat?" he asked.

"Anil, I am fine. Thank you," Rose said. Rose wanted to hit him in the face. Could he be more obvious? Rose just wanted to get past the first trimester to make sure everything was fine with the baby before sharing the news.

"Honestly, Amy," Rose reflected. "I think that he did it on purpose. I think he wanted his family to know, and instead of him discussing it with me he just did this shit. This highly suggestive bullshit."

"Why do you think that? Maybe he was genuinely concerned," Amy said.

"No. He was being an idiot, because at home he wasn't like this at all. He didn't ask me if I had eaten nor did he ever question a cup of coffee. He didn't even bring in the groceries for me! He was being a jerk. I think he just wanted his family to know, and instead of talking about it with me, this is how he went about it because that night Anil blew it."

"Why do you think that he wanted his family to know?" Amy asked.

Rose puffed her checks as she held her breath for a moment. "I think he seeks their approval so much. Maybe he thought they would be proud of him. Both his parents always wanted to be grandparents."

The family was upstairs making dinner, and Rose could hear Samantha speaking with Amita. She went upstairs to hang out with everyone when Samantha offered her a glass of wine.

"She is fine," Anil answered for her. Rose shot him such a look, but it was too late. Amita may be the worst mother-in-law ever, but she isn't the stupidest one.

Amita looked over at Anil and said, "Geeze, Anil, you are acting like she is pregnant."

Ugh, great. This was exactly not what I wanted to happen, Rose thought. She just looked at Anil and shrugged her shoulders. *I mean what are we supposed to do now, lie?*

Anil looked at his mother and said, "She is pregnant. We just found out."

Judging by the look on Amita's face, it looked like she heard "Rose and I are joining the Peace Corps and moving to Nigeria." She looked like she had eaten a giant turd. Her reaction confused Rose. She'd always talked about wanting to be a grandmother and how she couldn't wait to have little Anils running around. Rose didn't understand.

"Seriously?" Arjun asked. "That's great!" He gave them both hugs. "When are you due?"

"September," Rose said. "The end of September."

"Wow," Samantha said. "Congratulations. So, are you going to find out the sex of the baby?"

"I think so," Rose said. "We have to wait until I am further along. I don't know yet. Anil and I keep going back and forth about it. I mean we want a surprise, but at the same time we want to prepare."

It was weird. Amita didn't say a word, and for the first time she was actually silent. Everyone else was talking and asking questions, but not Amita.

Later that night, Rose was downstairs getting ready for bed. She had just pulled out her latest vampire novel to read when Amita walked into the room.

"Hi," Rose said. "Everything okay?"

"Oh, yes. I just wanted to apologize for not looking happy when Anil said that you are pregnant. I am very happy." She jumped up and down twice and clapped her hands.

"Oh, okay. Thank you," Rose said. Rose felt awkward in the situation, she did not know what to make of what just happened.

Things changed when they returned home. People say that having a baby changes a relationship. Rose wasn't expecting for these specific changes to occur, but really she should've known they were coming. The signs were there, and she ignored them. She looked back and thought that she was in love with the idea of being in love, and at the same time, the thought of leaving Anil made her so sad.

Rose didn't know if Anil was stressed having a new house and a baby on the way, but he came home every night late. Rose would wait up for him, and he would come home with what seemed to be a buzz almost every night. When he didn't come home with a buzz, he had a box of beer, and he would drink it all before the next day. Rose didn't know how a person could drink so much and stay alive. She couldn't really talk to him anymore either; he was never actually present.

Their lives went on like this for a while. By Memorial Day weekend, Rose was about five months pregnant. She was concerned because she wasn't gaining any weight. She tried to talk to Anil, but he just acted like it wasn't big deal. She felt like he had checked out. Her doctor set her up with an appointment with a specialist to check the baby. Rose's mom and Daniel flew into town to be by her side during the visit.

They all sat in the doctor's office waiting for the doctor to call her into the room. Rose sat next to Anil, and her mom and Daniel sat on the other side of her. Rose was nervous, and even though she had people with her, she felt alone.

A nurse called Rose. Rose took a deep breath and she and Anil got up and went into the room.

Rose put on a gown and laid down on the examining table. Another woman came into the room and told her that she would be conducting the ultrasound. She rubbed the jelly on Rose's stomach and began moving the scope around. Rose must have been holding her breath, because the technician looked at her and said, "Just breathe. Your baby looks perfect. Everything looks wonderful. You may be a tiny thing, but your baby is fine."

"Thank you," Rose said. She looked over and Anil looked frozen.

The technician looked over and smiled. Her smile spoke of the hundreds of times she must have seen a husband with the face Anil was wearing. "Would you like to know what you are having?" she asked with excitement.

"Yes," they both said at the same time.

She took the instrument and ran it over Rose's stomach. She looked up and said, "See there? That is a boy. You are having a little boy."

Rose could feel my eyes well up. She could hear his little heartbeat, and she could see that he was well and safe. She looked at Anil, and he looked sick. He had gone pale. This wasn't what Rose was expecting.

"Would you like me to go get your parents?" she asked.

"Yes, please," Rose said. The technician left the room to grab her mom and Daniel. Rose looked over at Anil, who had seemed to have lost all his blood.

"What's wrong? Are you okay?" Rose asked Anil.

"I just don't want him to be like me," he said. "I was hoping it was a girl so she would be like you." Rose could hear his voice shaking. She was so confused.

"What do you mean? You are so smart and wonderful. You are talented. Don't say that babe. You are going to be great father, and he will be lucky to be like you."

"I realize now, Amy, that I wasn't listening to him. I didn't hear what he was saying. I didn't hear what he was *really* afraid of our son becoming. It would not be until years later that those words would haunt me. I get now that he was worried about his mind—about our some becoming an addict. He was worried that our son would have racing thoughts and self-medicating and the drinking."

Rose's mother and Daniel walked into the room and stood at her side. Rose looked up at them and said, "The baby is fine." Rose looked at the technician and said to her, "Please show them."

The technician took the instrument and said, "This is the baby, these are toes and legs, and look it is a boy!" Rose's mom giggled and hugged her. She seemed happy and excited. "I am taking you both to a celebratory dinner! See I told you this little peanut is fine," her mother proclaimed.

After seeing their baby, Rose and Anil decided on the name Enzo, the Italian version of Henry. It just seemed to fit their little guy. They agreed to keep the name a secret until Enzo was born.

Anil called his mom and dad later that night. Rose could hear him tell his parents that the baby was fine and that it was a boy. He put his parents on speaker.

"Maybe the next baby will be a girl," his mom said. Rose guessed she was hoping for a granddaughter, so she was a little disappointed that they were having a boy. Her statement irritated Rose, so she got up and left the room. Making his parents happy was just too exhausting. Anil got off the phone and sat next to Rose. She looked up at him and asked, "How about a babymoon?"

"What?" he responded.

"A babymoon?" Rose said. "You know, where you and I take a little trip before little man comes. We could go for the holiday and just get away for a few days. Sit on the beach, relax, eat, and just hang out."

"That sounds good," Anil said. He sounded almost relieved, and Rose wasn't sure why. "I'll look for a nice beach spot close by, and we can go away for the long weekend."

"Great," Rose said before giving him a kiss. "It will be nice to take a small break before the baby comes. Who knows when we will have a little break again?"

The next morning, Rose walked into work and Dara was sitting at her desk. She had her usual "we aren't making any money" look on her face.

Rose looked at her and smiled. "It will be okay," Rose said.

"How are you feeling today?" she asked.

"I am fine. The doctor said everything is okay. I am having a little boy," Rose shared.

"That fits you," she said. "Funny, people who don't want or care if they are having a baby have them so easily." Rose just pretended like she didn't hear her and turned on her computer. She had a barrage of emails.

The first email was from Vishwa. *Hello Everyone, Rose and Anil are having a little boy. Now it is time to help them pick a name. Maybe each of you could send a list and then we can narrow it down.*

The next email came in from his cousin, Aahna. *My sister and I put together a list of names. We tried to pick names that would be easy to say in the States. Here you go, Neil, Advik, Arin, Daksh, Isaac, and Jai. We both like Daksh the most.*

Anil had responded: *Haha, guys! Great names.*

Vishwa weighed in with: *Great job! I think Neil is great. You both should name the baby Neil. I like Neil. What do you think, Kalpit?*

Kalpit said: *I like Daksh, but Neil is good.*

Rose felt her blood begin to boil. She could not believe that they were trying to take over the naming of her child. They had *no* boundaries.

Rose sent her own email. She knew Amita had instructed him to send this. Just like she had tried to have the girls push her to pick the red sari. Rose took a deep breath and wrote to everyone, *Hello, thank you so much for trying to help us pick a baby name, but Anil and I have already chosen a name. We are keeping it a secret. We need to have some surprises!*

Anil wrote Rose back in a private message: *Geez babe, you can't let my family be a part of anything. They just wanted to have a little fun.*

Then his cousin Yash replied to the group: *Nice. You tell them! Can't wait to hear what the baby name is going to be.*

Anil saw Yash's reply and said: *I guess I was wrong, and what you said isn't bad.*

Rose found it interesting that Vishwa never responded again. He didn't email her after that either. He just kept telling Anil that he liked the name Neil and kept sending Anil job opportunities in the DC area.

Rose got home from work, and, as usual, Anil was out. Rose felt exhausted. Not just from the pregnancy, but also from the constant picking of her in-laws and Anil's drinking. They had to have a say in everything, and instead of Anil and Rose living their lives, they were battling their lives, and worst of all, this caused them to battle each other.

Anil and Rose found a nice little place along the beach for the holiday weekend. It was a historical hotel on the water, and they were excited to take a few days and head out of town. A few days before the trip, Anil was on his computer, and Rose began to pack a little early and clean the house when Anil's phone rang.

"Hi, Mom and Dad," Anil said, putting the phone on speaker.

"Hello, Anil," they both said. "We were thinking that we could come visit you for the holiday weekend."

"Well, Rose and I are going to the beach. We are having a babymoon, but maybe when we get back," Anil responded.

"What? Why won't Rose let us see the home? She is trying to keep us from the baby's life. You have been in that home since the end of December, and we still have not seen it," Amita said in her usual squawking tone.

"Mom, Rose has not been feeling well. We visited you in February for a week. We wanted to get away for the weekend just the two of us. Rose isn't keeping you from anything," Anil explained.

"Why can't you come here to visit your family?" she asked. "You should be coming home," Amita continued. "She has stopped you from everything. Dad sends you jobs in DC every day. Do you call? Are you looking?" Rose could hear her voice getting louder. "Dad got you a job interview here with the university. You didn't call."

"Mom, Rose does not want to live by the university, and she does not want to move to DC. She likes it here and has started her career. She is pregnant, and she is tired. She and I are going to the beach," he said. "I will talk to you later. Love you guys." He hung up the phone.

Rose looked up at Anil and said, "Thank you. Why doesn't she come for the Fourth of July? Maybe I will feel less exhausted by that time. Also, the house will be completed, and I will feel better about that too," Rose said. It was true that Rose didn't want to move again, but she also didn't want to live near his family.

"Okay, thanks babe. I know she just wants to see the house and be a part of everything," he said.

Rose thought that would be the last of Amita acting like a complete crazy person, but it wasn't. She didn't get her way, so she must have called Arjun and given him an earful, because Arjun sent Anil a harsh and critical email. In his email he claimed that Rose was trying to keep them out of the baby's life. He questioned Rose's motives as to why they had not been to the house. He felt that his mother should be spending more time at the house helping her get ready for the baby. He asked *What is Rose trying to do, take over and not let the baby be a part of their lives?*

Anil called his brother. "Arjun what are you talking about?" he asked. "My wife has done everything that Mom and Dad have asked. She is pregnant and has been going nonstop."

"I know, I know," said Arjun. "Mom has been driving me crazy, and I just wrote that letter without thinking. I was frustrated listening to her. I know Rose would never do that and Mom is just acting crazy."

Rose felt better knowing that Arjun didn't buy into his mom's crazy ass behavior. She was worried that she might have convinced him otherwise and ruined their relationship.

Rose's pregnancy was progressing, but she was still small and not gaining much weight. She was eating and the baby looked fine, but the doctor wanted more tests. Rose went in for a day of testing and found out that she had gestational diabetes. The doctor said that she would feel much better once she started the insulin and that she would maintain better weight. She was happy that there was a solution to her problem, and that the baby was doing well. Her sweet little Enzo.

Fourth of July came sooner than she had hoped, and Amita and Vishwa came to the house. By this time, Rose was seven months pregnant and had a little belly. Enzo's room was almost complete. Rose's mom's friend, Laura, had come to their home and painted a safari on his walls. Laura was so talented that the animals looked real. Enzo would have a giraffe looking over his crib with these big loving eyes. A toucan sitting on a tree sat next to the giraffe. A baby orangutan playing with a butterfly by his bed. An alligator looking after her eggs sat next to his dresser, and a baby hippo played in the water. She had painted turtles and frogs hidden in the grasses. Rose smiled as she looked around his room; it was so very precious.

Amita looked around the room. "Wow, your mom's friend is very talented," she said. "I am really surprised with this house. You did a good job. I was worried that you would not know how to pick a home." Rose just looked at her.

Amita had brought snacks and dinner, so Rose started to set the table. Amita handed Rose some napkins and said, "Try these. They are just as good as the expensive ones you use, but they are cheaper." Rose took the napkins and placed them on the table, although she was resentful "Thank you," Rose said. *Seriously, has she really been stewing over my napkins all this time? It is absurd and fucking insane.*

"I am glad you did the room neutral," Amita said. "When you have the next baby, they can share the room easily."

"I am just trying to have the first one," Rose said. "I do not know if we will have any more after this." Rose wanted to say, *Your son comes home late every night. Sometimes he does not come home at all. He drinks himself blind; the last thing I need is another pregnancy.*

"Two children is best," Amita continued. "You should have them two years apart," she said. "Also, I was thinking that I could come out before your due date to help you. I can also be in the room when you have the baby," she said.

Rose looked her dead in the eye and said, "My mom is coming to help me. You can come when she leaves. She will be here for about three weeks. My doctor said that I need to be relaxed and that I should not have any stressors. Thank you for offering."

"I can help," she said.

"Mom, Rose's mother knows how Rose likes things done. The baby and Rose come first. You can come to the house when Rose's mom leaves," explained Anil. Amita got really quiet, which only meant that she would make Anil's life hell later on.

Rose got up and cleared the table. The nice thing about her pregnancy was that she could claim to be tired and go upstairs and watch television. The pregnancy gave her the excuse that she needed to spend as little time around Amita and Vishwa as possible. She didn't want to hear her comments.

Rose looked up at Amy and said, "I thought my pregnancy would be a happy time for Anil and me. I know that pregnancy can be a difficult time in any marriage, but it seemed much more so for us, and I felt robbed of experiencing the pregnancy like I wanted, one with joy."

Amy looked into Rose's eyes. "What stole your joy?"

"Well," Rose continued as her throat grew tight, "I had the pressure of Amita, Anil's drinking, and this disease. I had to give myself six shots a day for the diabetes. It was rough, and I needed my husband, but he was off at the bars. I remember standing in front of the window one night waiting for him to come home and I was crying."

"Because you felt alone, abandoned?" Amy asked.

"Yes," Rose said through a gulp. "I had to take these stupid injections, and I was having Braxton Hicks contractions. My husband wasn't answering my texts and was nowhere to be found. I was alone,

I was scared, and I could not tell anyone what I was going through."

"Why do you think you could not tell anyone?" Amy said.

"I did not want to upset my mom or friends. I did not want to be the loser. I had to suck it up and put on a brave face. That might have been the loneliest point in my life. I was good at hiding it, Amy; not one person knew. On the outside and to everyone else, life was good. I had everything. I had a smart, good-looking husband, I was a lawyer with my own business, and I smiled and laughed all the time."

❧

Rose's mom came into town as promised, one week before her due date. She was great. She cleaned and cooked. She washed all the baby's clothes and took care of Rose. Anil would come home drunk, but he was such a good drunk that only Rose could really tell, at least that is what Rose assumed at the time. Rose would find out later that her mom knew, but she didn't know what to say or do about it.

Because of the diabetes, Rose's doctor made her pick a date to be induced on. He said that she could not wait past the due date and that if she went into labor naturally before the due date, that would be fine, but if not then he would induce her. Rose wasn't afraid to be induced. She figured, *Well, if it hurts worse than going naturally, I wouldn't know the difference. I never had a baby before, so I won't have anything to compare it to.*

On September 24, Rose went into the hospital to prep for the next day. She walked into the hospital to check in, and the nurse greeted her with a big smile. She had gotten lucky and was given a birthing suite. The room was huge and had a place for Anil to chill out and relax. The room had a Jacuzzi in case Rose wanted to use it along with a television and Bose sound system. Rose didn't get to use any of the stuff in the room, because she was prepped and given a sleeping pill.

When she woke up, she was greeted by a young nurse who hooked her up to an IV. She smiled. "Good morning. How did you sleep?"

"Well, thanks," Rose said. "Can I eat something? I am really hungry."

"No, I am sorry. We have been given strict orders. I am going to start the inducement. I will be back to check on you in a little bit." She stuck a needle in the IV and started up the medication. As she walked out the door, Anil walked into the room.

"Good morning," he said, and he gave her a kiss.

"Morning." Rose smiled. "I am hooked up to so many machines. How am I supposed to move around?" Rose said to him. "Do I have to lay in bed all day? That kind of sucks."

"I brought some movies for you," he said. "Maybe that will help pass the time."

"Thanks. I am hungry and they won't feed me," Rose said.

"Why?" he asked. "I can run and get you something if you want," he said.

"I don't think they will let you come in with it," Rose said. "The nurse seemed serious."

"Okay, here, let's watch a movie." Anil put a movie in the player and laid down next to Rose.

By lunch time, Rose was starving. She begged the nurse for some food. She gave her a cup of clear broth and some Jell-O. Just as she was finishing, the doctor walked into the room.

"Hello, Rose. Sorry that I didn't get in here earlier, but I already delivered a set of twins this morning," Dr. Treconi said. "How are you feeling?"

"I'm good," Rose said. "I am just waiting for something to happen." Rose giggled.

"Wow, Rose you are in labor. You don't feel that?" he said.

"I mean, I feel crampy. Does that count?"

"Yes," he laughed. "Okay, we have a little bit of time. I will be back," he reassured her.

"I hope so, I would prefer not to do this without you." He laughed and then walked out the door. Rose could see her mom round the corner, and she came into the room.

Before leaving, the doctor said, loud enough for everyone to hear, "Remember, Rose, your mom and husband can stay, but if anyone stresses you out, then I will have everyone leave."

During one of Rose's visits, about six months into her pregnancy, her blood pressure was high. He asked Rose what was wrong, and she started to cry. Rose told him how Amita was stressing her out. How she would not let up about visiting and moving to DC or near her. Rose told him how she accused her of trying to keep the baby from her. She told the doctor about her husband's drinking.

The doctor became angry and told Rose that she should not have Amita around too much if she was going to only think of herself and act nasty. Dr. Treconi then went on to say, "As a matter of fact, you should wait to have your mother-in-law here at all. At least give yourself four to six weeks rest before she visits. It is important that you think of yourself, Rose. You can become very ill if you do not take care of yourself." Rose realized now she should have listened to her doctor and taken better care of herself, but she didn't listen, and instead she took care of everyone else.

Around three in the afternoon, Rose could really feel the contractions. The first hard contraction came in and knocked the breath out of her. She didn't scream or say a word, she just took a deep breath. Her mom looked over at her and asked, "Are you okay?"

"Yes, I am fine," she said. "No big deal." Rose smiled.

"Well, that machine is going crazy," she said.

"I guess that is a good thing," Rose said. "Enzo is being forced out." Rose laughed. The contractions got closer together, and before she knew it, her doctor had returned.

"How is my favorite patient?" he asked.

"I'm fine. I am just waiting for you to tell me it is show time," Rose said.

He laughed. "Rose, you are going to have this baby soon. Do you want an epidural?"

"I don't know. How much worse does the pain get?" Rose asked.

"Let's just say even with your high tolerance for pain, you won't be making jokes," he said with a serious look. "I need to know now because in the next few minutes or so I will not be able to give the medicine to you."

"I will take it," Rose said. It wasn't soon after that Rose was given the medication. The doctor was right, and by five o'clock Rose was pushing to deliver her son. She looked at the doctor after forty-five minutes of pushing and said through a laugh, "This is really exhausting."

He looked at Rose and said, "This is labor. You didn't think it was going to be easy, did you?"

"No, but this is a lot of work," Rose said in between pushing. "How much longer is this going to take?" Rose asked the doctor. "I could really use a break."

He started to laugh and said, "Rose, the last patient took three hours of pushing to have the baby. I am here all night. It is up to you."

Rose looked at him and said, "Fuck that." She gave two more pushes, and her peanut was born with the loudest scream she had ever heard. Anil cut the cord, and little Enzo was handed to her. He was perfect. He had all his little fingers and toes. Enzo had a full head of hair and the whitest skin. His eyes were chocolate, and his nose was like a button.

The second Rose took him into her arms, she knew pure love. The kind of love that is totally unconditional and irrevocable. She knew that this little person was a gift, and she was lucky to call him her son. She was so happy that her little man was doing well that she didn't even notice that it took the doctor forty-five minutes to stitch her up or that she had lost so much blood that she was actually a gray color. She was so happy; she just held her sweet little boy.

CHAPTER 8

Rose was in the hospital for about a week before they let her go home. Enzo slept in her room next to her in a little baby bed. The hospital kept the babies with their moms and not in another room.

Rose's doctor had kept her in the hospital longer because he had concerns about her loss of blood and sugar levels, but as soon as everything stabilized, she was wheeled out of the hospital and she headed home. Rose remembered that day so well. She held Enzo in her arms as they wheeled her down the corridor and onto the elevator. Anil had the car seat in the middle of the car, and the staff double checked the seat for good measure. As soon as Enzo was placed in the car seat, he began to scream. He hated that thing.

Sweet Enzo was home at last. Rose held Enzo all the time. She could not put him down. She was in awe of this little person that took so much energy and time. Rose's mom laughed because she said that she knew where Rose was by listening for the kisses that she gave to Enzo. Rose couldn't help it; she held her Enzo all the time. He was perfect; he had that sweet baby smell and little button nose with huge brown eyes. Rose could still feel his tiny fingers grabbing onto her hand.

❧

Rose looked up at Amy who had been listening intently. "You know, my mom was actually a huge help. My mom stayed with me after the delivery for about three weeks and legitimately did everything she could to help me. When I woke up in the morning, there was breakfast. My mom cleaned, cooked, and did the laundry. There was so much laundry. She was amazing, and I really needed the help. Anil was hardly around, he said he had to work. I know now that he wasn't working the hours that he said that he was working." Rose looked at Amy as her eyes welled up. "I know now that he lied all the time and was off to the bars. I was a fool. I believed him so easily."

Amy handed Rose a tissue. "Why did you believe him?"

"Hmm, I wanted to believe him. I wanted a real relationship." Rose shifted uncomfortably.

"Real?" Amy's head shifted to the side as she asked Rose.

"I wanted to believe he would not do that to me, but he did. Doesn't that make me a fool?" Rose asked.

"No, that makes you human." Amy smiled.

❧

"Morning, Mom," Rose said as she walked down the stairs with the baby.

"Good morning." She smiled as she was cooking breakfast.

"Smells good," Rose said to her. "What are you making?"

"I didn't do much. I'm making breakfast sandwiches with avocado. Is that okay?" she asked, and she leaned over and kissed little Enzo's head.

"That's great. Thank you, Mom." She handed Rose a cup of coffee, and she sat at the table. "It smells good, Ma. What time did you get up?"

"I couldn't sleep. I thought I heard Anil go in and out of the house last night. Was he up all night too?" she asked me.

"He is usually up all night," Rose said. "He works from home too." Rose didn't say a word to her mom, but it bugged her that Anil was up all night and in and out of the house. It aggravated her that he would forget to lock the doors when he came back into the house. It didn't matter how upset she got with him; Anil always managed to leave a door unlocked. The worst part was how much he drank at night; she could smell the booze coming off his skin when he came to bed.

"Are you going to decorate?" her mom asked, bringing Rose back to reality. She was so far away in thought, thinking about how far away Anil gotten. *I just don't know how to pull it together.*

"Oh yeah, Halloween," Rose said through a half smile. "Sure, have at it. The bins with decorations are in the garage." Her mom was so funny. That day, she was in the garage pulling out the decorations.

Rose watched her whirl around with amazement. It is always hard for her to remember her mom's age, because she had the energy of someone twenty years younger. Within three hours, Rose's home looked like she lived in a Halloween village.

"What do you think?" her mom asked as she started pulling food out for dinner.

"It looks great, Mom. You always do such a beautiful job. I think you missed your calling. You should have been a holiday decorator."

"Well, at least you will have Halloween. I organized all your decoration boxes to make it easy for Thanksgiving and Christmas decorations," she smiled.

"Thank you," Rose said. Rose looked around and thought about how she was leaving in a few days and Amita was coming. She must have had some kind of look on her face because her mom looked at her and said, "Do you like it? Is everything okay?"

"It looks beautiful, like a Halloween village. I like it a lot," Rose said with a smile.

Her mom's flight was early in the morning. It was warm outside, and Rose was feeling sad. She drove her to the airport with a lump in her throat. Rose didn't say a word, and her mom didn't notice because she was playing in the backseat with the baby. It was nice because the baby would normally scream in the car, but with her in the back he seemed to be soothed.

When Rose got home, Anil was already gone. He didn't get home until late that night. He said that he stopped to watch the game with friends. Rose could smell the beer and she was upset, but she was tired, and she didn't want to argue, so she went upstairs and went to bed.

The next morning, Rose said to Anil, "Did you remind your parents to get the whooping cough vaccine? The pediatrician said that everyone who touches the baby needs to take that vaccine."

"Yes, I told them," he said.

"Okay, did they get the vaccine?" Rose asked. Rose was beginning to learn that she had to be specific.

"Look, I told them that they needed to get it. I am sure that they did," he said walking out the door. It seemed like every word out of his mouth sounded like irritation. Rose felt as though he blamed her for his parents not liking her. She felt like he blamed her for his drinking.

Amita and Vishwa arrived with a vengeance. She came into their home and immediately began filling the refrigerator with her groceries. She began to move items on the counter and place her spices everywhere. Within minutes, Rose's home was messy and disorganized.

She grabbed the baby from Rose's arms and took over. Rose could feel her stomach flip over, but she was hopeful that with Enzo maybe the relationship would get better with Amita and she would accept Rose finally.

"Hello," Rose said, giving both of them hugs.

They sat down and held the baby for a few minutes. Then Amita got up and began to make snacks and heat water for their tea. "Would you like some tea?" Amita asked Rose.

"No, thank you," Rose said as she just stared at her blankly.

Enzo started to scream, and Rose went over to pick him up. "I can feed him," Amita said.

"I am breastfeeding him," Rose said to her. "He only feeds for a few minutes, so I will be back down shortly. When did you and Vishwa receive the vaccine?" Rose asked. Amita and Vishwa looked away and didn't answer the question. She just asked another question.

Rose knew that Amita did not like to take medicines. The bitch had never smoked a cigarette or had a drink in her life. There was one time her boys gave her pot brownies because she had cancer and she wasn't eating. They were worried so they tricked her. Rose thought that story was hilarious.

"Where is Anil?" Amita asked, still not answering the vaccine question.

"He is at work," Rose said. "I am worried because I think that he has been drinking too much, and he spends every night at the bar." For some stupid reason, Rose thought she might have some insight or maybe be helpful. She was wrong.

"He doesn't sound like he is drinking when we call," she said stretching the words. "He works very hard, and you should not be so difficult. Maybe you just want the baby to yourself."

"Well, he is drinking, a lot. I live with him, and I am telling you. He is getting mean when he drinks, and I need you to talk to him." Rose was desperate. Her nerves were fried, and she needed someone to reason with him. She was worried because he was becoming so mean and she was concerned that it would escalate.

"I think you just want Enzo to yourself," she said.

Rose didn't even know what to say. She couldn't breathe. She took the baby and went upstairs and began to cry. She just needed someone to help her get her husband back, but his parents were so deluded. Rose was alone. She would have to do this alone, and she resented that.

Anil walked in the door at around eight. Rose knew he had been drinking. She could see his glossy eyes and hear his slurring words. She thought for sure he was busted, and his parents would notice, but that hope was dashed in an instant.

His mother looked at him and said, "Hello, Anil. You look so tired. You work so hard."

"Have you been drinking?" Rose asked.

"I only had a beer after work," he said.

"You don't sound like you only had a beer." Rose was pissed, and she would be damned if his parents weren't going to see it.

"He does not look drunk," Amita said with conviction.

"He is fine," Vishwa said. He gave Rose a look like she had lost her damn mind. Then they sat Rose at the table and began telling her that she needed to be more easygoing. Their words echoed in her ears. She could not believe what she was hearing, and she just wanted to turn the table on end.

"It doesn't matter if the dishes are in the sink. You can get to them in the morning. You need to relax. Who cares if he does not put his shoes in the entry closet. Anil is working so hard," Vishwa said. "He lives here too."

"What? Don't you see that he has been drinking?" Judging by the looks that they were both giving her, they didn't see at all that he had been drinking. She felt like they blamed her too.

Anil ate and then went into the office to "work." Rose knew he wasn't working. She knew he was drinking, and she was right. He went to bed, got up, and threw up. He was slurring his words. He grabbed Rose by the neck and told her to get him something to eat.

Rose shocked herself when she just got up and did what he asked.

She felt like she wasn't a strong woman, but a shell of who she used to be. Rose never told anyone about the interaction.

Rose woke up to Amita drinking her tea in the kitchen. "Good morning," Rose said with a smile. She was tired from feeding the baby all night, and she was annoyed that she had to take care of Anil. She felt sick that his parents were useless.

Rose started toasting some bread when Amita looked at her and said, "I could hear you this morning playing with the baby. I was very jealous. You are very selfish with the baby."

Rose smiled at her and took the baby upstairs. She was so over the bullshit at this point. Couldn't she see what was going on with her son? Couldn't she see how worried Rose was and that all she wanted was a normal family? Nope, she could not see anything, because at the end of the day, her son was like her. He was selfish.

Rose didn't eat her toast, and by lunch she was starving. She got herself out of bed and went downstairs again. Amita was sitting on the couch reading a book. She gave her the baby and went into the fridge and began heating up some leftovers. She looked up and smiled.

"I didn't think you would name the baby Enzo. I thought you would pick a traditional Indian name," Amita said.

"Well, I figured since his last name is his dad's, that it would be nice to have a name from both cultures," explained Rose.

"He looks more like Anil," she smiled.

"Agreed. I think Anil is a beautiful man. That is one of the reasons I married him." Rose smiled.

As soon as Rose started to eat, the baby began to cry; she had to get up and feed him. *Fantastic, another cold meal. Maybe I will begin to enjoy the taste of cold food.*

A few days later, it was Halloween night, and Enzo was dressed as a monkey. Rose started to take some photos.

"Amita and Vishwa, hold the baby and I'll get a picture. Guys, smile." Rose had to show them how to smile. She wasn't sure if they just hated smiling or what. They looked miserable in every photo they were in.

This Halloween was different. Anil didn't hand out candy. He was barely present, and Rose was frustrated. This was the man who loved the kids trick or treating. He loved giving out the candy and seeing the costumes, but not this year. He was up in his office "working."

Anil's parents didn't stay more than a week, but they came back for Thanksgiving. It was an easy drive for them so they came back and forth. As usual, Rose had prepared a full Thanksgiving dinner, but this year was different.

This year, Anil continued drinking and started popping pills. This year, Rose would cover up for him and cook. He was smart. He made it easy for her to lie for him by buying the little bottles of vodka that he could keep hidden. Honestly, it wasn't hard to cover up for Anil. His mother and father didn't want to acknowledge his drinking and behavior. It would take something monumental to make them see that Anil had a problem and then they would blame Rose. Any respect that Rose had for Anil's parents began to disappear.

"I realized that I was becoming a little nasty," Rose explained, looking at Amy.

Amy looked up, "What do you mean?"

"Well," Rose said through a devilish smile, "Amita is a vegetarian, right? I make a soup every Thanksgiving meal. and I always make sure that it is vegetarian. That year, I used chicken stock, and I enjoyed watching her have a bowl and eat every last drop. I used chicken and turkey stock in almost every dish that year. That might have been my best Thanksgiving with her ever!"

"Other than me sneaking meat-based broth into my mother-in-law's food, the holidays weren't much fun. Anil kept drifting further and further away. After Anil's parents left, Anil had a million reasons why he had to join me later for Christmas. Amy, I didn't know it at the time, but Anil would begin bailing on me every Christmas thereafter. So, the baby and I got on the plane and took a flight out of town. I was surprised, my Enzo was an angel. He slept almost the entire flight."

"How did you feel when Anil started to cut his visits short?" Amy asked Rose.

"At first I was upset. The first year it really hurt my feelings, but by year six it became a relief," Rose said matter-of-factly. "I mean traveling with a small child isn't easy. I had to hold him the entire time. Not to mention, I had his stroller and carry-on bags and then checked bags too. It definitely wasn't easy, but at least when Anil wasn't around, I could relax. I didn't have to worry about his drinking and pill popping. I didn't have to stress out trying to cover for him and hide his drinking."

When Rose got off the plane, she and Enzo were greeted by Rose's mom and Daniel. It was great because Rose could relax. All Rose had to worry about was herself and feeding little Enzo. She rested and hung out with her family.

Anil would sometimes call Rose to check on her, but mostly he didn't call. When he did call at night, he was wasted. Rose could always tell he was out drinking because it would start with a text message, *Hey, I am out with Scott. We are gonna watch the game.* Then a few hours would go by and the text would start again, and Anil would say, *You're bugging me.* However, by the end of the night the text messages became abusive and he would say things like, *My eyes bleed when I am with you. You are a cat that came to my door looking for scraps.*

"What went through your mind when Anil sent those texts?" Amy asked softly.

"At first, my stomach would turn. I would feel hurt, and I wondered if he meant all the cruel things that he texted, but when he was sober in the morning he would always apologize and tell me that he never meant any of what he said. I worried so much about him. I knew he was drinking and driving, and it scared me to death."

"My mom let me relax in the morning while she and Daniel played with Enzo. I woke up to giggles and the smell of coffee. My son's laugh was so cute. He still has the sweetest little laugh and smile. That little baby laugh that is infectious." Rose smiled thinking of Enzo's laugh. Rose looked at Amy and said, "Having that little guy makes everything that happened next worth every moment of every day with Anil."

"Anil did came to my mom's house on December 23. He drank so much every night that he could barely stand. I did my best in covering for him, but of course my mom went all cloak and dagger. She marked Daniel's liquor bottles to see if any had been taken. I felt the room spinning after she told me," Rose explained with a pained expression. "Amy, how many times can a person be betrayed? I felt betrayed by my mother again. I guess it was at that point that I knew I was on my own. It felt like it was gossip to my family, a fun game. This was my life, and all they cared about was being right, knowing the truth, and showing me that I was defending the enemy."

"How did that make you feel?" Amy asked. She looked so concerned.

"At first, I was angry. I just wanted to scream and yell at them. Then I felt like they had made a fool of me. I knew what my husband was doing, and I didn't need an intervention. However, my mom loves the dramatics, and my life was nothing less than dramatic. I think, in some way, it was exciting for her. I don't know. All I do know is it was painful and hurt me more than helped. I just felt ambushed. I felt so, so alone," Rose explained.

"Do you think they wanted to hurt you?" Amy asked.

"No. I just think they would do anything to prove their point, and it didn't matter that it hurt me. I mean, the reality is that I knew but he is my son's father. I didn't want everyone talking about my husband like he was a piece of shit. It was never about me. It is always about Enzo. So, no. I was never really protecting my husband, but I was trying to protect my son. It didn't work though. They told everyone and talked about it like it was a soap opera." Rose just stared at her feet.

"I think you are correct. It does not help your son to speak ill of his father. It only hurts him," Amy said.

"When my parents were divorcing, all my mom did was speak bad about him. Hell, she still does, and the man is dead. It didn't matter whether it was true, she just had to speak her truth. That is what she calls it—her truth. It didn't matter that it hurt so much to hear those ugly words. It didn't seem to matter to her that people treated us differently, like there was something wrong with us. All that mattered was her side—her truth. That is what I didn't want for my son. I didn't want him to feel like a part of him is bad," Rose explained.

When Anil became verbally abusive over Christmastime, Rose walked him upstairs.

He was so loud. "You did this to me!" Anil snarled. "You see me, what I have become? You did this. You pregnant cat scratching at the door," he said as he crawled into bed. Rose remembered running downstairs and getting him food and water, but he was so angry, and it made it worse. Rose laid him down and prayed that he would just fall asleep. He ended up passing out after he walked her around by her neck.

Christmas morning was nice though. Anil woke up and, as usual, apologized for his behavior and said he was going to take a break from drinking.

"I'm sorry. I think I need to take a break from drinking," Anil said with no emotion. It was like he was dead inside.

"I know," Rose said as she kissed Anil. "We will figure it out. I love you." He looked so defeated, and Rose felt bad for him.

"Did you believe him?" Amy asked Rose.

"Did I believe him? I would say yes. I think I believed him, or at least I wanted to believe him…No. I was a fool, and at first, I believed him," Rose laughed uncomfortably. "I'm an idiot, right? I really believed him."

Amy smiled. "No, you are not an idiot. I think you did know. I think you chose to ignore all the signs. You were trying to keep your family together."

"Was I? I hurt so many people trying to protect my family. I became someone that I do not even know anymore. I am so numb, I feel nothing and I don't think I ever will again," Rose shared.

"I guess I have been lying to myself this whole time. I just thought I could fix him, but that is silly. You can't fix anyone." Rose smiled through her tears.

Rose changed the baby and the three of them went downstairs. As she walked down the stairs, she could smell the coffee brewing. She looked over at the Christmas tree that was decorated like it was out of a magazine. Rose didn't count, but she bet there were over seventy-five presents. It took them all morning to open their gifts. It was always so much fun to see what everyone received. Most of the gifts were for Enzo.

Anil left Rose's mom's home three days later. He went home to his family's house to spend New Year's there. Rose knew he really went to go drink with his friends. Somewhere deep down, Rose thought that maybe he didn't want to be with her, almost like an inconvenience.

Rose always felt sad when Anil left. She kissed him goodbye. Her family always seemed happy when Anil left and that made Rose angry. Anil called a few times, and every time he called, Rose could tell he was drunk or high.

When Rose got home, Anil got even worse, which Rose didn't think could happen. It was the same routine every time. He would drink, text Rose sweet messages, then progressively get nastier. It became unbearable, but somehow, she tolerated it.

February came—a time for love. Rose always hated Valentine's Day. Nothing good ever came of Valentine's Day for her. Arjun, on the other hand, was having a great year. He became engaged to Samantha. So they were off to visit Anil's parents again. Enzo cried the entire trip.

The pair walked into Vishwa and Amita's home. It was about eight, and Rose was totally fried. She held Enzo in her arms, and he was just exhausted from screaming. Amita went to grab Enzo.

"He cried the whole way here," Rose said.

"He will get used to it," Amita said. Rose was annoyed by the comment.

"Hello, Vishwa. You don't happen to have any red wine, do you?" Rose asked.

"Yes. It is right here." Vishwa handed Rose a glass and wine bottle.

"Thank you," Rose said, and she filled her glass to the top.

"How was the ride?" Vishwa asked.

"The baby cried the entire way. I don't know what it is about being in the car, but he hates it; it is terrible," Rose said with clear frustration in her voice.

They sat down on the couch and immediately Amita began talking about Samantha. Rose liked Samantha. She was harmless and seemed okay, but it did give Rose some joy that Amita didn't like her.

"So, when are Samantha and Arjun getting married?" Anil asked.

"I don't know," Amita said to Anil. "They haven't picked a date yet. Samantha wants to have the wedding by a lake that she likes. I can't remember which one."

Rose could barely make out what they were saying about the wedding plans. She was so tired; she decided to turn in for the night. "Good night. I am tired," she said. She scooped up the baby and went downstairs.

Rose could hear them talking upstairs, and if she had the strength she might have driven back home. She could hear Amita say, "I think Rose is drinking too much. Maybe she needs to take a break." Rose put Enzo in the crib next to her and pulled the covers over her head so she didn't have to hear the bullshit. Unfortunately, she could still hear them.

On the drive back home, Anil made a pitstop at his friend's house and picked up a bag of weed.

"I don't think it is a good idea for Enzo and I to be in the car when you have this shit," Rose screeched while Enzo was screaming. "I mean seriously, don't you care at all?"

"It will be fine, Rose. You are so dramatic," Anil said though his teeth.

Rose climbed in the back of the car. She couldn't do the screaming any longer. She unbuckled the baby and held him the rest of the way home. She knew she shouldn't have held him in the car, but she could not take the screaming anymore.

The next morning, Rose walked into her office to see Dara.

"We are going out of business. We have no money," Dara said.

"Okay," Rose said.

"I am serious," she said. "We are going to have to shut this place down." Then she got on the phone and started screaming at her husband. She was yelling at him for all the affairs he had on her. She was screaming at him for leaving his job. Rose just sat in her office with Enzo and began to type. She didn't know which was worse: working with Dara or going home to someone who drank himself stupid.

Rose got home, fed Enzo, gave him a bath, and went to bed. After a while, the door opened and Anil came into the room. Rose just laid there and pretended to be asleep. She did this day after day, night after night. Dara by day, and drunk husband by night.

Rose looked into Amy's eyes. "I just felt beat up."

"I bet that was exhausting," Amy said. "You were trying to keep it all together."

Rose smiled. "You are being kind Amy. I was told by Anil's therapist when he was in rehab that I was an enabler."

Amy laughed. "It may be enabling, but you had so much going on and you did what you had to do to survive. You were in full blown survival mode. I think it is more complicated than saying you are an enabler."

"Yes, but things were going to get a lot worse. It seemed that Amita tried to occupy more and more of our time. It felt like this weird competition, but a one-sided competition. Amita seemed to want to have more of Enzo's time than my family had. She sucked up every holiday with us. The worst part was Anil became worse, and his mother didn't even notice. I was hoping that Samantha and Arjun's engagement would preoccupy her, but it didn't. Amita didn't even flinch. She kept up her attitude and what seemed to be a hatred for me."

"Are you sure it was hatred?" Amy asked.

"It didn't feel like hatred, I guess, but it was *something*. I really don't know. Maybe she was insecure. I mean, when I think about it, I feel so sad for her. I feel sad that she has never had someone who loved her unconditionally. We are all searching for that kind of love in the world, but at least some of us have it with our parents. Amita never had it. She never felt a kind touch or loving hand. I think that is why she held on so tight to her boys, but they are boys. Boys fly away. The tighter she held those boys, the more they seemed to run.

Anil did it with booze and pills, but he still took me to Florida on Fourth of July weekend with his family to celebrate."

❧

The plane landed and Anil, Rose, and Enzo got off. Rose was carrying Enzo. He had fallen asleep in her arms. Rose was impressed with herself; she was carrying Enzo and two oversized bags, which was no easy feat. Many people told her she was weak, but here she was. They grabbed a cab and gave the driver the name of the resort.

"I forgot to tell you," Anil said. "My parents and brother asked us not to drink on this trip."

"Us?" Rose asked. "Why am I being told that I cannot drink? I am a grown woman! It really bugs me that your family believes they can honestly tell me what to do."

Rose thought Anil didn't tell her because he knew she was stubborn. He knew the request would get under her skin and she'd want to do the exact opposite. They ended up stopping at a liquor store and bought a stash of small liquor bottles for Anil and three bottles of wine for Rose.

When they arrived at the condo, everyone was there. Amita immediately shared that there would be no drinking, but she was kind enough to give them the master suite. So naturally, they went into the master suite and had a drink. Rose felt like she could have just gone along with the request because she knew it would be best for her husband, but at the time she was too stubborn to be told what to do. She would always feel guilty for that; she enabled her husband for years.

"I did enable him. I know now that I played a part in his disease. I helped," Rose gulped. "I contributed. I'm not a fool, you know? When a marriage falls apart or a person falls apart in a marriage, that takes two players. Maybe that is why I will always feel a soft spot for him, a pain in my heart. Maybe that is why I will never let another person in again. I don't know, I just know that I can't hurt him anymore."

Amy just listened as Rose went on with what happened. Usually, Amy had something to say but this time she was quiet. Maybe she was taking it all in and listening, or maybe she had some insight that she thought Rose wasn't ready to hear yet. Either way she remained still and quiet in an unnerving way.

It was early that day, so they all decided to go on a walk and see what attractions were available. Rose had a small bottle of scotch, so she was feeling no pain. Anil guzzled two bottles, but it didn't seem to have an effect on him. Rose changed Enzo, and they went downstairs to look at brochures. Amita tried to make small talk.

"Enzo is eating food now?" she asked.

"Yes," Rose said. "But I am not giving him grapes, peanut butter, or any foods he can't mush up on his own. The peanut butter is just a precaution in case he is allergic."

"What about some chola? I think he should eat more than just Italian food," Amita said.

"Yes, well that is fine. I just think you should keep the spiciness to a minimum." Rose ignored her apparent dig.

"Maybe we should go to the beach tomorrow?" Amita suggested.

Everyone liked Amita's suggestion. Her suggestions always gave Rose a pit in her stomach, but maybe it would be fun. Maybe she was going to be nice for one day. *I could put the baby's toes in the water and splash around with him. That might be nice*, thought Rose.

The next morning, off to the beach they went. They packed some snacks, and Rose put on a ton of SPF and a T-shirt over her bikini. Her white skin couldn't bear the sun.

When they got to the beach, Vishwa and Amita said they would watch the baby while Anil and Rose were in the water. Rose got a strange feeling that she shouldn't leave Enzo with them.

"Come on," Anil shouted. "My parents raised my brother and I; Enzo will be fine."

Rose reluctantly went into the water with Anil. She wasn't in the water long when she left to check on the baby. She walked up to her in-laws feeding Enzo grapes. Rose lost it.

"Get it out!" Rose screamed. "I told you no grapes!"

Amita looked up, "I told him that you said no grapes, but he did it anyway." She looked at Vishwa.

"What do you mean? This could kill him if he chokes!" Rose said.

Vishwa laughed. "You are so dramatic. He can't die from grapes."

"Really?! Well tell that to my best friend who lost her two-year-old nephew to choking on grapes. Please tell her," Rose said through her teeth.

"You worry too much," Vishwa said with what seemed like dismissiveness.

"He is my son. I adore him," Rose said as she grabbed the baby and walked away.

"What's going on?" Anil asked. It was more of a scolding than a question.

"I told your mom that I didn't want Enzo eating grapes. You know Jessica lost a nephew to grapes, but your parents gave him grapes."

"I think you are being dramatic, Rose," Anil said with resentment.

"I am not being dramatic. The pediatrician also handed us a list of foods that we are not supposed to give to Enzo due to the risk of choking. Why do you question everything I do? The doctor gave us the list," Rose said frustrated. "Why don't you ever take my side? What is in her cooch juice that you can't just stand up for me for your son?"

It was like Amita had some sick hold. Every time Anil was around them, he became neurotic. He wasn't himself. He paced the floors and acted like a beaten child.

Rose started playing with the baby in the water when Vishwa came over and asked to play with Enzo. Rose reluctantly handed the baby to him. He started playing with him in the water, then he started taking the baby out farther and farther. But Vishwa couldn't swim. He kept falling in the water and Enzo kept going under with him. Vishwa was laughing and little Enzo was screaming. Rose grabbed Enzo and pulled him from the water. She walked away and started packing up the bags when Amita came over. She picked up Enzo, but the wind kept taking her sunhat off her head, and she went to grab it and dropped the baby. She started to laugh.

Rose didn't think either one of them really wanted to hurt the baby. She just thought they were both careless. They had no common sense, and it was always about them asserting what they wanted rather than what was right. *I said no grapes, so they gave my baby grapes. I want my home clean, and they tell me to let it go. I like nice napkins and they judge them*, Rose thought. She took the baby and went back to the condo.

Anil got to the condo and he was pissed. "What is wrong with you? My father was playing with the baby. Enzo was fine," he screamed.

"Enzo was crying. He was scared! What is wrong with you? Why can't you defend your family?" Rose screamed back.

"Do you honestly think that they would hurt him?" Anil asked through his clenched teeth.

"Not on purpose, but they have to prove this twisted point. Don't you see that?" Rose asked.

"I think you are dramatic, Rose. I think you can't be happy and that you always have to be negative," Anil said with all sincerity. "I think no matter what my parents do you will always find fault."

When Anil said it, Rose believed him. She thought maybe he was right. Sometimes, she still thinks he is right. *What if I am just being negative and I can't be happy?* Rose thought.

The next day they went to the Everglades for a boat ride. They walked through the gate in the park. Rose was holding Enzo when Amita asked to carry him. She gave the baby to Amita, and within about five seconds, Amita handed Enzo to Vishwa. They walked over to where the boat departed. It was fenced in with a chain link fence. The fence was an average fence, but there were signs posted every fifty feet or so that said, "Do not climb fence. Do not sit on the fence." The signs were placed there to protect guests from potential alligator attacks. Rose looked and she saw Vishwa sitting Enzo on top of the fence. She could hear her heartbeat and the blood drain to her feet.

"There are gators in the water. You are not supposed to sit him on the fence. He could fall in or a gator could jump up," Rose said. "There are signs!" Rose was in shock.

Vishwa started to laugh and mock her. "They can jump? Right."

Rose ran to the attendant. "Look! They have my son on the fence. Please do something," Rose said excitedly. "Please tell them."

The attendee rushed over and said, with what seemed complete irritation, "Sir, you need to hold that baby. You cannot put him on the fence. Didn't you read the sign? If I have to ask you again, it will have to ask you to leave the park. Thank you."

Vishwa laughed. "There are really alligators in the water," Rose said. She just looked at him like he was stupid. He is a professor, and by all accounts a smart man, so how could he be so dumb at the same time? It seemed that Amita just goes along with what Vishwa said blindly. Rose was glad when the boat ride was over, and they got back to the condo. She could not wait for that nightmare vacation to end. They were leaving after the Fourth of July.

The next morning, they had breakfast and headed out to walk the boardwalk. They went in and out of the shops. They stayed out all day and waited for the fireworks. Finally, it was dark, and they all walked onto the beach to find a spot to watch the fireworks. It took them a while to get through the crowd and find a place where they could watch comfortably.

It took about thirty minutes for them to find a decent spot to stand. The fireworks began. Enzo was so excited, and he enjoyed the fireworks. He was giggling and pointing. Then, just before the finale, Anil's family said it was time to leave; they didn't get to see the finale.

"Okay, everyone, let's go," Vishwa exclaimed.

"But the fireworks just started, and we just found a spot where we can see them," Rose said.

"Well, they are all the same and we should go," Vishwa said as he was walking away.

"Anil, I don't understand," Rose said with a very confused look.

"I don't know," Anil said with what seemed to be a grumble.

Anil was equally as irritated that they didn't see the show. They had a few drinks at the condo and then the next morning, they flew home.

Once they got home, Rose started making plans for Enzo's first birthday. Making the plans for his birthday kept her from having to think about Anil's late nights home and drinking. She emersed herself in party plans and work. She called her mom every day and discussed the birthday. It was all she could do to keep what was really happening hidden. She just wanted a boring, normal life, but her life was anything but boring and normal.

"Where were you?" Rose asked Anil as she bit through the words. "You can't even walk."

"This is all your fault," Anil grumbled.

"You are going to get a DWI! What are we supposed to do then?" Rose screamed. "You are going to humiliate me in front of my peers. You need help!"

Rose didn't know why she stayed. Maybe it was the glimpses of her funny, sweet Anil. Maybe it was that she was a fighter or maybe she felt stuck. Whatever was the reason, she tried to make everyone on the outside think her life was perfect and they all believed it.

Rose's mom came into town early to help with the birthday party. Rose was happy but terrified that she would see how bad off Anil was. He was blasted every fucking night.

"Hi, Mom," Rose said as she hugged and kissed her. "Hi, Daniel! I am so excited you are here. Let me take your bags upstairs." Daniel didn't let her.

Rose's mom and Daniel began helping her prepare for the party. Poor Daniel became Rose's handyman. He started hanging curtains and ceiling fans and patching up nail pops. He never complained. At least, he never complained to Rose.

They were there about a week when Vishwa and Amita barged into town.

"Hi, Rose!" Amita exclaimed, and she grabbed Enzo out of Rose's mom's arms. "Oh, here is my baby, my little pig," she said.

Rose's mom stood there and just looked at her. Vishwa began unloading and taking over the counter spaces. Within minutes, they had destroyed her clean little home.

Enzo's party was a Mickey Mouse theme. He loved the mouse so much. Rose's mom made trays of baked ziti, and Rose made the smash cake. Enzo's cake was a bright Mickey cake that they got from the baker down the street. It wasn't a big party, but they decorated like it was a huge bash. There were probably only twelve people over, but they made it an extravaganza.

After Amita and Vishwa left, Rose's mom stayed behind for an extra week. When Amita realized this, she stalled.

"So when is your mom leaving?" Amita asked.

"She is staying an extra week," Rose said. Rose realized then she should've just said she was leaving shortly after them.

"Well, we should stay too. Everything should be fair," Amita squawked.

"I don't think that is a good idea," Rose said as she guided Amita out the door.

After they left, Rose's mom busted her ass cleaning the house. Anil came home late, and Rose's mom and her watched a movie before bed.

Then it finally happened, the moment that Rose had been dreading, Anil exposed to the world what was really happening behind closed doors. He began texting Rose nasty messages.

You are a bitch! Whore! Then before Rose could text back, Anil started sending her mother vile messages. He called her a voodoo witch and other crazy names.

"Rose?" her mom asked quietly. "Anil is texting me really mean messages." She showed Rose her phone.

"Amy, I couldn't breathe," Rose said, looking like she was about to lose her breath again. "It was like the walls were closing in around me. I could feel my heart begin to race and my hands sweat. I thought I was going to have to run to the bathroom and vomit, but amazingly with all those feelings, I said quietly back to my mom without missing a beat, 'Mom, I am sorry. We should probably stay at a hotel. Anil is being mean, and, well, I just don't want to deal with it.' My mom didn't act surprised or scared, she just agreed. She helped me pack for the night."

"Your mom helped you pack?" Amy asked.

"Yup," Rose said.

Amy sat back and crossed her legs. "Why did your mom respond in such a manner?"

"She wasn't surprised. My mom knew he had a problem. She isn't an idiot." Rose cleared her throat. "I think she just wanted to help me. I think she felt bad for me, and I imagine she was probably wondering what the fuck I was really going through."

"We got in the car, and I picked out a hotel that was near my home. My mom helped me with Enzo, and when we got inside, she picked up the cost of the hotel. I thought for sure I was going to hear it, but instead my mom laughed and said, 'Well shoot, if I had known we were going to need a hotel, I would have taken us on a nice trip this weekend.' I thanked her for her help."

"What was going through your mind?" Amy asked.

"I guess it was sadness, fear, and terror. Amy, I left because he had become so unpredictable that I didn't know what he was capable of doing. I mean…" Rose trailed off as she cleared her throat. "He started walking me around the house by my neck. What if he did something else? I mean, holy shit, what if he touched me in front of my mom?" Rose began to laugh uncomfortably.

The next morning, when Rose woke up she noticed Anil had called her phone at least eight or nine times. She called him back.

"Hey," Anil said. "I got into an accident, and I could not reach you, so the neighbor brought me home."

"Oh," Rose said.

"I rolled the car three times," Anil said. "Are you coming home?"

"Yes," Rose said. "We are on our way now."

Rose was almost relieved. She was relieved because she wasn't going home to a trashed house. She was relieved because now maybe he would get help. She was relieved because he could not drive anymore. When she got home, he looked pitiful. Rose didn't say much. Rose had Anil call his father and tell him what happened. Rose thought his parents might help her convince Anil he needed help, but they just came into town and blamed her. They enabled him.

"Anil, we love you," Vishwa said while walking and pacing around the house.

"Yes," Amita parroted as she bobbed her head up while sitting on the couch.

"We are proud of you," Vishwa said.

"Yes, very proud," Amita repeated as she continued to bob her head.

Then they began to tell Rose how she could make Anil's life easier. *Is this really happening?* The next thing Rose knew, Vishwa was cutting a fifty-thousand-dollar check and paying off Anil's loans to alleviate the stress he was under. They left him another car to help with the situation. One would think that this would make things better, but it got terribly worse.

He still drank and went out, but he did it on foot. So he would call Rose and tell her to pick him up at a bar or restaurant, but he could not remember the name. Rose would get in her car and drive around looking for him. She was terrified. One night, Anil called her.

"Hello?" Rose answered.

"I am at the restaurant. Come get me," Anil slurred. "Be useful for something," he continued.

"Where?" Rose said.

"You know!" Anil screamed and hung up.

Rose was scared out of her mind. She knew how bad he popped off at the mouth. What if he started being an asshole to a patron and they beat him up? Rose called the nanny for Enzo and asked her to bring Enzo to her home. Then Rose called Arjun.

"Arjun, I don't know what to do. I cannot find Anil and I am scared," Rose said fighting tears.

"Call the police," Arjun said. "You are a lawyer, you should know what to do," he said with what seemed to be irritation.

"I can't. That could ruin his career," Rose said.

"Well, I don't know what to tell you." He hung up.

Rose received another call from an unknown number.

"Hello?" Rose answered.

"Hi, yes. I have a young man here, and...Well...I am the waitress at Jay's... I don't know what happened, but he just got really drunk all of a sudden. I was worried about him. He is picking fights with customers and I have him outside. He almost walked out into traffic, but he fell down the stairs, and...I saw 'wife' next to your number so umm, can you come to Jay's and get him?" she asked.

"Yes, I am on my way. I will be there in five minutes. Thank you for calling," Rose said with relief.

Rose would never forget that waitress. She helped Rose put Anil in the car. "Thank you again," Rose said. The waitress just smiled and walked away.

On the way home, Rose realized Anil wasn't the same person she married. She was afraid for her life. Rose tried to walk him into the house, but he kept saying how it was all Rose's fault. He grabbed onto her neck again. Rose could tell Anil didn't even realize what he was doing, which made it even scarier for her.

"Anil," Rose said softly. "Why don't you relax; I will go grab Enzo."

"Where is Enzzzo?" Anil said slurring his words.

"He is on a playdate, remember?" Rose lied. "I'll be right back."

Rose had no intention of going back to the house until she knew he was sober. Rose told the nanny what was going on, and she kindly offered her place to stay. The next thing Rose knew, the police were trying to talk to her. Apparently, Anil in his drunk stupor had called the police and told them Rose had kidnapped Enzo. Rose pulled up the security camera footage from the house; she could see at least ten officers there. Rose was frantic. Her phone rang suddenly, and she answered.

"Hello?" Rose said softly.

"This is Officer Roake. Is this Rose?" the officer asked.

"Yes. This is Rose."

"Is the baby with you?" Officer Roake asked.

"Yes, officer. He is with me," Rose answered.

"Where are you and the baby?" Officer Roake questioned.

"We are at the nanny's house, but I don't want my husband to know where we are, officer. You see, my husband is a drunk, and I was afraid, so I am hiding until he is sober. I'm not coming home until tomorrow," Rose explained.

"I can tell he is intoxicated, ma'am. Frankly, I am glad to hear that you are safe. We were afraid that we might be at a crime scene. We thought something happened to you and the baby. Thank you for answering the phone. It is a good idea to stay out of the house tonight."

Rose was shocked. Anil was so off his rocker that the police thought he had hurt Rose and Enzo. Of course, this event didn't provoke Anil to get sober. Anil apologized again, and Rose accepted his apology.

The next day, Rose went into work and Dara quit unexpectedly.

"Good news for me, bad news for you. I'm leaving. I got my dream job working with kids," Dara laughed.

Although it was sudden, Rose was relieved. Dara was so negative. Dara quitting actually made Rose feel like things were looking up for her. *Life is good,* Rose thought. She took over the business, and she was happy until about two weeks later when Anil came stumbling into the house.

"Anil?" Rose asked. It was as if a match had been lit. Anil stood with his hands in fists and started screaming in the middle of the room.

"Are you okay? Maybe you should lay down," Rose trembled.

Anil screamed again. "This is your fault!" He picked up a chair and slammed it to the ground. The chair splintered. Rose ran upstairs and into the bedroom and locked the door. Anil began to pound on the door, and he got it open. Anil grabbed Rose and threw her to the bed and began to choke her. He sunk his nails into her scalp and pinned her to the mattress. She could feel the blood in her hair. Rose knew she had to get Enzo out of there. She managed to break free, and she grabbed Enzo from the crib next to the bed and ran out of the house. It was raining, and Rose was terrified for Enzo. Luckily, she had grabbed the car keys. She got Enzo in the car, and she closed the door. She locked it. Rose ran down the road. As Rose was running down the street, a police officer jumped out and drew her weapon on Rose. Anil had called the police. Rose immediately raised her hands above her head. Rose told the officer that she had locked her baby in the car; Rose asked if she could reach into her pocket to give the officer the car keys. She said yes; another officer went to get Enzo from the car. The officer brought Rose into the home; they were starting an investigation. They were going to arrest Anil. Oh my god, Rose thought. *He will lose everything. I am an officer of the court and I will have to tell the truth, and everyone I know will be there.* Rose looked at that officer and said, "Please. Don't arrest him. You know me. We are in court all of the time, and I promise I am calling his parents and he is going to rehab. I promise."

"Okay," she said. "You promise?" she asked, seeming unsure.

"Yes. Please. You know what will happen if you arrest him. DSS will get involved, and they are a nightmare. I will have to stand in court. Please."

"Okay," the officer replied, "but I am taking him to the hospital. I am not leaving him with you."

Rose agreed to that. She called his parents and told them that if they didn't come and take Anil to rehab, then Rose would file for a divorce.

They came to the house in the middle of the night. Amita went up to check on Anil. He was passed out in bed. Rose sat on the couch and told them what had happened, and the next day, they began looking at rehab centers. They found one about two hours away that had an opening. They planned on taking Anil to the center the next morning. Rose helped him pack.

"You look happy," Amita said. "You know, you are not so perfect yourself—" she started saying before Rose cut her off.

"I am happy. My husband is going to get help," Rose said.

"Well, you do not look hurt. Anil looks banged up. I think you hit him," Amita claimed.

Rose hated her. Her comment made her go numb. She felt like a small part of her died inside. Rose kept on packing.

Anil woke up and chimed into the conversation. He told Rose his mother was right about her. "That's right," Anil said as he stumbled into the room. "She charged five thousand dollars on our credit card."

This didn't happen. They had saved exactly five thousand dollars. Vishwa and Amita made Anil use that money to pay off the credit card. They would not help pay for his rehab treatment unless he used that money to pay for the card. This meant that Anil was going into rehab and leaving Rose with a baby, bills, and only one stream of income with no savings.

After they took her husband to rehab, Vishwa texted Rose, *Don't be offended, but Amita and I think you need therapy too.*

Rose texted back: *I think we all need therapy.* Once Rose sent that text, they never brought up therapy again to her.

Anil's therapist called Rose from the center. Dr. Hug was straightforward and didn't hold back. He didn't want to speak to Anil's parents. Dr. Hug said that he didn't care for them after accessing the questionnaire that Vishwa and Amita were given. He said that every question that they answered on the questionnaire, Amita and Vishwa made it about themselves. *Big surprise.* Dr. Hug told Rose that his parents were enabling Anil, but she was too. Dr. Hug suggested that Anil stay in the center for ninety days and Rose agreed.

CHAPTER 9

Rose wasn't allowed to speak to Anil for the first week. Rose thought cutting off contact for a short time at the beginning was beneficial. It helped both sides get space and time to breathe and think.

Vishwa and Amita didn't call or ask how Rose was doing. They didn't see if she needed help. They didn't ask for their grandchild.

Rose also didn't hear from Anil almost the entire time he was away. Maybe they blamed her; maybe they thought she wasn't supportive enough. The truth, Rose would come to realize, would be worse than that. It would always make Rose feel this empathy toward Anil, this loyalty, a sadness.

Rose was alone with a baby, and the house was finally quiet and still. At first, the quietness of the house was terrifying, and Rose kept having nightmares of the bedroom door being kicked in by Anil. She would wake up in a sweat crying, screaming in her sleep night after night, all to look at the door and see nobody screaming or calling her names. Those dreams still haunted her. Once she'd calmed down, Rose would just look over at little Enzo sleeping and kiss him. She knew they were safe and still. She knew Enzo was safe.

The first time Rose heard Anil's voice, he seemed different. He seemed so far away. The phone rang, and Rose saw Anil's name on her phone. Her hands grew sweaty and her throat became dry.

"Hello, Anil," Rose said.

"Hi," Anil answered.

"Are you okay? Are you feeling okay?" Rose asked, keeping it together.

"I am fine. I miss you," Anil said. "We can start having visitors every Sunday for two hours," Anil said. "You can bring Enzo too," he said.

"This Sunday?" Rose asked.

"Yes."

"Okay, I will bring him. What time?" Rose asked.

"We can have visitors from noon until two," Anil responded.

"We will be there," Rose said.

The drive was two hours one way. Enzo was remarkably quiet. Rose pulled up to what looked like a large home and parked the car. She got Enzo out of the car. Her legs felt so heavy; she could hear her heart beating. Rose opened the front door. The room just inside looked like a living room with a couch and two chairs. It looked like a grandmother's home. The furniture faced the unlit fireplace.

"Hello. Can I help you?" a woman's voice chimed.

"I am here to see Anil, Anil Ahuja," Rose said in almost a whisper. "I'm his wife, Rose."

"Oh, yes. Nice to meet you. We have heard so much about you," she said with a smile. "You can walk down that hall. Anil is waiting for you."

"Okay, thank you." Rose turned the corner. Anil was in a large room, and he looked over at them. Rose put the baby down, and he waddled on over to his father. Anil picked up the baby and little Enzo put his little arms around his father and laid his head on his father's shoulder. Enzo was so quiet and still. They just hugged for a few minutes.

"You look good," Rose said through a gulp.

"I think he missed me," Anil said. "Thank you for coming. It means a lot to me. I'm glad you came."

"Me too. How are you?" Rose asked as she hugged Anil.

"I'm doing well," Anil said with a half-smile. "Come on, I'll show you around."

They walked down the hall. The center looked just like a huge home. They walked down a hallway with tile floors and floor-to-ceiling windows that let in the sun from outside. Rose could see why Anil was so calm. He had a beautiful space to heal in. They turned a corner and Anil showed Rose a small room with two twin beds.

"This is my room. I share it with my roommate," he smiled. "Come on let's take a walk. There is a small pond with ducks that Enzo might like to see."

"Okay, that sounds nice," Rose smiled.

Anil and Rose barely spoke. They walked through the woods in almost complete silence. She could hear the ground under her feet. She didn't know if he just didn't know what to say or if they didn't have anything to say to one another.

"My parents are going to India for four months. They said that they wanted to see family and friends. My parents want to travel now that they are retired," Anil said. "They are leaving after Christmas."

❧

"Amy, I was relieved that they were leaving, and I kept thinking to myself that it was time to turn over a new leaf," explained Rose. "Maybe we all just needed a break and some time to heal, then we could finally be a family. After this first visit, I went every week with Enzo to see Anil. I went to a four-day seminar on healing and how to begin the healing process with my husband. Every time I went to visit, I came home alone to face everything alone, but I learned something too. I now knew that I could be alone, and I could take care of the bills, my son, the business, and my home—alone. I also learned who my friends were and who I could trust. You see, Amy, people really show you who they are when you are down. My neighbor friends deserted me. They felt above me and superior. They made fun of me. You would think that it would hurt my feelings, but instead I felt like I dodged a bullet. I could see clearly for the first time. I was happy that I didn't have to deal with such assholes anymore," Rose shared.

"How did that make you feel about what you learned about yourself?" Amy asked.

Rose looked straight into Amy's eyes. "I felt new, like I was different somehow. I wasn't dependent. I got rid of every asshole in my life, and the people who were in my life now are real. I love living in reality." Rose looked off with a soft smile.

"Anil was gone for three months, and when he came home, I don't know Amy, it was different. Anil had changed but so had I. We were not fun together anymore, and Anil seemed to resent me or maybe he realized that he never really loved me. Every day seemed the same. It was boring. Anil went to work and so did I. We did the same thing day after day, and I felt stagnant. Either way, we changed. Then one day, about a month after Anil's parents left while Anil was at work, he called me.

"Hey," he said. "My mom has cancer again."

"What?" Rose said. "Are you sure?"

"Yes. She was having pain in her leg and so she went to the doctor. Apparently, the cancer ate through the bone. My dad got a flight home. She is going to see her doctor," Anil said with zero emotion.

"I'm sorry. I really am," Rose said as a pit grew in her stomach. She knew that this was bad.

Rose's first thought was *What if this triggers Anil's drinking?* Then she felt shitty making it about Anil.

When Amita returned home, they learned that the cancer was all over. Her ovarian cancer had returned and spread throughout her body. The doctors were going to try an aggressive treatment. The next morning, she was having surgery on her leg. The doctors were going to take the destroyed part of her bone and replace it with a metal one. They were all relieved it didn't need to be amputated. Rose had hoped that Amita being ill would bring their family together.

They went to visit Amita for Memorial Day. It was their hope that seeing Enzo and having the family around would cheer her up and raise her spirits. It took them about six hours to drive to the house. Enzo had gotten used to the car and was good. He just sat in the car and sang his songs. They also had a small video player that Rose's mom bought them to help with the trips. When they got to the house, Amita and Vishwa were acting as if nothing had happened. It was the strangest thing. Rose didn't know how to deal with that or how to react.

Apparently, their closest friends didn't know how to deal with it either, because the next afternoon they had their friends come for lunch. Rose enjoyed Mary's and James's company. They are both eccentric, kind souls. Mary was a counselor. She had long salt-and-pepper hair, big brown eyes, and a slim figure. Her preferred style was hippie. James was a brilliant doctor with a dry sense of humor. He had more of a disheveled look. They both came in with warm hugs.

"Hello, Mary," Rose said, excited to see her warm face. She gave Rose a hug and smile. James was beside her and he smiled and gave Rose a hug and said, "We can't wait to see the little one. Wow, he is getting so big," he laughed.

"Do you want something to drink?" Rose asked Mary. Rose was excited for some normal conversation. They walked into the living room and sat on the couch.

"They didn't tell us she was sick," Mary said with sadness in her eyes. "We just found out."

"I am sorry, Mary. I am sure that it is just because they don't know how to tell everyone," Rose said.

"James kept saying that Amita didn't look well. Maybe we should have said something."

"It isn't your fault," Rose said. "This is no one's fault."

Amita walked in the room with snacks. Mary and Rose smiled awkwardly.

Anil and Rose hung out with Amita and Vishwa that weekend. The weekend went by fast, but Rose noticed Amita became more bitter, and she tried to stay out of her way. Rose didn't blame her for being angry about her situation.

Anil wasn't really dealing with his mother's illness. They spent the next few holidays with his parents. They went to Williamsburg, Virginia, with her for the Fourth of July. His parents had a time-share there, and so they went on trips with them often and enjoyed the condo. The whole family was there.

Amita had a hard time walking with the metal leg, so they didn't go walking much. Vishwa was frustrated because he wanted to walk more, and he pushed Amita to walk even though she didn't feel like it. Vishwa enjoyed walking, taking hikes, and seeing waterfalls. Rose could tell that Amita was in pain, she kept wincing, but she kept going only stopping to sit on a bench to take short breaks.

It amazed Rose that she pushed through it. She always did what Vishwa wanted, even when it caused her pain.

Rose remembered Amita talking about being a physical therapist one day over a year ago when they were visiting their house.

"I wanted to be a teacher. I really wanted to teach students, that's what I wanted to do, but Vishwa said no." She seemed sad as she recanted the story. "So, I never became a teacher. That is it."

Rose wasn't sure why Amita didn't tell Vishwa to fuck off. Vishwa seemed so insensitive to her condition, her needs, and wants. He just wanted to take walks and hike that trip, so they all did. Thinking back, Rose wasn't sure why she hadn't said anything to him. She watched Amita suffer and she didn't say a thing. It was obvious Amita was in pain the whole trip. Everyone could see it, but everyone acted like normal, like it wasn't happening.

Amita loved that timeshare and Vishwa kept talking to her about selling it, either at that time or if she died. She didn't want to sell it. She looked sad when he spoke about selling, but no one seemed to notice. Anil eventually mentioned it seemed like it made her sad, but he never told his dad to shut up. Rose felt frozen from shock. But like everyone else, she didn't.

"Anil, why don't you tell your dad to stop?" Rose asked.

"If I stand up for my mom, she will just make excuses for my dad. It's just not worth it," Anil said like he was merely recited a fact.

I guess she did it to herself, Rose thought. *But why, when it is something so important, no one says anything? Does anyone get it? She is probably going to die! No one gets it!*

On that trip, they didn't do much. Amita could barely walk. The next time they would see Amita was for Enzo's birthday. She didn't stay for long. It was hard for her to travel. Her chemotherapy made her so sick. She had sores in her mouth, so it made it hard for her to eat. She would pass out and bleed when she went to the bathroom. I don't know what was worse, the chemo or the disease. That chemo even changed the color of her skin. Rose was horrified and the whole experience softened her toward Amita. Unfortunately, it didn't work the other way; Amita still clearly disliked Rose. To Rose, it seemed so unfair for anyone to have to suffer so much.

Enzo's party was at an art studio. It lasted two hours, but they went early to put out the food. There were only eight children at the party, but there were so may activities for them. The children had several art stations that they could visit. It was so interactive.

Amita didn't have anywhere to sit at the party. She had to stand almost the whole time. Vishwa found a seat, but he didn't offer it to her. Amita looked exhausted. She'd started to take on this grayish color.

When the party was over, they went back to the house.

Rose made it a point to check in on Amita, because her family wasn't doing it. "Amita, do you want me to get you something?" Rose asked. In true Amita fashion, instead of answering or asking for help, she got up and began cooking an Indian meal. Rose knew she liked to cook, and she was a great cook, but she had to be tired. She definitely didn't look well. It seemed that Amita never complained.

Vishwa continued to order Amita around the house. That poor woman could never sit down, because the second she sat down, Vishwa was right there giving orders. "Amita, can you please get me some tea? I would like some snacks." Rose could see where Anil got it from, because every time she sat down he had a request.

Rose had really expected things to change, but they didn't. She thought her and Amita would become closer. She thought they would bond, and she would soften. She thought Anil would appreciate her because she stood by him. She really believed he would partner up; be a team. That didn't happen at all, not even a little bit. Anil said he appreciated Rose, but he didn't show it. Rose still did all the cooking, cleaning, and taking care of the baby. Anil was a slob; Rose would clean the sink, and he was right there to leave a dish. Rose felt like a hamster in wheel. She would ask for help, but he didn't care.

Amita she just became angrier; and it was like she'd been given a green card to be a huge asshole. She had no problem saying how she really felt. They went through the holidays, but during that time Amita had put pressure on Arjun to have his wedding. They were supposed to have their wedding about a year later, but Amita kept saying she was worried she wouldn't make it. Rose thought it was strange, because they didn't even like Samantha. Amita began helping plan a spring wedding for them, which was nice because the wedding planning took some of the focus off Rose and her family.

When the wedding date arrived, Rose, Anil, and Enzo drove to his parents' house for the wedding. Samantha and Arjun were having their wedding in Samantha's backyard. It was the same house Rose and Anil had had their party. They had a very large property.

When they finally arrived at Anil's parents' house, Amita was sitting at the table with Gitamami and her husband. It wasn't too late, but the drive with Enzo always takes longer.

"Hello," Rose said as she walked in the door. Gitamami and her husband greeted her with hugs and a smile. Gitamami loves children, and she was so excited to meet Enzo. She scooped him up and immediately began to play with him and give him kisses. Enzo began to giggle. Rose went back out to the car and finished bringing in all the bags.

The next morning, Rose got up early to feed Enzo. Amita was in the kitchen preparing snacks for the henna party.

"Good morning," Rose said. "Can I help you with something?"

"You can chop these vegetables," Amita responded. Rose could hear Enzo playing with Gitamami in the living room.

"Okay, sounds good. What is the plan?" Rose asked Amita. She was sautéing some onions with spices.

"Tomorrow we are going to Samantha's parents' house for the henna party. I am bringing the snacks, and her mother is making pizza and providing wine," Amita said.

"Okay, sounds good," Rose said. "How many people will be at the wedding?"

"Not many," Amita said. "I think they are inviting about seventy-five people to the after party. The wedding is only family," Amita said. "There will only be about fifteen people at the ceremony."

"That is nice," Rose said as she chopped vegetables. Amita and Rose worked on the cooking for a few hours. She finally got hungry, and they decided to heat up leftovers. Amita had to stop several times to catch her breath.

"Why don't you sit down?" Rose suggested to Amita. "I can heat up our lunch and set the table. Maybe it would be good for you to just relax for a few minutes." Rose began to heat the food. Gitamami sat with Amita at the table. It wasn't long before Vishwa and Gitamami's husband sat down too. They were all chatting about the wedding when Amita said, "I don't know why he picked Samantha."

Rose could hear them all shushing Amita, but she continued. "Sarah would have been the best daughter-in-law. I am very serious. Sarah was the best." Rose could hear everything she was saying, despite the table's efforts to silence Amita.

What a bitch! Rose thought, *She knows I can hear her*. Rose could see Gitamami looking at her, but she just kept chopping like she heard nothing. She chopped those vegetables like she was chopping up her heart. Rose was so angry.

When they arrived at Samantha's parents' home, there were

pizzas lined up on the counters and Amita's snacks were there too. Rose could see Samantha getting her henna put on her feet. "Hello, Samantha. Wow, that looks beautiful," Rose said.

"I'm over it," Samantha said.

"Oh," Rose responded. "Do you want a drink? Food?"

"Seriously, Rose. I am over it. Yes, please get me a drink." Rose had never seen Samantha look so irritated. She was usually chill and easygoing. Not this time. Rose returned with drink in hand and she smiled. Samantha took the drink and gulped it down.

"Have you eaten anything?" Rose asked her. She looked like she was drinking way more than she was eating.

"No, no one has gotten me anything to eat," Samantha snapped. "I have been sitting here for two hours, and no one has brought me anything."

"Okay, I'll go get you some pizza," Rose said.

"No, I'm fine," she bit back. Rose knew she needed food, so she went over and put a slice of pizza on her plate and several snacks. "Look," Rose said. "I'll set this here. They are here if you want them." Rose smiled. She understood how Samantha felt. You have to sit still for hours like a damn statue and it sucks. Everyone around you is eating and drinking, and you are just sitting there. God forbid you have to use the bathroom.

Rose got up to see where Enzo was playing. She was concerned because there were so many people at the house, and it wasn't child proof. Enzo loved to get into everything, and Rose didn't want him to get hurt.

Rose began to walk around the home looking for Enzo. Enzo was outside with Arjun and Anil. They were talking, but they were not close to Enzo. The had their backs to him on the lawn. Enzo was playing in the driveway; it was large enough to hold about eight cars. There was a huge barrel filled with rainwater. Enzo started to pull himself up onto the barrel.

"No. No. Enzo," Rose said. She was worried he would topple into the barrel.

"Yeah, I'm going to let him die," Arjun snapped.

"I just came out to check on Enzo," Rose said carefully.

"Right, because I am going to watch him die," Arjun said. Anil just looked at him. Anil was as shocked as Rose was; Arjun wasn't usually this mean. It was at that moment that Enzo began to run down the hill. He was still wobbly, and Rose was worried he was going to face plant. She ran after him and caught him.

"Jesus Christ, Rose! Let him be free and have a moment to himself. He needs to learn and have his independence without you hovering," Arjun snapped.

"He is two years old," Rose said as she picked up Enzo. "I hardly think a two-year-old needs independence." Rose shot Anil a death look as he stood there. She took Enzo inside with her. *He is ridiculous*, she thought.

Anil came inside about an hour later. "Hey," he said. "Arjun is just a little stressed, and he has had way too much to drink. He isn't ready to get married, and he feels rushed. He didn't mean anything by it. He is taking out his fear and frustration on you."

"I guess." Rose put her head on Anil's shoulder.

"You know my mom pushed him into this," Anil said.

"I know, it sucks," Rose said. We left the party shortly after that and went back to Anil's parents' house and to bed.

The next morning everyone was getting ready for the wedding in the afternoon. Rose decided to wear a cute blue dress that made her eyes pop. Amita had bought Enzo and Anil an Indian outfit. She had even picked out Samantha's wedding sari. Rose walked up the stairs to meet everyone, and Amita immediately started in on her. Admittedly after the night before, Rose wasn't in the mood.

"I have Indian clothes for you to wear," Amita said.

"Thank you," Rose said, "but I like this blue dress. I am going to wear this." Amita didn't speak to Rose the rest of the day because she didn't wear the sari. To Rose, it was the best day ever. She completely avoided her.

The ceremony began with Arjun on a horse. The family followed the horse up the walkway to the stage that was set up for the ceremony. The priest performed a short ceremony. Samantha had written sweet vows. She looked at Arjun with such love. It seemed like Arjun made his up on the spot.

When the ceremony was over, Samantha's sister took the wedding pictures. They all gathered for a group picture and then a family picture. The family picture naturally featured Amita and Vishwa in the middle with the bride on the end.

Rose started to look around and noticed the priest was leaving. Samantha was running around looking for Arjun.

"Hey guys, did you sign the license?" Rose asked. Surely, they must have signed.

"What license?" Amita asked.

"If you don't sign the license in front of witnesses, then you have only had a ceremony. They are not legally married," Rose said.

Rose had never seen a woman make such a dash in all her life.

They yanked that priest out of his car, and before she knew it, they had gathered everyone back around. They all stood and watched the signing of the license.

They went back to the house for the after party. The party was at Amita and Vishwa's home in their basement. They had a band in the backyard and tables were set up in the basement and outside on a stone patio. The tables were covered with white linens, and each table had a tea light and plant. Lights were strung above the patio and over the band. The band had set up a small stage.

It was unusually warm, and Enzo was sweating up a storm in his little outfit. Rose could tell he was getting fussy. The material was rather scratchy, and his skin was reddening. She took Enzo into the bedroom and put him in a cotton shirt and shorts. His face brightened up quickly. *Crisis averted.*

Rose walked over to the wine and beer table and poured herself a large glass of wine. She handed Enzo a bottle of water. Vishwa made his way over to her and said, "Watch Anil tonight. I am worried with all the alcohol around that he will drink."

"He will be fine," Rose said with clear irritation in her voice. "Anil has been doing great. If you sat down and talked to him about what he has been through, you would be proud of him and not worried," Rose said. They never gave Anil the credit he deserved. It drove her nuts.

The party started, and people started to pour into the house. Samantha and Arjun were dancing, and Rose wanted to dance too. She picked up Enzo and started to dance with him. They were dancing when she heard Amita say, "Let Vishwa hold the baby." Vishwa came and took Enzo out of Rose's arms.

Rose felt like everything was a struggle with them. If she watched Enzo, they let him free. If she kept Enzo clean, they made him eat dirt. If she was close to Enzo, they made him far. So Vishwa walked away with Enzo. Maybe an hour went by, and Rose saw Vishwa, but she didn't see Enzo. She walked away and started to look for him. She didn't know where to begin; the home backed up to woods. The front of the house wound around onto a main road. Rose ran through the home. It felt like five hours had gone by, but it must have been only twenty minutes or so, when she finally saw Enzo crawling up the stairs.

"Oh, good. I was worried that we would not find his mom," a young man said to me. "I have been watching this little boy for about thirty minutes. I didn't want him to fall down the stairs."

"Thank you so much," Rose said. Her heart was beating a million times a minute. "Thank you."

Rose was so upset with Anil's parents. She was so happy to leave their house. She wanted to scream. The more she looked at the situation, the more she felt like she was crazy. Maybe ignorance is really bliss. Arjun was freaking out the entire time. He didn't want to go through with the marriage, but in the end, he did get married. Samantha seemed to have no clue. She seemed happy. All night she went around calling Arjun her husband happily, all while Amita bitched that he didn't marry Sarah. Rose felt like she was watching a movie.

They went back and forth to Anil's parents' home that summer. Amita looked worse and worse, but nobody seemed to notice. Rose would tell Anil, and he would say, "She is fine." But Rose knew she wasn't fine. And they kept pushing her too hard.

Amy looked at Rose and said, "Amita set the tone. She set the stage."

"What do you mean?" Rose asked.

"Amita didn't set boundaries. She never said, 'I do not feel well. I need a break.' She sucked it up, and as a result, she didn't teach her boys empathy. She taught them how to be selfish. She didn't teach them how to be in a relationship. Rose, I do not know that I can help you save your relationship, because Anil would have to acknowledge that he has to change, and I do not believe he will. I am not saying that it isn't possible but, in this situation, it may not be possible," Amy explained.

Enzo's birthday came, and this time Amita and Vishwa didn't come. They got angry because Rose waited too long to make plans. They said it was too late. Rose thought it was really because Amita didn't feel well, and it was easier to blame her. Anil became angry. "Jesus all they wanted was a cup of tea and a fucking cupcake, but you didn't let them have it!"

They went to his parents' home for Thanksgiving. The entire family went to Samantha's home. Amita looked so gray. Rose remembered the day after Thanksgiving, they went out to dinner and she could barely eat. That Sunday, Amita wanted Chinese food but Vishwa would not spend the money.

"Amita, if you want Chinese food, I will buy it. What do you want?" Rose intervened.

"Oh no. It is okay. We ate out once this week. I should not eat out again," she said.

It broke Rose's heart. She loved Chinese food. She looked so bad. She would just lie on the couch and rest. We were all sitting around, and Amita was feeling so sick. Arjun and Anil were talking so loudly, and they had all the lights on and Amita looked like death.

"Hey, guys. Lower your voices. Your mom looks so bad," Rose said.

"She is fine. If she isn't feeling well, she will go in the other room," they said.

"She wants to be with us. God. Just lower your voices," Rose said. They didn't.

Rose just looked at her, and she could see death. Rose didn't know how no one else noticed but death was everywhere. You could feel it. Rose told Anil that she was worried, but he ignored her and said she was exaggerating, but Rose knew what she saw and felt. She didn't have much time.

When Anil and Rose got home from that Thanksgiving, it wasn't long before they got the call. Amita had only a few months left. The cancer had riddled her body. She died on December 29. She never made her sixtieth birthday.

"We drove into town for the funeral and arrived on December 30. The service was three hours long. Amita's family was there, including the family she didn't like. I remember walking up to Amita's casket. I never thought I would cry at the funeral so hard. I cried for my husband. I cried that she died, and we never made peace and that she never approved of me. The worst part is a part of me cried in relief. Oh my God, Amy. I cried and cried." Rose paused and collected herself.

"Amy, can you help my marriage? Can you help me heal?" Rose asked through her tears.

ABOUT THE AUTHOR

Sofia Bella Roma is a lawyer in North Carolina. She has been practicing law since 2009. She was first licensed to practice law in Massachusetts and then went on to become licensed attorney in North Carolina. Sofia has spent most of her career telling stories. She regularly performs to judges when litigating her cases. *Mother Knows Worst* is Sofia's debut novel. This book tackles common problems in relationships and takes on mother-in-law drama with a quirky point of view. Sofia knows firsthand about difficult relationships since she has been practicing law as a divorce attorney. She currently lives with her son and their pet lizard. She has a love for the arts and enjoys making people laugh.